I0554096

LETHAL PASSAGE

AN ALLISON HART NOVEL
BOOK 2

ROBIN MAHLE

HARP House Publishing, LLC.

Published by HARP House Publishing
January 2020 (1ˢᵗ edition)

1

The rumble of the vessel's diesel engine echoed inside the hull as it traveled just below the ocean's surface. What it carried was worth far more than the lives of the 4-man crew navigating it through the hostile seas. Cocaine—3 tons of it, wrapped in plastic and encased in waterproof bags worth an estimated $80 million.

The 25-foot narco-sub that took a year to build at a cost of $2 million was on its maiden and probably only voyage. Built-in scuttling valves would be deployed at the first sign of the Coast Guard. The vessels were never meant to last, just built to make it near enough to US shores for the cargo to be unloaded onto faster boats for the final leg of the journey. The cost to build was insignificant in comparison to the drugs' street value and the crew was expendable.

The seas rolled and water seeped into the air vent, which was the only exposed part of the semi-submersible. A crewman spotted the leak coming from their only source of air. His eyes revealed what his face couldn't. Worry. He cast his sights to the cargo shoved deep inside the hull and then to the man at the helm. "How much longer?" The Columbian spoke in his native Spanish. "I have to piss."

The 1,400 nautical mile journey across the ocean was treacherous enough but was made worse by the fact that there was no toilet. Fishing boats were posted along the route that provided food and water for the crew, sometimes fuel if necessary. They also kept a lookout for the Coast Guard to warn of potential danger ahead.

"Hold it or piss in the container," the man replied without taking his eyes off the GPS that guided him through the black seas in the middle of the night.

The crewman grabbed an empty milk container and did his business, replacing the cap and shoving it under the bench where he sat. "You didn't answer my question. How much longer?"

"200 kilometers. We should be there before dawn." The man at the helm turned back. "Keep listening for boats."

The other two crewmen each slept on a 1-inch thick mat and a small pillow. There was hardly room to move inside the rudimentary hull that looked like it was built for a high-school science fair. Many lives had been lost on these trips. However, the money that awaited the crew on their return, should they survive, would set them up for future success. For them, it was worth the risk.

The puddle of water grew larger beneath the air vent as the hours passed. But they were so close now. The final hurdle was to navigate near enough to Haven Key for the shipment to be unloaded onto a boat that would traverse into Cove Harbor.

The pilot slowed the vessel and shouted, "Pendejos, despierta." "*Wake up, assholes.*" He peered through the small window, squinting to see in the darkness as he set his course through the difficult waters. "Por radio vamos a venir." "*Radio them we're coming.*"

The engine whined as it slowed to a crawl. Water trickled faster through the vent as the sub bobbed in the pitching seas. The narrow channel was lit with buoys deployed by the recipients of the shipment.

One of the crew picked up the radio. The young man was barely 5 feet tall and had made this journey before. "Be ready. We're almost there." He had proven his worth as the only crew member who spoke English.

The arrangement was for the shipment to be unloaded from the boats onto moving trucks and driven into Tampa where it would be dropped at a warehouse. From there, it would be distributed and sold throughout the city.

"Veo la señal." *"I see the signal."* The pilot checked the GPS and slowed further.

Two small boats decelerated as they neared the vessel. A pounding on the hull sounded inside.

"Abre la escotilla." *"Open the hatch."* The pilot turned off the engine and watched as the English-speaking crew member ascended the ladder and unlatched the lock.

He pushed it open and emerged.

"Raise your hands! Let me see your hands!" A Coast Guard officer trained his gun on the man.

Weapons clicked into position as a spotlight flashed in the crew member's eyes. The light blinded him, but he knew what was happening. "I'm unarmed!"

Inside the vessel, the other three scrambled as if there was a place for them to go. One reached for the valves, ready to sink the sub and the drugs inside.

An officer jumped onto the sub and pulled out the man. "You're under arrest for trafficking narcotics. Who's inside?"

"Three others. They don't speak English."

"How much coke?" The officer pressed on.

"2700 keys."

"Son of a bitch." He turned back to his colleagues. "They got 6,000 pounds of coke inside."

———

ALLISON HART STOOD BACK AND EXAMINED THE SIGN ON THE door of her new office. Her head cocked and her brassy blonde hair, usually worn in a pile atop her head, rested against her back. A smile teased her lips. "ACL Investigative Services." She turned to Charlie. "Has a nice ring to it, doesn't it?"

Charlie looked at the sign with a raised brow. "Sounds like a place to go for knee surgery."

"Don't listen to her, Allison. I like it. I think it's perfect," Lucy replied.

"Thank you. Allison Charlie Lucy. ACL." She turned to them. "Because if it wasn't for you two, I wouldn't have crossed the finish line."

"Far be it from me to refuse credit, but in this instance, it was you, my friend. You got the license, the loan. This is your baby and I'm just happy to be a part of it."

"You always sell yourself short, Charlie." Allison inserted her key. "Let's go take a look inside." She opened the door and a waft of stale air spilled out. "First thing we need to do is open the windows."

Charlie shuffled inside wearing a bulky sweater that didn't suit her already stocky frame. She set down her box on a nearby desk. "It's not so bad in here. A little cleaning, a little disinfecting." She walked around and gazed at the carpet. "Might need some new carpet, Alli. There's a blood stain over here."

"What?" Allison rushed to her side. "Where?"

"Right there." Charlie pointed to the dried spot.

"That's not blood. That's wine," Allison said. "Look at it."

Charlie squatted for a closer look. She shook her head of black hair that was styled short and spikey. "No way. I know a blood stain when I see it. I have two boys who like to pick fights with each other."

Lucy approached. "Let me see." She leaned over and studied the deep red spot. "Charlie's right; it's blood."

"This was a lawyer's office. Why would there be blood on the floor?" Allison pressed on.

"Maybe someone didn't like their settlement?" Charlie laughed. "Relax, Alli. I'm just giving you a hard time. It's wine. Come on. We have a lot of unpacking to do."

It had been nearly four months since Allison Hart was abruptly fired from her job as a Worker's Compensation investigator for the State of Florida. She blew the whistle on a senior member of staff she had witnessed taking part in a fraud scheme. At the age of 48, the rest of her life had suddenly become a blank slate. Her 18-year-old son, Nolan, still lived at home and went to community college. Her 20-year-old daughter, Micah, attended Florida State and there were a ton of bills to pay. Through a series of extraordinary events, Allison found herself knocking on the door of a private investigator named Tommy Boyce. He gave her a job and wound up dead. Now Allison was a P.I. and had dragged her best friend, Charlie Wells, into this new life.

Lucy Boyce, Tommy's daughter, was the "L" in ACL. The 19-year-old with long dark hair and petite build wanted to continue her father's line of work and someone needed to take over his clients. She offered to come on board. Tommy had been in the business for a long time and had been a cop before that. People trusted him and now it was up to her to earn their trust.

Then there was Charlie. She was the shoulder to lean on and the tell-it-like-it-was best friend. Allison needed Charlie more than

Charlie could ever know. They'd met when their kids went to the same grade school. Years later, both would end up divorced. It was Charlie who got Allison the job with the State. It had been 20 years since Allison had worked and employers weren't exactly pounding down her door when she decided to go back. Well, it wasn't a decision so much as it was a necessity. Her ex-husband, Leo, was a high school baseball coach. It wasn't like Allison got his money in the divorce because he didn't have any.

Now here they all were. Thrown together by circumstance. And Allison couldn't have been happier.

"Knock, knock." Shane Sullivan rapped his knuckle on the open door. "It's starting to shape up in here." The 40-year-old detective for the Tampa Police Department was slender and fit. With deep brown eyes, a sharp jawline, and a full head of dark brown hair, he was also easy to look at.

"Shane." Allison set down a box of files on her desk. "Come on in. We're just getting unpacked. I didn't think you were stopping by today."

"I had a spare few minutes and wanted to see how the newest private investigating agency was coming along." He continued inside.

"Hey, Shane," Charlie said. "Not too shabby, huh?"

"Not shabby at all. It's good to see you." He offered a friendly hug.

"You too. Alli says you've been keeping busy at the station."

"Busy trying to get noticed."

Shane "Sully" Sullivan worked counterfeit merchandise cases and small-time robberies. But where he wanted to be was in Major Crimes, working Homicide. He and Allison met shortly after her divorce at the courthouse during one of her fraud investigations. They'd been friends ever since and helped each other out once in a while. Most recently, he'd been a big part in uncovering a corruption and murder scandal that catapulted Allison into her current line of work.

"Well, I'm glad you could find time to check in on us ladies," Charlie said.

"Since when do you need anyone to check on you, Charlie?"

He smiled. "Hey there, Lucy. How you doing?"

"Doing all right, Detective. Thanks for asking."

Allison approached him. "You want the nickel tour?"

"That's why I'm here. Show me what you got."

———

THE COLUMBIAN DRUG RUNNER, WHO WAS THE ONLY member of the crew who spoke English, was so far refusing to answer questions. Special Agent in Charge Erik Markham of Homeland Security sat in the interrogation room along with DEA Agent Dominic Pierce, and Tampa Police Detective Anton Baylor.

Agent Markham leaned against the wall and shoved his hands in the pockets of his tailored pants. The 52-year-old DHS agent had been after the cartel for years, mostly in Mexico. But since the recent rise in demand for cocaine, he shifted his focus to Florida where shipments were coming in like it was the 1980s all over again. He raked over the kid with stern dark eyes and a lined face. "We know this isn't your first trip to Florida. The cartel has put a lot of faith in you. But they can't help you now. We need to know who was supposed to pick up the shipment on the boats."

The young man not more than 25, rolled his eyes and slouched deeper into the chair, ignoring the question.

"Not feeling up to talking today, huh?" Detective Anton Baylor was a veteran on the police force and a member of the Organized Crime Drug Enforcement Taskforce for the past 3 years, along with the other agents in the room. This was the largest bust of his tenure. The 45-year-old detective was polished with a slight paunch and was of average height. He'd worked his way up the ranks, which was tougher than it should have been thanks, in part, to the color of his skin. But he was here now. He was respected and had more than earned his position.

"I sure would hate for the rest of the crew members to find out you gave up everyone. Imagine if word got out that you talked." DEA Agent Dominic Pierce has been through this scenario plenty of times in recent years. He was young in comparison to his colleagues on the task force. The red-haired, fair-skinned man compensated for his recessive traits by bodybuilding in his spare time. No one ever called him a Ginger, unless they were looking for trouble.

"Look, kid. I know what you're thinking, but we can help you out. We can protect you," Detective Baylor said. "But you gotta give us something."

The kid peered at the men. "What can you do for me? You know how this works. You know how it will end."

"We do," Agent Pierce replied. "So give us a name and we'll work out a deal. Who was supposed to pick up the drop?"

"I'm dead anyway." The kid pulled upright again and released an exhaustive breath. "Can you guarantee the safety of my family? They will need to be brought here. They will be killed if they stay in Bogota."

Pierce looked to his colleagues and returned to the kid. "I have people there who will find them and ensure their safety. You have my word."

"The Southside Runners. That's all I know. They don't tell us more than we need to know. Please. Don't let them kill my family."

"We'll get them to safety." Pierce looked to Detective Baylor. "Southside Runners. I believe they're in your jurisdiction, Baylor. You and Agent Reddick will need to move fast."

Baylor nodded. "Agreed. I'm supposed to meet with him soon. His FBI field office is still on scene hauling in the drugs. I'll bring him up to speed."

———

LOGAN CARR ROLLED UP THE BLANKET ON HIS BED AND tucked it in his duffle bag. He pushed aside the dark blonde strands of hair that fell onto his face before zipping it up. The 23-year-old had been here for six months. A transition from the prison cell he'd lived in for the previous 5 years.

"Today's the big day, huh?" Dale Meek leaned into the doorway and eyed him. He scratched at his scruffy beard and placed a hand on his scrawny waist. "Lucky you. Getting out of this shithole half-way house is the best thing that's going to happen to you. Don't screw it up."

"I don't plan to." Logan tossed the bag over his broad shoulder as if it weighed nothing. "I already got me a place and a job. I ain't going back inside for nothing. Mark my words."

"Plenty before you have said that very thing," Dale replied.

"Yeah, well, they ain't me. I made mistakes. I was young and stupid and listened to the wrong people. Five years inside changes your perspective." He started toward the door wearing a wide smile and hope glimmered in his blue eyes for the first time in years.

"That it does, my friend." Dale Meek tugged on his sagging jeans and extended his hand. "You keep your nose clean. I don't want to see you back here."

Logan accepted the handshake. "You won't. You can count on that. No offense, but I hope I never see you again." He walked through the old house dotted with worn furnishings and dingy carpet and made his way outside. He unlocked his old

Toyota pickup and threw his bag onto the bench seat. Climbing inside, Logan keyed the ignition and stopped to take a last look at the transition house. He waved a final time to Dale and drove away.

A reformed convict himself, Dale Meek kept the other occupants in line until they got their acts together. He had hope for Logan. He was a good kid and Dale figured he was going to keep his word and never come back to that place again.

Tonight was his night to make dinner and he was feeding five others. Dale never was much of a cook, but people seemed to like his chili so that was what he was going to make chili and cornbread. The store-bought kind, not homemade. He pulled out the large pot and started dicing the onions when the doorbell rang. "Ah, hell, Logan. What'd you forget?" Dale wiped his hands on a dishtowel and started toward the door to open it.

"Evening, Dale. How are you?"

"Detective Baylor, I'm doing fine. What are you doing here, if you don't mind me asking?"

Baylor stood on the porch illuminated with a single fixture beside the faded red door. The painted wood railing was chipped and rotting, and his hand rested on it. He appeared like a man joining an old friend for a cup of coffee. Though his gray sports coat over a white button-down shirt and dark jeans spoke to his true identity as a detective on a mission. "I need to talk to Logan Carr."

"Man, I'm sorry, but Logan's gone," Dale said.

"What do you mean, gone?"

"I mean, his time was up. He moved out today. In fact, you just missed him by an hour, tops," Dale added.

"Any idea where he was going?"

"I suppose you'd have to ask his parole officer."

Detective Baylor placed his hands on his full hips. "Are you trying to tell me you don't know where he's moving to? I find that hard to believe, Dale."

"I'm just saying it ain't my place no more. Logan did his time. Besides, why are you looking for him?"

"I'll tell you that if you tell me where he went."

Dale folded his arms and eyed the detective, refusing to answer.

"Fine. I'll tell you out of the kindness of my heart. Then maybe you'll remember that kindness and return the favor. Logan Carr used to have dealings with the Southside Runners. One of them, in particular, I know was his buddy."

"Yeah, so?" Dale added.

"So, they're into some deep shit with the Columbian cartel. Coast Guard intercepted one of their shipments late last night. They were the designated recipients of that shipment. You get where I'm going with this? We managed to get one of the crew in custody to open up to us. You and I both know Julius Hardin runs that gang right now. And I know Logan and Julius were buddies at one time."

Dale shook his head. "Doesn't mean that's the case anymore. Besides, shouldn't you be looking for Julius then?"

"Everyone's out looking for him. But we're also looking out for his associates. Past and present. I'm sure you understand why it is we'd want to talk to Logan. And by 'we', I mean, the entire Drug Enforcement Taskforce."

Dale peered at the detective. "I'm sure Logan would like nothing more than to clear up whatever it is you think he's gotten himself into. So, I'll tell you where he's going. But that kid don't know nothing about no drug bust or the cartel. Just 'cause he ran with the Southside Runners back in the day, don't mean he is anymore."

"I thank you very much for the cooperation, Dale."

2

The Northern Breeze trailer park in North Tampa was where Logan Carr now called home. The furnished one bedroom single-wide was still better than the 6 x 8 jail cell he had occupied for the past five years.

Channel 9 aired a basketball game while Logan sat on the worn yellow sofa with his feet on the table. He wanted nothing more than an ice-cold brew right now, but that was against the rules. No drinking while on parole. He'd been sober for five years so what was another two? His initial sentence had been for 7 years, meaning his parole would go on for two. So, rather than a beer, he popped open a can of Coke and chugged it down.

As evening settled in and the early January air seeped into the poorly insulated trailer, Logan reached for his hoodie and slipped it over his head. Then the knock came. Call it a side-effect of prison, but surprise visitors were generally considered ominous. The knock sounded again, this time it was louder.

Logan pushed off the couch and opened the aluminum front door.

"Mr. Logan Carr?"

"Yeah?" He peered at the man. No uniform, but it was pretty clear he was the law. "Who are you?"

"I'm Detective Baylor with Tampa PD." He displayed his badge. "I'd like to talk to you about a man I think you know pretty well."

"Well, that didn't take long," Logan replied.

"I'm sorry?"

"The cops harassing me. It didn't take long."

"I'm not here to harass you, Mr. Carr. I'm here to ask you about your association with a man by the name of Julius Hardin."

"The fact that you're here suggests you are already well aware of my former association with Julius."

"Mr. Carr, may I come in?" Detective Baylor pulled his sports coat around him and appeared to suffer from the cold night air.

Logan studied him. "Sure. Why not?" He stepped aside and closed the door behind him. "Although, it isn't much warmer in here, but be my guest." He walked to the refrigerator. "I'd offer you a beer, but I'm not allowed to drink. I have water and Coke."

"Nothing for me, thanks. I won't be here that long."

Logan returned to the sofa. "Have a seat and let's get this over with so I can get back to watching the game."

Baylor sat down. "Late last night, we intercepted a large cocaine shipment coming in from Cove Harbor. And when I say large, I mean, record-breaking."

"Good for you," Logan replied. "What's that got to do with me? I've been out six months. Kept my nose clean and I just moved out of the half-way house into this awesome place. So, I'm not sure why you're coming for me."

"I'm not coming for you," Baylor replied. "But we both know the Southside Runners never really let anyone off the hook."

Logan stared at him with a blank face.

"You did some serious time for Hardin. I can't believe he wouldn't come back at you with a peace offering."

Logan eyed him. The detective clearly didn't know the entire story behind the reason he served time and Julius Hardin hadn't. "You think he came to me asking if I wanted a piece of the action? You're wrong. I don't know shit about a drop. You can check with the house, Dale Meek. He knows I went to work and came home when I was supposed to every day."

"It's important we track down the distribution of the drugs and break the connection to the Columbian cartel."

Logan chuckled. "Good luck with that."

"When was the last time you spoke to Hardin?" Baylor asked.

"You know I'm not allowed to hang with former associates. I haven't talked to him since before I went in."

Baylor nodded. "So you haven't seen or heard from Hardin since back in the day?" He didn't wait for a reply. "I hope you aren't lying to me, Logan. Serious heat is coming down on the Southside Runners."

"You got questions about them, why don't you just ask Julius yourself?" He held the detective's gaze. "Ah. You can't find him, can you? And you think I know where he is. Look, Detective, if you read my file then you'd know the deal I made. And if you think Julius Hardin would come to me after that, then you must be buyin' what they sellin'."

"I'm just trying to help you out, son." Baylor pushed off the couch. "I thank you for your time and I'm sure I'll be seeing you again soon." He stopped and turned back to Logan. "You hear from your boy; you be sure and give me a call."

Logan showed him out. "He's not my boy and you're sniffing up the wrong tree, Detective Baylor. I'm done with all that shit. I paid my dues. I served my time. You got no right to come harass me like this."

Baylor stepped outside onto the wooden landing. "I'm not harassing you, son. I'm trying to save you from getting lured back in."

"Sure you are. Good luck to you then." Logan closed the door and walked to his kitchenette. A pack of smokes lay on the counter and he shook it until one raised up. With his lips, he pulled it out and reached for the lighter. The flame tickled the end of the cigarette and Logan took a long drag. He exhaled a thick puff of smoke and stared into the room. "Son of a bitch."

———

Downtown Tampa was still adorned in lights of gold and silver as the holiday season drew to a close. The air was crisp and the breeze coming off the bay sent goosebumps crawling on Allison's skin. Wearing a gray sweater with leggings and black boots, she regretted not bringing a coat.

Shane opened the door to the restaurant. "After you, ladies. Let's have ourselves a drink to celebrate the newest detective agency in the city."

Allison walked inside. "The three of us can have a drink." She turned to Lucy who trailed her. "Sorry, kid. It'll have to be ginger-ale for you."

"Gee, thanks. I'm so excited," Lucy replied.

"Don't rush these things, Lucy," Charlie began. "What I wouldn't give to be 19 again."

Shane followed them inside and approached the podium. "Table for four, please."

"Right this way." The host emerged from behind the podium

and led the way. "Will this do?" He pointed to a round table near the back.

"Fine by me." Shane turned to Allison. "You good with this?"

"Sure." She took a seat.

Charlie sat next to her. "Will the kids be joining us, Alli?"

"Nolan is meeting with a prospective manager. Leo's with him. He needs to get signed before he starts in the Spring."

"What about Micah? She's still home from school, right?" Charlie continued.

"Yep. She's home. But she's out with her friends tonight trying to squeeze in a few last visits before going back to school."

Shane sipped on a glass of water. "How's all that going? Her being home, I mean."

"It's been hit and miss," Allison began. "She hasn't said much. Claims to be excited about the agency but hasn't come down to see the office yet."

"In all fairness, we did just open it up today," Lucy said.

"Sure. Yeah, I know. I'm giving her the benefit of the doubt." Allison picked up the menu. "I'm starved and would love a glass of wine."

Shane traded glances with Charlie before he shifted the conversation. "So, Lucy. You're still on Christmas break, too, isn't that right?"

"I am. Which is great with the office getting set up and everything. Perfect timing. But I'll have some tough decisions to make now that we're up and running."

"You haven't decided if you'll be returning to school?" Shane asked.

"Not yet. It sort of depends on the workload here," Lucy replied.

Lucy had quickly become an integral part of the agency. Without her, there would be no agency because Allison had no clients. Several of Lucy's father's clients had agreed to call them up if they needed anything. Right now, however, it didn't appear that anyone needed them. And now Allison had a two-year lease on an office, utility bills and salaries to pay. Someone better need something fast or they weren't going to be in business for very long.

Shane clinked his pint glass with his fork. "Attention. Attention, please." He raised the glass. "Today marks the first day ACL Investigative Services opens its doors. Allison Hart, Charlie Wells, and Lucy Boyce. You three made this happen and you should all be proud. Allison, this was your baby and you made it through the training, the tests and most importantly, pulled it all together. I'm so proud of all of you and I hope this marks the beginning of a new phase in our relationship. To ACL Investigative Services and to Allison Hart. Cheers."

"Cheers." Allison raised her glass and toasted to her friends. "This was our success. Not just mine. And I can't wait to get started."

———

LOGAN STEPPED OUT OF HIS TRUCK AND WALKED UP THE driveway of the house he moved out of only hours earlier. It was almost midnight, and all was quiet in the old rundown neighborhood. He tossed away his cigarette, pushed his long hair into place, and shoved his hands in the pockets of his black hoodie. The front door was only steps away and the porch light was off. He knocked. "Come on, man. Come on." He could see his breath in the cool night air as he stood beneath the overhang.

The porch light flickered on and the door opened until the pull chain drew taut. "Dude, what the hell are you doing here?"

"Dale, I need to talk to you. Can I come in?"

17

Dale closed the door and unlatched the chain before opening it again. "Get inside. It's cold as hell out there."

Logan walked in. "Man, I need some help."

"Christ, Logan, you just moved out today. What the hell happened?"

"I know he came here first, Dale. How else would he have known where I moved to? I'm not pissed. I just need some help."

"Right. Yeah." He closed the door and started into the kitchen, pulling his robe around his skinny frame. "You want some coffee or something?"

"Sure. Thanks." Logan followed him. "When did that detective show up today?"

"Not long after you left. An hour, maybe." Dale started a pot of coffee. "He was going to talk to your parole officer, and I thought maybe it was best not to alert her. So I told him where you moved to. I'm sorry, man."

"Don't be. Like you said, he would've found out anyway. Listen, you remember the cop that busted me?"

"Boyce, wasn't it?" Dale placed a mug of steaming coffee in front of Logan.

"That's right. Detective Tommy Boyce."

"What about him?" Dale asked.

"He helped me cut a deal with the D.A.'s office," Logan replied. "Boyce had some contact there. I can't remember, but anyway, it reduced my sentence by a few years."

"Right."

"When they let me out and I came here, I remember getting a call from him. I never bothered to return it, thinking, what the hell, right? But now I'm like maybe I should have. I'm wondering if he can help me 'cause I'm pretty sure this detective—the one who knocked on my door earlier tonight—I think someone told him I'm still talking to Julius Hardin."

Dale shook his head and thin strands of hair stuck to his stubbly beard. "No way, man. Julius is bad news."

"No shit. I told Detective Baylor I haven't had anything to do with him since back in the day. He didn't believe me though. Said some big drug shipment was intercepted and the Southside Runners were supposed to distribute the drugs."

"Damn. Wouldn't surprise me if Julius had his hands in that deal," Dale replied.

"Wouldn't come to me as no surprise either," Logan said.

"What's any of this have to do with you and that Detective Boyce?"

"When I was arrested, Boyce and his partner tried to get Julius, but they didn't have enough. I gave them what I could, but you know. Maybe Boyce would like a second chance and he could help keep me out of the other detective's sights in the process."

"Whatever you have to do, man. You gotta protect yourself. These guys, Julius and his crew, they're dangerous. You been inside five years and he's only gotten stronger. But you know, the cops don't have anything on you. Maybe it's best you let this lie."

"Nah, man. You didn't see the look on Baylor's face. He's made up his mind already. I think he'll try to get me to help him bag Julius. He won't care if he throws the net over me too. I'm just an ex-drug dealer scum bag."

"That ain't who you are no more, man," Dale said.

"Doesn't matter. I gotta do something. I'll try to get in touch with Detective Boyce and see what he can do to help." Logan stood. "Thanks for the coffee. I should let you get back to sleep. Sorry to come so late. I just needed to talk to someone."

"Hey, you do me a favor and keep me in the loop on this, yeah?" Dale said.

"You know it."

After Logan left, Dale grabbed his phone and typed a message.

"We might have some trouble with Logan Carr and a detective on his ass. Might need some help on this one."

The text message was sent to a man by the name of Sam Childers who ran a private subcontracting firm that operated the half-way house. A reply quickly arrived. *"Let's meet tomorrow. Fill me in then."*

———

HAILEY CRUZ WALKED INTO THE STATIONHOUSE TO THE aroma of coffee and donuts. The 22-year-old willowy woman looked older than her age. Drug use tended to have that effect on people. Hailey had been clean for the better part of 5 years, mostly since her now ex-boyfriend, Logan, had been in prison. Now that he was out, he called on her for help. And the money she had kept hidden for him.

Hailey had moved on long ago, opting not to wait for Logan and was now married with a 2-year-old little girl. But she held a soft spot for him. He had been her first love. Probably true love at that. But they were young and stupid and they both knew that they weren't right for each other. Now they were no longer clouded by their addictions.

She wanted to help him, though, and even felt obligated to help when he called on her early this morning. He needed to know how to contact Detective Tommy Boyce. It had been six months since he had heard from the detective and Logan had no idea if he was still with Tampa Police, but it was his only lead. However, walking inside the police station while on parole and after being visited by another detective, well, Logan didn't think going inside himself would do him any favors. Word might get back to Detective Baylor and Logan didn't need to raise any more red flags. So he called on his ex and here she was, ready to help.

"Good morning." Hailey approached the desk. "Can you tell me if Detective Boyce is in today?"

"I'm sorry, who?" Officer Cook sat behind her desk and scratched at the ponytail pulled tight at the back of her head.

"Um, Detective Tommy Boyce," Hailey said again.

Cook turned to a nearby colleague. "Hey, Fletch, you know Detective Tommy Boyce? Does he work in this district?"

"Boyce? Oh man, he hasn't worked here in years." The officer approached Hailey. "You're looking for Tommy Boyce?"

"Yes, sir." Hailey grew nervous from the growing attention.

"I'm real sorry, ma'am, but um, he passed a few months' back. I mean, he retired from here and started up a P.I. agency long before that. I went to his funeral. Heart attack. How do you know him?"

"Through a friend." Hailey felt her pulse rise. "So, he's gone?"

"Yes, ma'am."

"Well, thank you. I don't want to take up any more of your time." Hailey turned and hurried toward the exit.

"You know," Fletch began. "I hear his daughter was taking over the family business. You could touch base with her if you need more answers."

Hailey turned back. "Do you know her name?"

Officer Cook shot Fletch a concerned look before turning to Hailey. "I don't think we have that information handy."

"Okay. Thank you both for your help." Hailey smiled but on turning back, the smile faded, and she continued toward the doors of the station nearly running into someone. "Excuse me."

"Whoa. Hey, no problem." Shane blocked the tackle. "You okay?"

"I'm fine. I'm so sorry." She pushed through the doors.

"She in a hurry or something?" Shane asked Officer Cook.

"She was looking for Tommy Boyce. You had something to do with him last year, didn't you?"

He whipped around and peered at the exit as Hailey walked outside. "Yeah. Who is she?"

"Didn't give a name," Cook replied. "Hey, where you going?"

Shane was already through the doors and hustled to catch Hailey before she pulled away. "Excuse me, miss?" He jogged toward her. "Miss? You're looking for Tommy Boyce?"

Hailey stopped at her car and turned to Shane. "Yeah. They said he died."

"He did. About 4 months ago. Why are you looking for him? Was he an old friend or something?"

"No, sir. I'm sorry. I clearly made a mistake." She inserted her key into the driver's side door.

"No, wait. Hang on. What's your name?" Shane asked.

"Hailey Cruz."

"Ms. Cruz, why are you looking for Tommy? You're not in any trouble, are you?"

"No. It's nothing like that." She sighed. "I was just doing a friend a favor. He's looking for Detective Boyce."

"Well, Tommy retired a few years ago and started his own agency before he passed away last Fall. This friend of yours, why was he looking for Tommy?"

"Look, I don't want to get anyone in trouble..."

"Who's talking about trouble? Your friend obviously doesn't know that Tommy passed away."

"They said something about his daughter taking over the business?" Hailey asked.

"Sort of. It just so happens I know his daughter pretty well and the people who run the agency are helping out some of Tommy's old clients. If you'd like, I can put your friend in touch with them. If you think it would help."

Hailey studied Shane before continuing. "I guess that would be all right. Um, can I get your number and have him call you?"

"You got it." Shane pulled out his wallet and handed her a business card. "That's my cell. Your friend can call me any time."

She peered at the card. "Thank you, Detective Sullivan. I should probably get going."

"Sure. Yeah. You have a nice day, Ms. Cruz." Shane watched as she pulled away and he picked up his phone. "Hey, Allison. Listen, I might have a lead on some work."

3

DHS Agent Erik Markham entered the conference room. "Sorry, I'm late. There's coffee in the back if anyone's interested." He sat down at the table where the rest of the taskforce had already arrived. "Where are we at with identifying known associates of Julius Hardin, or Hardin himself?"

Detective Baylor pulled upright in his chair. "I spoke with an old associate of his named Logan Carr. He was released from prison six months ago after a plea deal was bargained down to a five-year stint for drug smuggling."

"Sounds promising," Markham replied.

"He just moved out of a half-way house and into a trailer park in the north part of the city. I paid him a visit last night to see if he had heard from Hardin recently."

"And?" Markham sipped on his coffee.

"Says he hasn't talked to Hardin in years. Insists he's trying to keep his nose clean and move past his incarceration."

"But you don't think so?" FBI Agent Dave Reddick was in his

mid-thirties and a rising star at the Bureau. He monitored gang activity in the city and had been at the site collecting evidence just after the bust. "Any idea why Logan Carr would risk going back to see Julius Hardin? It would likely be a parole violation if he had." He pushed his hands through his thinning brown hair and the lines on his high forehead deepened.

"Hard to say. Guys like Logan Carr don't usually stay on the straight and narrow for long. They see how hard it is to get a decent job. Figure they could make more money going back to their old ways. It's a vicious cycle. Now, I can't say for sure Carr is that guy, but I'm going to keep an eye on him. He and Hardin, from what I gather, were pretty close back in the day. And, come to find out, Hardin might be looking for payback since Carr cut himself a sweet deal that led to him serving less time while he pointed the finger at Hardin. Something I wasn't initially aware of when I made contact."

"Did it hurt Hardin, though? Enough to warrant said payback?" Agent Markham asked.

"I'm still looking into what the deal entailed. I have to pull the old case files. But in the meantime, I'd like to keep an eye on Logan Carr. See where he goes, who he talks to. He served serious time for drug trafficking. He has to know who's still in the game and what game they're running."

Reddick crossed his long legs as he shifted in his chair. "A lot's changed in the five years since he's been on the inside."

"Not as much as you might think. Coke has made a serious comeback." Baylor glanced at DEA Agent Pierce, who had thus far kept quiet. "I'm not the only one who sees that. The only difference now is how they're getting it here. The cartels keep tweaking how they're building these narco-subs and pretty soon, we won't be able to detect them at all."

"Then it's in our interest to stay on top of the distributors," Reddick added.

"If Julius Hardin knows his old buddy is out, and I'm sure he does, then I have no doubt he'll send people to him. If that happens, then I'll have leverage to use against Carr," Baylor added.

"Good. You keep working that angle," Markham said. "In the meantime, Pierce, what have you learned from your team?"

"Word's out about the bust and most think it was a snitch inside the Southside Runners. Which presents a bigger problem for me."

"Are your people protected?" Markham asked.

"So far. We'll keep working to find out if and when the cartel will trust the Runners to make another pass. They might be on the lookout for a new partnership. These gangs talk to each other," Pierce added. "According to my operative inside a rival gang, he says there's been a whole lot of chatter about the Runners."

"He came through for us on the tip that led to the bust," Baylor said. "You think it's time to pull him out? You don't want to risk exposure."

"No way he'll want out. Not now, when so much is going down."

"Then let's get back to work," Markham said. "We have a lot of ground to cover."

———

ALLISON UNLOCKED THE DOOR TO THE OFFICE. "WELL, today's our first official day." She walked inside and flipped on the lights.

Three desks were positioned inside the rectangular room. Allison's desk was in the far left corner nearest to the window. Not that it was much of a view. She overlooked the parking lot. Then there was Charlie's desk toward the middle, against the back wall. And finally, Lucy's workspace. Her desk was on the right nearest the door. The place still needed a personal touch and the smell hadn't quite cleared out. But the lease was affordable.

"Our first full day." Charlie cupped her hand around her ear. "Nope. Don't hear any phones ringing."

"Give it time. They'll come." Allison dropped her things onto her desk. "Let me go put on a pot of coffee."

"I'll do that," Lucy replied. "It's closest to me anyway."

"Are you sure? I don't want you to think you're the gopher around here because you're not," Allison said.

"I know I'm not. I want to." Lucy walked to the cabinet where the coffee maker sat. Below it was a bar-sized refrigerator. "We should put water and stuff in here for potential clients."

"Good idea," Charlie said. "Maybe some vodka too. Although, that'll just be for me."

"Not a chance. I'll want a piece of that action, too," Allison replied.

"Then I have nothing left to teach you, Grasshopper." Charlie smiled before dropping onto her chair. "What's on the docket for today?"

"Interestingly enough, I got a call from Shane earlier this morning. He might have something for us." Allison pulled out her chair to sit. "He's coming here in a little while to talk about it. But he's not sure if the person will call or not."

"So he's coming here with nothing?" Charlie asked.

"Not nothing. I just said..."

"You said he thought he had something. Not that he actually had something." Charlie switched on her computer. "I'm just saying. If he's got a lead, fantastic. If not, then he's coming here for you."

"What is that supposed to mean?" Allison asked.

"It means, ever since we started this thing, he's been in constant contact with you. Haven't you picked up on that?"

"I don't know. No." Allison creased her brow. "He's excited for us. And frankly, it's good for us to have someone on the force who can help us out. I won't turn him away."

"I have a feeling he's counting on that," Charlie replied.

"You're crazy. But then I already knew that."

Lucy handed Allison her coffee. "Here you go."

"Thanks, Lucy." Allison noticed the look on her face. "You think she's right, don't you?"

Lucy shrugged. "What do I know? I'm just a kid."

"Oh sure, use the kid card now when I need you to back me up," Charlie said.

"Well, Charlie might have a point, but who knows? I haven't been on a date in like a year. I have no room to talk when it comes to guys," Lucy replied.

The door opened, capturing their attention.

"Good morning, ladies." Shane walked inside. "Oh, coffee. Mind if I grab a cup?" He walked to the pot.

"Good morning, Shane." Charlie glanced at Allison with a toothy grin. "Alli says you might have a lead for us?"

"As a matter of fact, I do." He poured coffee in a mug and started back toward Allison's desk.

"See? I told you," Allison replied to Charlie before offering Shane a pleasant smile. "Take a seat. Tell us all about it."

"How about I do you one better? I'll let him tell you about it." Shane turned toward the door that was still open. "Come on in, Logan."

Logan Carr walked into the office. He kept his eyes on the floor letting his dark blonde hair dangle in his face.

"Mr. Carr. Welcome." Allison approached him. "I'm Allison Hart. Over here is Charlie Wells and this is Lucy Boyce."

"Boyce?" He looked at her. "You're Tommy's daughter."

"Um, yes, I am. You knew my dad?"

"Why don't you come in and have a seat." Allison led him to her desk. "Charlie, Lucy, grab a couple chairs and let's huddle up over here." She turned back to Logan. "Please excuse the furnishings. We just moved in here and don't yet have a conference table."

"No problem. Thanks for seeing me," he replied.

"Our pleasure." Allison sat down. "I'm afraid Detective Sullivan hasn't filled us in on why you've come to us."

"I thought you should hear it directly from him," Shane said.

"Okay, then," Charlie began. "Tell us what it is you need, Mr. Carr."

He shot a glance at Lucy. "Detective Boyce arrested me for drug trafficking almost 6 years ago. I spent the last five in prison."

Lucy appeared concerned. "Okay. Why would you come looking for him now?"

"Cause he tried to help me. I know it sounds funny, but I think your dad felt bad for me. I got caught up with some shady people when I was just coming out of high school. Don't get me wrong, I knew what I was doing was bad. But it didn't stop me. Anyway, Detective Boyce busted me. Kept saying I should give up whoever was running the show because I'd be the one doing the time otherwise. But what I had—it wasn't enough."

"This person he wanted you to give up. What was his name?" Allison asked.

"Julius Hardin."

"He's the suspected leader of a gang called the Southside Runners," Shane began. "They're known distributors of most of the coke that comes in from Columbia—for the southern part of the state anyway. There was a huge bust the day before yesterday. The Drug Enforcement taskforce is handling it. A detective upstairs in Major Crimes is working it with them."

"Their sources tell them it was the Southside Runners that were supposed to pick up the shipment that night," Logan added. "They came looking for me since they knew I used to call myself one of them."

"Do they think you've been in contact with Julius Hardin?" Charlie asked.

"Yes. But I swear to you I haven't. I have a job now. I got my own place. I'm cleaning up my act. I don't want anything to do with Julius Hardin or his crew. I don't know why Detective Baylor tracked me down. I didn't do anything."

"He thinks you can help him," Shane said. "I don't know Baylor personally since we aren't in the same department, but his reputation precedes him. And he's on the Drug Enforcement Taskforce. It's kind of a big deal. All the agencies have a hand in it. Just to give you a little background, I was aware of the bust. Hell, everyone was. And they brought in the four-man crew—Columbians—running the drugs to shore. One of them talked and corroborated that the Southside Runners were scheduled to pick up the shipment that night, had they made it to shore. Everyone's looking for the suspected leader, Julius Hardin."

"That's why I wanted to see Detective Boyce. I figured he could keep the cops off my back, you know? They got plenty of people. They don't need me." Logan looked away. "I'm sorry Boyce is gone. He was a good man."

"Thank you," Lucy replied.

"What is it you think we can do for you, Logan?" Allison pressed on. "We're a private investigative agency. Lucy was good enough to reach out to Tommy's clientele and let them know we're here to help them out. But what I'm hearing from you. Well, I'm not so sure we can help, as much as I hate to admit it."

"Before you shoot him down, I think you can help." Shane

turned to Logan. "You need someone to prove you haven't been in contact with the Southside Runners or Hardin, right?"

Logan nodded.

"Okay. And you also need someone to prove you've been where you say you've been. Work, the half-way house and so on."

"Sure," Logan replied.

"Well, that will require some details you can get for yourself, but with the help of ACL, they can gather character statements from your co-workers and others at the half-way house. They can also make sure Detective Baylor doesn't try to use you as bait."

"How can we stop that?" Allison asked Shane.

"By making sure Baylor doesn't drum up anything to hold over his head in exchange for cooperation. Have a solid case in favor of his personal and professional ethics. If Baylor tries to pull the rug out from under him, you'll have plenty of evidence to disprove whatever he might've drummed up," Shane replied.

"Let me get this straight," Charlie began. "We lay it out that you haven't talked to any of your former cohorts. Prove you're telling the truth about your whereabouts since leaving the pen. Talk to a few people and make sure the cops don't find a reason to use you to lure Julius Hardin out into the open. Does that sound about right?"

"Sounds about right, I guess," Logan replied.

"Well then, I'd say that was doable. Wouldn't you, Alli?"

———

LOGAN STEPPED OUT OF THE CORRIDOR OF THE ACL OFFICE building and surveyed the parking lot before making his way to his truck.

Detective Baylor gazed through the windshield of his car and spotted his target. "He's leaving."

"That didn't take long. Who do you suppose he was meeting with?" FBI Agent Reddick sat in the passenger seat and looked on.

"We'll have to find out." Baylor furrowed his brow. "Wait. Who's that guy? He's trying to get Carr's attention."

"Isn't that the guy who we saw pull in about the same time as Carr?" Reddick asked.

"Maybe. Let's see where this goes," Baylor added.

The men watched Carr as the other man approached him and the two began speaking. Detective Baylor turned to his FBI counterpart. "It looks friendly enough. They must know each other."

Reddick held up his phone and took pictures of the two standing at Carr's vehicle. "Are we following him or what?"

"Carr, yes. We'll figure out who the other guy is. I'll tell you one thing; he looks like a cop."

"Then it should be easy to identify him," Reddick replied. "The other guy's leaving. What do you want to do?"

Baylor pulled his seatbelt across his chest. "We're staying on Carr. I'm not letting him out of my sight." He waited for Carr to pull away and started to follow.

"Why do you think Logan Carr, after a five-year stint, would even consider getting back into the game?" Reddick asked.

"I'm not sure he would, but Hardin might not give him a choice," Baylor replied. "Hell, I have no idea if Hardin's even been in touch with him. But if he tries to, we'll be right there watching."

"Look, we both know that the Columbians aren't going to take this lightly. They'll take out everyone. Hardin, and his entire entourage. If we don't find him before they do, this will all have been for nothing and another gang will replace the Southside Runners."

"And we'll be starting from scratch," Baylor said. "Yeah, I get that. Don't worry. We'll get to Hardin before the cartel does. Even if we have to use that kid to do it."

―――――――

SHANE RETURNED TO THE OFFICE AND SAT DOWN ACROSS from Allison's desk. "So? Did you three talk about it?"

Allison looked at her colleagues and then to Shane. "Setting aside the aspects of this case, drug trafficking, dangerous gangs, Columbian cartels. How is Logan going to pay us? Look, I'm all for helping those in need and this man is undoubtedly in need, but we're running a business. We don't have the luxury of doing this pro bono."

Charlie meandered toward them. "Alli has a point. Logan's in trouble. The kind that brings a whole new level of problems. I know what I said earlier about taking this on, but we did talk it over when you were outside with him. We need to be compensated."

"If I told you he had the money would that settle it?" Shane asked.

Allison turned her sights to Lucy. "This man was arrested by your dad. And yet he wanted to turn to him for help."

"He trusted my dad," Lucy said. "That means something."

"It does. So, if he could pay us and we do our best to keep down the costs, would that make a difference to you two? With the understanding that there is an elevated risk for us."

Charlie shook her head. "Why couldn't this just be some guy spying on his ex or something?"

Allison snickered. "Trial by fire, Charlie. Trial by fire."

"I suppose it would just be pulling records, which I know Shane over here could help us out with," Charlie began. "Getting his employment history and attendance at work. Basically, just seeing to it that we have enough evidence to hand over to the detective who's interested in Logan to show that he's been keeping to the terms of his probation, making it harder for him to try to rail-road this kid."

"Right. That's all this is," Allison said. "We have no reason to get involved in the other stuff. The Southside Runners or whoever. We'll leave that to the cops."

"And you say he has money?" Charlie asked Shane.

"He does. Logan made a plan for himself for when he got out. Money won't be a problem for him."

Allison nodded. "Well, then, if you two are good with it, I say let's move forward."

"I'm good," Charlie said.

"Me too," Lucy added.

"Then ACL Investigative Services has its first client."

———

DETECTIVE BAYLOR'S CAR ROLLED TO A STOP SEVERAL FEET behind Logan's old white pickup. "You gotta be shitting me?" He turned to Agent Reddick. "What'd I tell you, huh? I knew it."

"Before you jump the gun, let's be sure about what we're seeing right now."

"He's sitting in front of the house of one of Hardin's guys. I know because I already checked out this place. Got nothing from it. Logan Carr is making the rounds, Reddick. I'm telling you."

They waited a few houses down the street inside a neglected neighborhood and peered at the house ahead.

"It's one of his guys, not Hardin himself," Reddick added.

"Well, how much more direct do you want him to be?" Baylor watched as Logan remained in his truck, looking at the house. "Come on, man. I know you want to go inside."

"No way is he going to risk it," Reddick continued. "He can't be that stupid. He has to know we're watching him."

"Maybe he does. And maybe he's proving a point," Baylor replied.

"And what point might that be?" Reddick squinted as he gazed through the windshield. "Someone's coming out. It isn't Hardin."

Baylor reached for his phone and took pictures as the man approached Logan's truck. "Seems a friendly enough convo going on. They look like old pals."

"Now the guy's leaving and Carr is getting back in his truck. That's it. Conversation over," Reddick said. "What now?"

Baylor kept his eyes on the truck and waited for Carr to pull away. "We keep following." As he started, still several feet away, concern masked his face. "Wait. Did he just look at us?"

Reddick laughed. "He's giving us the finger, so I guess we've been made."

"Nah, man. Carr was making a point. He's showing us who to look at."

"What do you mean?" Reddick pressed on.

"I mean, whoever that guy was who came out of that house, Carr was telling us we should be looking at him." The detective dropped back and lost sight of the truck. "Guess we better find out who he was."

"If that's the case, maybe we're looking at this kid all wrong. Maybe we can use him to help us identify all known associates of Julius Hardin's."

Baylor continued along the road. "Kid's been out of the game for 5 years. He might still know some of the big players though. Let's see what he can offer us."

4

When department brass called in a detective it usually meant one of two things. That detective was about to be promoted or fired. Shane "Sully" Sullivan had just been summoned to Lieutenant Loretta Cooper's office. Shane had been working hard to prove himself this past year as a detective in Investigations and Support. The goal was to be assigned to the Major Crimes Unit.

As he started toward the lieutenant's office, he tried to recall anything that might dissuade the lieutenant from promoting him. Okay, maybe he hadn't had the experience just yet, but he never missed a day and had zero unsolved cases. That had to stand for something. At the very least, it should mean his current job was safe.

"Hey, L.T. You wanted to see me?" Shane started inside when he noticed a man in the guest chair. "Oh, I'm sorry. Should I come back?"

"No. Come on in, Sully," said Lieutenant Cooper. "This is Detective Anton Baylor. He works in Major Crimes, Narcotics."

"Oh. Detective Baylor." Shane offered his hand. "Nice to meet you. I've heard the name, but..."

"Detective Sully, is it?" Baylor returned the greeting.

"It's Sullivan, but everyone calls me Sully. What can I do for you?"

"Have a seat, Sully." The lieutenant gestured to a chair next to Baylor. "Baylor here is working on that big drug seizure that went down the other night."

"Oh, right. Yeah, I heard about that. Biggest one in something like six years?"

"Something like that. I'm assigned to the Drug Enforcement Taskforce with Homeland Security, the DEA and the FBI," Baylor replied.

"Congrats. That's a huge collar." Shane shifted in his seat. "What do you need from me? I work in Investigations and Support. That's a far cry from drug busts."

"That it is," Cooper said. "That's why Baylor wants to know why you were meeting with a man currently under surveillance for his association with the Southside Runners who, incidentally, were the intended distributors of the drugs from that bust."

Shane's brow knitted and he cocked his head. "I'm sorry. Who are we talking about here?"

"Sully. Is it okay if I call you Sully?" Baylor asked.

Shane nodded.

"Sully, I saw you with the man myself and so did FBI Agent Reddick from the Tampa Field Office. You were coming out of some office building and had a little chat with him. How do you know him?"

"Look, I'm not trying to sound like a jerk here, but can you give me a name? I talk to a lot of people."

Baylor turned in his chair to face Shane and his expression

hardened. "I'm not screwing around. How the hell do you know Logan Carr?"

"Sully. Come on. We're all on the same team," the lieutenant said. "Tell the man what you know."

"Oh, Carr. Right, yeah. Funny enough, I met him completely by chance. A friend of his came into the station looking for Detective Tommy Boyce."

"Boyce?" Cooper said. "He hasn't worked here in years and he passed a while ago."

"That was what I told the woman," Shane replied.

"What was her name?" Baylor asked.

"Um, I think it was. Oh hell, now what was her name?" Shane rubbed his chin.

Baylor shot around to the lieutenant. "Lieutenant Cooper, is this how you run your detectives?"

"Sully. Answer the man."

Shane peered at his boss and then back to Baylor. "She said her name was Hailey Cruz. She was a friend of the man looking for Tommy."

"And that man was Logan Carr," Baylor said.

"Yes, sir."

"So how did it turn out that you were talking with him earlier today outside that building?"

"He was asking for some guidance and I referred him to a friend of mine." Shane raised his hands. "That's all I know."

"Somehow, I think there's more to the story," Baylor said. "Sully, your lieutenant's right. We're on the same team. I'm tracking Carr to see if he goes back to his old ways. Visits his old friends. That sort of thing. You feel me?"

"Oh, I feel you." Shane flashed a phony grin.

"Good. Then you know how important it is that I understand Carr's intentions and if he plans on making any visits to his old cohort, Julius Hardin. He's the man in charge of the Southside Runners. We've been on the lookout for him too. Although, that could very well change if the cartel has a say in the matter. Believe me, they're plenty pissed off about their shipment being seized."

"So, you're not out to get Carr?" Shane asked.

"What do you mean, out to get him?" Baylor replied.

"I mean, look, I know how the game is played. I know you'll do what you have to do to get your man, regardless of who else you take down."

Baylor smiled and nodded. "I see you have no idea who Logan Carr really is." He pushed off the chair. "Because if you did, you would know he's a bad apple and you wouldn't be defending him." He turned to Lieutenant Cooper. "I thank you for your time, Lieutenant. I do hope I can count on your department's continued cooperation."

"Whatever we can do to help, Detective Baylor. Say hello to Lieutenant Tacada."

"Sure thing. Just do me a favor and keep your boy over here away from my suspects."

"Oh, Carr is a suspect now?" Shane interrupted.

Baylor glared at him. "You have a good day, Sully. I'm sure we'll be in contact again soon."

Shane waited for Baylor to disappear and turned to the lieutenant. "I didn't solicit Logan Carr, Lieutenant. I hope you understand that. He came looking for help, not the other way around."

"Why do you suppose he was looking for help from Tommy Boyce in the first place?" Cooper replied.

"Because Boyce believed in him. And I think Logan's looking for someone to believe in him now."

Lucy was assigned to pull Tommy's old files from his time at the Tampa Police Department. Tommy had kept copies of most of his case files from those days and she had already put them in a storage facility along with the files from his P.I. office.

Tommy had ensured Lucy's well-being after his death. The will she discovered disclosed that the house would go to her and the life insurance policy would pay off the mortgage and give her a small cushion to help launch her into a career after college.

She ultimately decided to put on hold school for the time being. At least until she figured out her place inside Allison Hart's agency. Over the past few months, Lucy had grown close to Allison and her family. Nolan had taken her out a few times, just as friends, of course. And she still had her own friends. But they couldn't understand why she decided to hold off on school. Then again, no one who hadn't been through the loss of both parents could understand how it changed her. She was alone. Sure, there was family in New York, but Tampa was her home. And the money her dad left gave her the opportunity to go to work with Allison and accept a small beginning salary, which would increase with each job they drew in.

The metal door for the climate-controlled storage unit unlatched and Lucy flipped the light switch. Boxes stacked on top of boxes lined the walls. Old computers from Tommy's office that had finally been released by the cops lay on a folding table, and filing cabinets were pressed against a back wall. For an outsider, it was chaos inside here, but for Lucy, she knew exactly where everything was. This was her system and it was time to find information on Logan Carr. They needed the job to get the agency off on the right foot, but this could prove dangerous and they needed to be armed with every bit of information Tommy had. They also needed proof that Tommy had offered help to Logan, as Logan had insisted.

The files from Tommy's days as a detective were in the boxes on the left wall all the way at the back. There were 15 of them. He served with the Tampa Police only a few years before he retired. The early retirement came along with the realization that his wife was dying of cancer.

Lucy didn't have any of the files from his days as a cop in New York, though his brother might. Right now, she didn't feel they were necessary. Lucy was on a mission to find the case on Logan Carr. And as she stepped back to view the labels on each box, she found the one.

"It should be in here." Lucy peeled away the boxes and worked her way down to the one she needed. "Right here." She set it on the folding table and sliced open the tape that sealed it and opened its flaps. The inside was packed with manila file folders, each with a label tab at the top. Lucy thumbed through the files marked TPD, 2012. It was one of three, and was marked A through F.

"Logan Carr. This is what I need." Lucy pulled out the file and opened it on the table. She noted the picture resting on top of the other papers. It was of the same man who arrived at the agency this morning, only this version was six years younger. He looked like a high schooler.

Lucy double checked the rest of the box to make sure there wasn't another Logan Carr file inside. She returned the box to its original location and left the storage room, securing the lock once again.

As she returned to her car, Lucy picked up her phone. "Hey Charlie, it's me. I'm on my way back to the office. I have the file."

"Awesome. I'll tell Alli. See you soon." Charlie ended the call as she sat at her desk. "Lucy's on her way back. She found the file."

"Perfect. I have no doubt Tommy would've kept notes in that file that we won't find in any criminal background check."

"No doubt," Charlie replied. "Oh, hey, what did you find out about Nolan? Did he sign with that manager?"

Allison smiled. "He did. Leo drove a hard bargain and got it done."

"Well, I suppose you have to give him credit," Charlie began. "At least he fought for his kid."

"He always has," Allison replied.

"I wonder why Micah still holds you responsible for the divorce then? You'd have thought Leo would've stepped up and made clear who should be held accountable."

"I don't lay all the blame at Leo's feet," Allison replied. "And now that Micah has been home for a little while, I feel like we've been able to work it out—some. She's a stubborn kid, but she has a good heart."

"Stubborn like you?" Charlie smiled.

———

THE SAYING "HEADS WILL ROLL," TOOK ON NEW MEANING when it came from a Columbian drug lord. Said drug lord might not fully understand the idiom and perhaps take the phrase too literally. That was an almost certainty. Which was why Julius Hardin was currently keeping a low profile. He wasn't directly responsible for the seizure of 6,000 pounds of Columbian cocaine, but his people were. Someone talked to the cops. Someone knew that shipment was going to be dropped at Cove Harbor the night before last. It was now up to Hardin to sniff out the virus before it infected the entire body.

"Have you tracked down everyone?" Hardin asked.

Mateo Figueroa was Hardin's right-hand man and appeared reluctant to answer the question. "They're all playing dumb, Jules. But we both know someone's lying."

Hardin meandered inside the warehouse that, by day, was used to ship machine parts from China. By night, it was where his people kept the cocaine shipments and divvied them up among the sellers whose territories covered the southern part of Florida.

"What about the cartel members who were arrested? Have our people talked to them?" Julius asked. "Maybe they know something."

"They're all being held by the Feds and the Feds are keeping a tight rein on them. They know what would happen if the cartel guys were released into gen pop."

"They'd be dead in minutes." Julius tossed his cigarette to the ground and smashed the butt with the heel of his Doc Martens. "They'll send someone else to find out who talked. And if we don't get to them, we're as good as dead too."

"How do you want to move forward, boss?" Mateo asked as he smoothed down his thick black hair.

Julius perched on the edge of his desk. His thin legs crossed, and his palms pressed behind him against the desktop. His receding brown hair that reached his shoulders blew against his hollow cheeks from an open window. "First off, I'm going to have to talk to Esteban. If I don't, he'll think I was in on the bust. I can't have that. Then, he'll want assurances that we've found the mole and fixed the problem." He pushed off the desk. "I need you to find out who talked. I need to know who that is, and I want him dead."

"You got it, boss." Mateo nodded and walked away.

Julius returned to his chair and picked up his cell phone. "I need to get a message to Esteban. It's urgent."

———

THE LOOK ON ALLISON'S FACE SUMMED UP WHAT THE OTHERS were thinking. "The Logan Carr in these files can't be the same man we met with this morning."

Charlie grimaced. "He was not a nice guy. What do you think your dad saw in him, Lucy?"

She shook her head. "After reading this, I'm not sure. There must've been some redeeming qualities that we aren't seeing here."

"Did your dad keep any recordings?" Allison asked. "Like interviews possibly?"

"I don't know. I'm pretty sure I have everything in that storage room. I don't remember seeing any digital recorders."

"Okay." Allison gazed at the ceiling. "You know, I'm wondering if Tommy worked with anyone."

"You mean like a partner?" Lucy asked.

"Yeah. Did he have one during his time with TPD?" Charlie added.

"Well, I do know he kept in contact with a detective by the name of Benny Asher. I think he might be retired too; I don't know. I only heard him mention the man a few times. So if he was his partner, I don't think they were that close."

"What are you thinking, Alli?" Charlie asked.

"Well, if he had a partner during this time, that partner could shed light on Logan Carr. Even if the two weren't that close, Tommy might have confided in him."

"Should we ask Shane to look him up?" Charlie asked.

Allison picked up her phone. "I'm way ahead of you." She waited for the line to answer. "Shane. Hey, listen, is there any way you can look to see if there's a detective still on the force named Benny Asher?" She waited while he spoke. "Lucy recalled the name and we thought maybe Tommy had a partner, or a close cop friend who he talked to about Logan Carr during that time." She nodded. "That would be great. Thanks. Let me know when you find something. Okay, bye." Allison turned back to Charlie and Lucy. "He's going to check it out. It's worth a shot."

"What do you want to do until he gets back to us?" Lucy asked.

"We have Logan's criminal records. Let's get employment verification and I'll go pay a visit to his parole officer."

5

News of the major drug bust had been broadcast on every local and national outlet since yesterday. "The largest in six years," they said. All that proved to Allison was that the drugs were still coming, and the cartels had been emboldened to bring in larger quantities through more sophisticated means.

The opioid crisis was still at the forefront of the country's mind and especially in Florida where enough pills had been distributed over the previous four years to create a state full of addicts. While law enforcement focused on that, the Columbian cartels saw a massive increase in the demand for cocaine. The 1980s called and they wanted their drugs back.

This wasn't exactly what Allison had envisioned for her first official investigation. Dangerous and deadly, the cartels weren't known for their compassion toward anyone involved in their trade. Law enforcement didn't seem to care much for those caught in the middle either. This was the reason Logan Carr came to ACL in the first place. Of course, he'd hoped to find

Tommy Boyce, but figured his daughter would be a suitable replacement.

Allison wanted to fight for Logan, but she needed to learn more about him. She had to make sure they weren't falling for his story like a bunch of neophytes. Even if they were exactly that.

The Tampa Parole Office appeared in the distance and Allison pulled into the parking lot. The late afternoon sun warmed the car and as she stepped outside, the reminder of winter came in the form of chilly gusty winds. She pulled on her thick sweater and walked toward the entrance.

"Hi there. I have an appointment with Parole Officer Rona Clark." She revealed a pleasant smile. "I'm Allison Hart with ACL Investigative Services."

"Of course. She's right over there." The receptionist pointed to a cubicle twenty feet away.

"Thank you." Allison walked in between the maze of workspaces, each with low cubicle walls that hadn't allowed for much privacy. She approached the one with the nameplate, "Rona Clark, Parole Officer."

The woman peered up at her with kind eyes, outlined by dark-rimmed glasses, and a round face with full lips. "You must be Allison Hart." She offered her hand. "I'm Rona Clark. Pleased to meet you. Have a seat. You're here to discuss Logan Carr?"

"I am, yes." Allison sat down. "Thank you for seeing me."

"Absolutely. What would you like to know about him?" She folded her hands and rested them on top of her desk. Her cleavage creased as she leaned in to pay closer attention.

"Well, I understand Mr. Carr is a former convict. He was very forthcoming with details about his past. However..."

"You want to know my take on him?" Rona asked.

"That pretty much sums it up, yes."

"Of course, I am required to disclose only certain aspects of my relationship with Logan Carr. Privacy concerns and all that. Having said that, I can tell you that he is one of the few, and I mean the very few, who I believe has done his best to turn around his life."

"He was released ahead of completing his full seven-year sentence, is that correct?" Allison asked.

"That's right. He was given early release for good behavior. Though he had served five out of his seven-year sentence. Which is why he is on parole and must check in with me on a weekly basis."

"I understand he moved out of the half-way house the other day," Allison began. "Have you seen his place?"

"We prefer not to use the term 'half-way house,' instead referring to them as residential rehabilitation centers. And no, I have not been to his new residence. I tend to keep those visits under wraps since they're supposed to be unannounced."

"Sure."

Rona studied her. "What is it that Logan needs from you, Ms. Hart?"

"Please, call me Allison. I'm not sure how much I can say due to client privileges and such."

"You're not his lawyer," Rona replied.

"No. I suppose not." She felt slightly embarrassed. "What I will say is that there are those out there who believe Logan might go back to his old ways and I don't think they care to find out whether that's true."

"And that's why he came to you?"

"In a round-about way, yes," Allison replied. "He was looking for Detective Tommy Boyce."

"That was the officer who arrested him," Rona replied.

"I understand that was the case, however, Mr. Boyce passed

away a few months ago. His daughter and I work together now. Logan was quite resourceful and managed to find us."

"I see." Rona nodded. "So you're trying to prove that he's been keeping his nose to the grindstone, so to speak? And you've come to me to corroborate his story."

"Yes. I'm building a character assessment."

"There isn't much I can provide to you on a professional level. But I think if Logan is coming to you for help, then he most probably needs it. In my experience, Logan is an honest man, even if he wasn't before. I read his case file. By all accounts, the investigating officer, Detective Boyce, believed Logan got wrapped up with some undesirables. I will say this, the people Logan knew back then are dangerous. He can't afford to get caught up with them again. He won't survive it."

————

It turned out that Detective Benny Asher had only recently retired. This information was gleaned by Shane after offering a favor in return. Said favor was for a woman in the personnel records department who needed a background check on her daughter's boyfriend. Regardless of the ethics involved, Shane obliged, and she proceeded to inform him that Asher was now in hospice living out his final days with lung cancer.

Shane was just about to pay a visit to Asher in the facility. He never was good at these things. Sick people and hospitals, it gave him the heebie-jeebies. It didn't help that as a kid, he was forced to visit his dying grandmother on a daily basis for a month. Each time he saw her, she looked worse and worse and he had nightmares that she would come back and haunt him. He was eight years old. Of course, she never did haunt him and passed away one night in her sleep after her long and painful battle with breast cancer.

"Evening. I'm Detective Sullivan here to see Mr. Asher. I spoke with someone on the phone earlier about it."

"That would've been me." The older woman, who looked like everyone's favorite grandmother, smiled at him. "He's not doing too well tonight, but I told him you was comin'. You can follow me back, Detective." She pushed off the chair with great effort and shuffled around the large reception desk. "I don't know how much help he'll be to you, seeing as how his memory isn't as good as it used to be. Something about all the painkillers they keep him on. Changes a person, you know?"

"Sure. That's okay. I just have a few quick questions for him and anything he can offer will be a great help," Shane replied.

The woman knocked gently on the door. "Hey, Benny? Your visitor is here." She pushed open the door. "Detective Sullivan. I told you about him. You remember?"

Shane followed her inside and the creeping sense of dread fell on his shoulders. He was a grown man now and there was no excuse for feeling this way, but it couldn't be helped. It brought back too many memories.

"I remember. I ain't senile, Louise. Let the man in," Asher replied.

She turned to Shane and raised her brows. "Good luck to you."

Shane nodded and waited for Louise to leave before approaching. "Mr. Asher. Thanks for seeing me."

"What else am I going to do? It ain't like I had dinner plans."

"I guess not," Shane replied.

"Take a seat, kid. I won't bite. You're here about Tommy? How is the old SOB?"

Shane sat down with his hands tucked into his jacket pockets. His 8-year-old self was telling him to get the hell out of there. But he couldn't listen. "Mr. Asher. I didn't want to mention this over the phone when I asked to meet with you, but I should tell you that Tommy Boyce passed away a few months ago. He suffered a heart attack."

"No shit? Well, that's a damn shame. We weren't partners for very long, but hell if I didn't admire the man. Well, I suppose I won't be far behind him in any case."

Shane glossed over the comment, not sure of how to respond. "When you two worked together, did you help him with a case, oh, I suppose it must've been when he first came on board with the Tampa Police. It was about a man named Logan Carr..."

"Arrested for drug trafficking and distribution. Oh yeah, I remember it well. Don't ask me why, but I can recall every case I ever worked on. It's like a damn filing cabinet in the back of my head. Can't remember what I ate for breakfast, but I can remember Logan Carr and his cronies."

"He's out on early release," Shane continued. "And he came looking for Tommy, but he found Tommy's daughter."

"Lucy? How is she doing? My God, she lost her mother and now her father." Asher turned to him. "What is she now, about 20?"

"19, I think. She's doing well, all things considered. Working at a P.I. firm."

"Like her daddy."

"Yes, sir. That's actually why I'm here. My friend runs that firm and Logan Carr came to ask for some help. Turns out, his old crew is still going strong and the cops think Logan might be running with them again."

"Carr? No, he ain't doing that. That kid, I don't know how he got caught up in that drug gang, but he shouldn't have been with them in the first place. Hell, he was all of 18 when we charged him."

"Did any of his buddies get charged?" Shane asked.

"A couple of them, but we never could get anything to stick on the leader of that gang. Justin Hardin, if I can recall."

"Julius Hardin. Yes. It appears he's still running the show and the cops think he's a part of that big drug bust the other night. Not sure if you saw that on the news."

"I don't watch the news no more. I mean, it ain't like it's actual news anymore now is it?"

"No, sir. I don't think it is."

"What is it you want from me, son?" Asher asked.

"I wanted to find out what you remembered about Logan Carr. And if you think it's a good idea for my friend to take on his case."

"Well, what case, exactly?"

"He needs help proving he's not with his old crew anymore. That he's not associating with them and that he's holding down a job and starting fresh. I suppose it's not really a case as such. More of a defense."

"Well, if I know Julius Hardin, and I do. If he knows that boy is out, he'll do his damnedest to reel him back in. He had Logan wrapped around his pinky finger. And if the cops want proof of Logan's participation, well, I'm sure they'll find it somehow." Asher looked at Shane again. "But I'll tell you, if your friend and Lucy Boyce think they can help keep Logan out of harm's way, that kid deserves it. Probably more than anyone."

———

ALLISON'S HOME WAS ON THE SMALL SIZE BUT WAS beautifully decorated and while some of the furnishings needed to be replaced, the interior had been updated prior to the divorce.

Inside the kitchen was a nook where a rectangle farmhouse-style dining table and six chairs sat in front of the picture window. The kitchen was good-sized and now boasted white cabinetry, quartz countertops, and a beautiful dark grey color scheme.

Allison and the kids sat around the table as the sun set below the horizon and the Queen Palms with yellowing fronds drooped outside the picture window in the front yard.

Nolan shot a glance to Allison and then to Micah while he shuffled the pasta on his dinner plate. "So, Dad got that contract from the manager we met with."

"Oh yeah? Was he okay with it?" Allison asked.

"He said he's got a lawyer-friend who offered to take a look at it," Nolan replied.

"Good. I'm glad he can do that for you."

"Yeah, wouldn't want you to sign away your life before you've had a chance to live it." Micah set down her glass and looked at her brother. "I'm happy for you, bro. You deserve this." Micah was the spitting image of Allison, save for the hair. She had left hers the natural-born deep shade of brown and wore it stick-straight to the middle of her back. Micah was also just a tad taller than Allison.

"Thanks, Micah," Nolan replied. "Have you been to see Mom's new office yet?" His eyes sparked with optimism. "It's so cool you're a private detective, Mom."

"Thanks, honey. It's nice to have your support."

"What? Because you don't have mine?" Micah interrupted. "I haven't been to the office yet, no."

"You should come down and I'll give you the tour. You can meet Lucy in the process." Allison did her best to keep her emotions in check. The tension between them had improved, but she wasn't out of the woods yet.

"Yeah, maybe. I still have some friends I want to see before I head back to school," Micah replied. "I only have a couple of days left."

"Sure. Yeah." Allison's attention was pulled away by the doorbell.

"Are you expecting someone?" Nolan asked.

"Shane said he'd stop by. I'll bet that's him." Allison stood from the chair. "Excuse me for a moment." She headed to the door.

"Sure. Don't mind us. We're just having dinner," Micah said under her breath.

"What's wrong with you?" Nolan asked. "Why can't you just get over it, huh? Geez. And besides, it wasn't about you anyway."

Shane followed Allison into the kitchen. "Hey, guys. I'm sorry to interrupt. I didn't know you were having dinner."

"Don't be sorry. Grab a plate. There's plenty of food," Allison replied.

"Thanks." Shane took a plate from the cabinet and dished out a healthy helping of pasta before sitting down next to Allison. "Micah. I haven't seen you in a while. How are you? You're looking well."

"Fine. Been busy. But I'm doing okay."

Shane nodded. "Good. That's good to hear. And what about you, Nolan? I hear you and your pops are looking into a manager who wants to sign you."

"That's right. It looks good so far, but we're waiting to hear back from the lawyer."

"Oh, lawyer. Sounds all professional." Shane took a bite. "This is delicious, Allison. Thanks. I was starving."

"Glad to have you." Allison was glad he was there if for nothing else than to relieve the tension at the table. She'd done her best to give Micah space and now awaited the fruits of her efforts if there were going to be any. "You talked with Tommy's old partner?"

"I did. Hell of a guy. It's a shame they say he probably won't last much longer."

"That is too bad," Allison said. "Did he offer anything helpful?"

"Oh, we can talk about all that after dinner. It's just nice to sit down for a homecooked meal."

"Don't you cook, Shane?" Micah asked.

He laughed. "Nope. Unless you count frozen meals in the microwave." He sipped on a glass of water.

"So, are you sleeping with my mom, or what?" She asked.

"Micah!" Allison looked to Shane. "I'm so sorry."

Shane choked on the water and dabbed his mouth with the napkin. "No, it's okay. You just caught me off guard, Micah, that's all. And to answer your question, no. Your mom and I are friends."

"Good. I'm glad to hear that because you know my mom, she's not over my dad yet. But I guess love wasn't enough."

"Okay, Micah, why don't you excuse yourself from the table," Allison said. "You're being very rude to my guest."

"You're right." Micah stood up and tossed her napkin onto her plate. "I'm really sorry for what I said, Shane. You didn't deserve that. Maybe it's best if I just go back to school a little sooner than expected." She began to leave.

"Maybe that's a good idea," Allison replied.

Shane peered at her. "Allison. Come on, she didn't mean..."

"Yes, she did."

"I think I'm done too. Sort of lost my appetite." Nolan stood up and pushed in his chair. "It was nice to see you, Shane."

Allison shook her head as Nolan left. "Ahh, kids. Now I know why you don't have any."

"She's obviously still struggling with the divorce, Allison. Cut her some slack," Shane replied.

"Oh, believe me, I have. I just can't win with her. I don't know what else to do. Sometimes, I think it's going great, and then there are times like this when she just goes off."

"Does she think you made a mistake in getting the divorce?" He took another bite of food.

"She thinks I should've forgiven Leo for his mistake. That everyone makes mistakes and Leo wasn't perfect. Well, no one's perfect, but I guess I just wasn't a big enough person to forgive him."

"He broke your heart, destroyed your trust. That's pretty tough to overcome."

"Yeah." Allison wasn't prepared to discuss this with Shane. "Anyway, since we're alone. I managed to meet with Logan's parole officer earlier this afternoon. And you know, she had nothing but positive things to say about Logan. Seems this guy just made a couple of bad choices and it changed his life."

"Does she think he's turned everything around for himself?" Shane asked.

"She does and she insists that he deserves a second chance."

"Well, that's not much different from what I heard from Benny Asher."

"Right. That was why you wanted to come over. How'd that go?" Allison asked.

"I feel bad for the guy. He's just waiting to die. But he's a character. And he remembers Logan Carr as if the arrest happened yesterday. He said pretty much the same as the parole officer. Although he did add that Julius Hardin would do what he could to try to pull Logan back into the fold. Guess he's something of a control freak."

"We can't let that happen," Allison replied.

"No. So does that mean you feel okay about this? About handling something that could be fairly dangerous if Logan's former associate finds out?"

"He's hiring us to help keep the cops off his back. That—we can do. As far as the rest of it, he might be on his own. I can't put Lucy or Charlie in that position."

"Or you, for that matter." Shane took another drink. "Then we're moving forward?"

"We're moving forward."

6

For an ex-con, finding a job was akin to playing the lottery. Both had staggering odds, but he held out hope that one day it just might happen. So when Logan Carr managed to get hired on as a busboy in a Cuban restaurant, he thanked his lucky stars to have won something, even if it was less than what he spent on the ticket.

It was a condition of his leaving the half-way house. Along with several other conditions Logan had to meet on a weekly basis. Because his incarceration was for a drugs charge, he also had to pee in a cup every week and wasn't allowed to have a beer, or any alcohol for that matter. And right now, he wanted nothing more than a beer to settle his nerves.

He pulled off his hairnet and hung the apron on the hook in the kitchen of the restaurant. "I'm clocking out."

"See you tomorrow, jefe," said another busboy who was actually a boy. He couldn't have been more than fifteen.

"Night." Logan walked outside and grabbed a cigarette on his way to his truck. He took a long drag and blew the smoke high into the air. A few stars twinkled as he gazed up and he was grateful to see them. Walking to his truck, Logan tucked his hair behind his ears and opened his driver's side door, tossing his jacket inside. He jumped in.

The restaurant closed at 10 pm, but it took another hour to help clean and lock it up. Logan had been on his feet for 9 hours. But it beat the shit out of sitting in a jail cell, so he wasn't going to complain.

This wasn't where he thought he'd be at the ripe old age of 23. He'd screwed up and paid the price. Unfortunately, he would continue paying that price for the rest of his life because he'd have to put on every application that he was a felon. Home loans, car loans, jobs. There would be no escaping his past. He had no one to blame but himself and he could admit that.

It was just bad timing when he found himself intertwined with the Southside Runners and Julius Hardin. The promise of money and girls and the good life was a powerful draw for the then-18-year-old kid who didn't have a clue as to what to do with his life and had barely finished high school. His parents didn't give a shit about him, but the older Julius Hardin had. He had been like a big brother and that changed everything.

There was no mistaking what Hardin wanted from him and Logan did it anyway. But when he wanted out, that was when problems arose. Hardin didn't take it well when Logan helped the cops dismantle his operation, albeit, only temporarily. Logan thought that would've been the end of Hardin, but he had enough friends in high and low places to see to it he stayed clean. In the end, Logan did the time, no one else. Getting revenge for something like that would be at the forefront of anyone's mind. But Logan tried hard to push away those damaging thoughts that would surely end badly for him. Hardin was Teflon. That was the real reason the cops wanted Logan—to give it one more try. Well, they weren't going to get him if he had a say.

He started up the truck and pulled out of the back lot where the employees parked. The dark night was crisp and clear, and Logan appreciated every moment of being on the outside.

As he made it onto the highway, he headed to the trailer park he now called home. It wasn't much. In fact, it was a stretch to call it a home at all. It was more like a one-room shoebox with a couple of windows for light. It was a little like the jail cell he once occupied but the bed was more comfortable, he had a TV, and a door on the bathroom. That alone was worth its weight in gold.

Headlights shone in his rearview and the glare hurt his eyes. "Come on, man. Turn off your brights." He squinted through the mirror again and flipped on the turn signal to change lanes. "Asshole." Logan slid over into the adjacent lane and switched on the radio. He was still getting used to the day's popular music because when he went inside, a song called *Gangnam Style* was all the rage. Now it was songs from someone called Cardi B who he didn't care much for and had no idea why she was so famous. It was that damn social media crap. He didn't like it then and it seemed to have gotten worse now. Luckily, a Maroon 5 song played. "At least they're still around."

The car with the bright headlights moved behind him in the next lane over. Logan peered again through the rearview mirror. "Son of a bitch. What's wrong with you, man?" It took a minute, but then it registered. "Freakin' cops. Fine. You want to follow me home, what the hell do I care?" He pressed on and tried to keep his eyes on the road ahead. His home was about another mile away. He would be there in a few minutes. But the glare from the headlights irritated him. "You're doing this on purpose." He switched lanes again and the car switched lanes too.

It was all Logan could do to keep his cool. If he sped up, they would pull him over for speeding. If he kept swerving between lanes, they'd pull him over for suspected drunk driving. "That's what you want, isn't it? Give me a damn ticket and cause me grief. Can't catch a damn break around here."

The trailer park was just ahead, and Logan pulled into his spot. He parked the truck and stepped out. The car was still coming. "You gotta be kidding me?" But when it drew near and slowed to a crawl, Logan got a good look at it. And the people inside. These guys weren't the cops. These guys were the South-side Runners.

Logan pulled back his shoulders and did his best to appear unafraid, though he was quaking in his shoes right about now.

The men stopped the car, blocking in his truck, and stepped out. There were two of them. Logan knew who they were and was grateful neither was Julius Hardin. He wasn't sure how that would play and didn't want to find out. But if Hardin wasn't here, then these guys were sent to only scare him. Nothing more. He could relax, a little.

"Evening." Logan took out another cigarette and lit it. "Care for one?"

"How you doin', Logan? Long time no see, my man." Mateo Figueroa offered his hand wearing a broad smile and a ridiculous man-bun.

"Doin' all right, brother." Logan returned the greeting and eyed the bun, desperately trying not to comment on it. "Keeping my nose clean."

"That's what we hear." The man from the passenger seat approached him. "Gotta stay clean when you're on parole, my friend."

"Yes, sir." He shook his hand. "I just got off work and was about to head inside. What can I help you two with?"

The men traded glances and Mateo turned back to Logan. "Not a bad little place you got here."

"Inside's for shit, but it's better than a park bench, or a jail cell," Logan said.

"I'll bet it is. Listen, man, you heard about that big bust the other night?" Mateo asked.

"Something about it, yeah. Was that you guys?"

"Was that us." Mateo laughed and turned briefly to his colleague. "You know Julius has been meaning to pay you a visit since you been out, but you know, house-rules and shit."

"Oh, I know. No problem, I get it. How's he doing, anyway?"

"Same as always. Except this deal that went down. It turned to shit, and Julius is cleaning up the mess," Mateo replied.

"I'm sorry to hear that. I really am," Logan added. "I don't mean to be rude, but why are you here talking to me?"

"Logan, Julius could really use your help," Mateo replied.

"I'm not sure what I can offer. They keep me on a pretty short leash."

"Sure. Sure. But you know, Julius thinks it would be a good idea to maybe set up a meeting in the near future. Someplace out of the way."

"Can I ask why?" Logan said.

"What do I know about how Julius thinks, huh? I'm just the messenger. Can you meet or not?" Mateo pressed on.

These men weren't going to take "no" for an answer. This was Hardin's style and if Logan pushed back, he'd find another, more intrusive means of communicating. The cops might catch on to that and then they wouldn't need to do anything to prove what they already suspected—that Logan was still working with Hardin.

"Sure. I guess so. I work odd hours, but I have tomorrow off."

"Well, all right. I'll relay that information to Julius." Mateo stepped back into the driver's seat. "You should get some rest. You look like shit, Logan." He started the engine while his partner stepped into the car. "We'll be in touch with a time and place."

Logan watched as the men pulled away and he felt the elephant rise up off his chest. He could breathe again. He was going to have to tell Allison about this because it would give the cops ammunition. Logan wasn't going back to the pen, that was just a fact.

———

"WHAT'D I TELL YOU?" DETECTIVE BAYLOR PEERED THROUGH the windshield. "I knew Carr was going to screw up and now he did. You can't tell me those guys weren't Southside Runners."

"I don't know what it was we saw, but I'll agree Carr was talking to people he knew." Agent Reddick turned to him. "Are we going to follow them or what?"

"No. Let's run the plates on that car and see what turns up. I'll bet you a dime to a dollar that car belongs to one of the Runners." Baylor pulled away from the road that fronted the trailer park and when he was out of the view, he turned on his headlights.

"Should we let Markham in on this?" Reddick asked.

"And Pierce. It could be exactly what DHS and DEA need to move forward. Although Pierce promised his man inside would find out where Hardin was hiding. Still haven't seen anything about that."

"I'll tell you one thing, Logan Carr didn't look happy to see them. Maybe we should give Pierce's insider a chance to tell us where Hardin is and back off Logan Carr until we know more," Reddick said.

"Even if he did that, we'd still need to catch Hardin on something before the cartel takes him out, which they will do if he doesn't answer for his mistakes. All I'm looking to do is get the

Southside Runners for trafficking. Logan Carr is the man to help us get that done."

"We will be putting his life in danger," Reddick said.

"Carr shouldn't have gotten himself tangled up with Hardin in the first place." Baylor continued driving toward the station. "Once we get back, we'll see just who it was he was talking to."

———

SHANE PUSHED UP FROM THE SOFA. "I SHOULD PROBABLY GET home. It's getting late. Thanks for dinner."

"Any time. I'll walk you out." Allison headed to the door and stood in the foyer. The house was quiet although she suspected the kids weren't asleep. Both probably had earbuds in, and their eyes glued to their phones. "Hey, about earlier. What Micah said."

Shane held up his hands. "There's no need to apologize. She's still a kid."

"She's 20," Allison replied.

"Micah will figure this out. She just needs time and support from you."

"You know, for a single guy with no kids, you make a little too much sense," Allison replied.

"What can I say? It's a gift." Shane grabbed her gently by the arms and kissed her cheek. "It'll pass."

"I'll have to take your word for it." She opened the door. "So, tomorrow. What do you think we should do?"

"It's your show. You tell me."

"I have one character statement. I feel confident that Logan Carr is a good kid who messed up, but he did his time. We'll start putting together his employment records and obtain details from the half-way house. I'd still like to get a statement from his employer. What about Detective Baylor? I want to do our job, but

I don't want to get in the way of whatever he's doing, unless it involves railroading my client."

"I'll do my best to keep him off your scent. But the sooner you get proof that'll keep Logan in the clear, the better for him. These guys, the taskforce, they want to see the Southside Runners go down for this."

"So would I," she replied.

"Yeah, but they need to go about it the right way. Not by hooking some ex-con who's trying to turn around his life just to bring in the bigger fish they're really hunting for." Shane stepped outside. "Night, Allison. Sleep tight."

"You too." Allison closed the door and locked it. "Oh, geez." She spun around at the tap on her shoulder. "Micah. You scared me."

"Sorry. I was going to the bathroom when I saw Shane leaving." Micah held Allison's gaze. "Mom, I'm sorry. I was way out of line earlier tonight. I was wrong and immature."

"It's not me who you should be apologizing to. It's Shane."

"Yeah. And I will. I promise."

Allison tucked her daughter's long dark hair behind her ear and held her gaze. "Micah, I don't know what to do about this anymore. About us. I know you think I should've stuck it out with your dad, but I just couldn't. I'm sure it's hard for you to understand..."

"No. It isn't. I understand. It's just that Dad tried so hard to make it up to you and it was like you just didn't want any part of it. Then I went off to college and it was just easier to ignore it. To ignore you."

"I get it," Allison replied.

"Then his stupid girlfriend came into the picture and I thought, well great. That's the end of that."

"I didn't want my marriage to end. I truly didn't. I was scared out of my mind. I wasn't sure if I could get a job to support myself let alone you kids."

"I know, Mom," Micah added. "Dad was the one who messed up."

"Now, that's not entirely fair. It takes two to tango, as they say."

"Well, you weren't the one who cheated. I'm sorry that happened to you. And if you wanted to date that cop, I wouldn't have a problem with it."

"Who? Shane?" Allison chuckled. "Oh no. No. I have no interest in him at all. First of all, he's much younger than me."

"He's not that much younger. Besides, I saw the way he looked at you just now when he was leaving. He likes you, Mom."

"He might like me but it's only because he can't have me. You'll find out there are plenty of men out there that once they get you, they lose interest. I can't explain it."

"Well, I'm sorry anyway and the next time I see Shane, I'll apologize. But, Mom, I don't want to go back to school yet if that's okay."

"Of course it's okay. I want you here too. We'll just keep talking and we'll work all this out okay?" Allison embraced Micah. "You're my baby girl. I love you."

"I love you too, Mom."

———

THE ONLY LIGHTS ON INSIDE THE WAREHOUSE WERE THE lights above the sorting table. It was 2 am and Julius Hardin had been summoned. The leaker had been found.

"You screwed up, man." Julius strolled across the concrete floor and peered at the man tied to the chair. "Esteban is someone you don't want to piss off. Did you really think you could get away with snitching?"

The man's left eye was swollen shut and his bottom lip dripped blood down his chin. "It wasn't me."

"I'm sorry, what?" Hardin leaned in.

"It wasn't me. I swear it."

"It wasn't you." He nodded. "Then who the hell was it, huh? This is the cartel. You are messed up in the head, brother, if you think you can get away with that shit, and under my watch?"

"I've been loyal to you, Julius. I'm not dumb enough to cross the cartel. I don't know who it was, but it wasn't me."

"I can't believe someone like you even works for me, man." Julius pulled out a gun from his waistband and cocked it, pointing it the man's head. "You're leaving me no choice, my man. Cause if I don't take care of this, Esteban will be putting a gun to my head, you feel me?"

He nodded.

Two men burst into the warehouse and marched toward Julius.

"What the hell?" He turned to them. "What's wrong?"

"We tracked him down like you asked," Mateo began. "He was playing all cool and shit, but he agreed to meet tomorrow." He shot a glance at the bloodied man in the chair and repulsion sparked in his eyes.

Hardin appeared to notice the look. "This is the guy. The snitch."

Mateo peered again at the man in the chair before turning back to Hardin. "How do you know?"

Hardin furrowed his brow and stepped closer to Mateo. "What the hell do you mean, 'how do I know?' I know because I have people who are loyal to me. Are you questioning me, bro?"

"No. No, man. It's just. Hell, I don't know. I don't know

anything about it." Mateo shed his gaze to the ground and shoved hands in his pockets. "You're the boss, Julius."

Hardin stepped away again. "That's right. I'm the boss." He studied Mateo. "Tomorrow, huh? Tell Logan 3 o'clock at the restaurant in St. Pete's. He'll know the place. It's our old stomping grounds." He turned back to the man in the chair. "Nobody likes a rat, brother." He fired the gun, point blank at the snitch's head.

He collapsed in the chair.

Mateo and his partner traded glances before he gazed back at the dead man.

Hardin wiped the splattered blood off his face. "Hey, do me a favor and clean this shit up, yeah?"

7

The idea hadn't fully rooted in Allison's mind yet. Going to an office every day again and knowing she was responsible for it and the staff inside. Taking on Logan's case, or rather, helping him prove he'd followed the rules of his probation to a T wasn't what she had in mind when they officially opened their doors only a few days ago. But it was a paying job and if they could help this kid get out from under the thumb of his previous life, then this was exactly as she had imagined it after all.

Allison walked inside and noticed Charlie was at her desk. "Good morning."

"Back at ya," Charlie replied. "Lucy brought in some bagels and put on a fresh pot if you're interested."

She eyed the credenza at the back. "Thanks for bringing food, Lucy." Allison started back toward the spread. "You know you don't have to prove your worth around here, right? We both saw your value the minute we met you. Not to mention, you're the one with the connections. Remember that."

"I just thought maybe you guys would be hungry. It was no big deal." Lucy returned to her desk with a coffee and bagel in hand. "Besides, I was starving."

"It's appreciated." Allison walked to her desk.

"Anyway, how was your night?" Lucy brushed off the praise.

"Shane stopped by and had some dinner. We discussed his meeting with your dad's old partner, Benny Asher," Allison replied.

"How is he doing?" Lucy asked.

"Unfortunately, Shane says he's in hospice care. Lung cancer," Allison replied.

"Oh no. That's awful," Lucy said.

"It is. Shane said he was a tough old goat, though. I bet he and your dad got along well. And he remembered Logan Carr, that's for sure. He made it pretty clear Logan was a good kid who got involved with the wrong people. It makes more sense as to why your dad would've tried to help him, despite some of the things we read in his file."

Charlie grabbed a coffee and a bagel, slathering on the cream cheese. "What we read in the file, though, Tommy didn't include any of his own opinions on Logan."

"It had nothing to do with the case, I imagine," Allison said. "I'm glad we were able to piece together the whole story."

"Maybe not the whole story, but enough for us to get going, right? We assume we're on the right side of this?" Charlie asked.

"I think so," Allison said. "And I think we should pay a visit to the man who runs the half-way house where Carr was living up until a few days ago. If we need proof Logan is on the right path, this guy should have it."

Charlie downed the last of her coffee and finished half the bagel. With a full mouth, she began. "We aren't getting any younger. Let's go." She grabbed her bag. "Lucy, you'll hold down the fort?"

"You got it."

Allison grabbed her purse. "Do me a favor and pull the employment records for Logan while we're out, would you? We'll review it when we get back."

"Sure thing. See you guys soon," Lucy said.

———

ALLISON WAS REMINDED OF PAROLE OFFICER RONA CLARK'S preferred term, residential rehabilitation center, as they pulled up to the half-way house. At first glance, it was nothing more than a Spanish Colonial two-story in need of repairs inside the less than desirable neighborhood near Ybor City. The success rates of facilities such as this were also less than desirable. However, Allison hoped that Logan Carr would not be a statistic and would find his way to a better life.

"Well, this is it." Charlie peered through the windshield of Allison's old Honda Civic. "Not much of a place but probably better than prison. What's the guy's name?"

Allison looked at the file. "Sam Childers. He's listed as the managing member of a company called Galway Rehab, LLC. There's a man living here who runs the place for him, but Sam is the one to talk to."

"How did you find this out?"

"Logan's parole officer gave me the information," Allison replied.

"Okay then. Let's talk to Sam." Charlie stepped out of the car and headed to the front door.

Allison followed and on arrival, she knocked. A man wearing an open flannel shirt with a tank top underneath and a pair of ripped jeans answered. "Mr. Childers?"

The man with long hair, a stubbly beard, and wary eyes peered at them. "What do you want with Sam?"

"He's expecting us." Allison offered her hand. "We're with ACL Investigative Services."

"What's that?" the man asked.

"We're here on behalf of a client. Is Mr. Childers available?" Allison pressed on.

From beyond the door, a man approached. "It's okay, Dale. They're here for me. Let the ladies in." Sam Childers approached the door. "Allison Hart?"

"That's right. I'm Allison and this is my partner, Charlie Wells. Thank you for meeting with us this morning."

"No problem. Come on in." He opened the door and they stepped inside. Childers stood nearly 6 feet tall and was too thin. His gaunt cheeks were dotted with acne scars, but for a man who appeared roughly in his late forties, he still had a head full of dark brown hair that was short and stylish. "You'll have to forgive the mess. The guys aren't much for cleaning up after themselves." He closed the door behind them. "Can I get either of you a coffee?"

"No, thank you," Allison said.

"All right then. Come with me and we'll have a chat." He turned to Dale. "I got it from here."

"Okay, boss." Dale eyed Allison and disappeared beyond the corridor.

"Don't mind him. He spent almost 20 years inside and doesn't trust anyone." Childers offered a pleasant smile. "And just so as I don't catch you off-guard, I'm a reformed man myself. Spent eight years behind bars."

"I don't blame him for not trusting people," Charlie said, not addressing Childers' previous comment.

"Let's have a seat at the kitchen table." He started ahead. "You want to talk about Logan, huh? You know he only just left here a few days ago. Suddenly, I'm getting a whole lot of interest in him. Six months of nothing, then poof! Everyone's here asking about him."

"Who else has been here?" Allison followed him into the messy kitchen, trying her best to withhold judgment.

"Oh, let's see." Childers pulled out a chair at the square oak table and sat down. "There was the Tampa police, some detective named Baylor. He and his FBI agent buddy. Can't recall his name though. And now you too."

"What did they want?" Charlie joined him.

"They wanted to know where Logan ended up. What he was up to."

"And did you tell them?" Allison was the last to take her seat.

"Course I did. They would've found out anyway just by talking to his parole officer. Besides, that kid's done nothing off-kilter since he got out. Hasn't even sneezed without excusing himself. I'd find it hard to believe they'd have any reason to keep their sights trained on him."

"I guess that sort of leads me to why we're here," Allison began. "Are there records of when Logan came in every night and left every day? You know, for work and stuff."

"Sure. Part of the deal of getting to stay here is that you basically clock in and out."

"Could we get those records?" She added.

Childers eyed them. "Well, I don't know. That's not usually public information."

"Even if we have Logan's permission?" Charlie asked.

"Why would he want his own records? He knew when he was here and when he wasn't," Childers replied.

"You're right," Allison began. "But we're looking to make a case as to Logan's character and prove his whereabouts to show he's been keeping out of trouble if you know what I mean."

He eyed her. "Maybe I do. And have you talked to his parole officer?"

"I met with her yesterday. Everyone seems to be under the impression that Logan is a good kid who got a bad rap."

Childers' lips turned into a frown as he nodded. "I'd tend to agree with that assumption." He stood up. "Let me pull his file. I'll be right back."

After he left, Allison turned to Charlie. "What do you think?"

"I don't know. He seems all right. A little resistant, but all right."

"Yeah, that's what I thought," Allison began. "Maybe his time behind bars made him more cautious."

"I'm sure it did. Still, it would really help our case if he turned over those records. Can't dispute daily reports, right?" Charlie asked.

"So long as it proves our point to Detective Baylor. Along with his employment records that Lucy is working on, we should be well armed." Allison peered around the kitchen. "I can't believe people live like this."

"Not everyone has such high cleanliness standards as you, Allison."

"High standards, sure. But I don't see any standards here at all." As she continued to examine the kitchen, her eyes were drawn to the window when a car passed by. Her brow furrowed and she looked at Charlie.

"What?" Charlie surveyed the room. "What'd you see?"

"We need to go." Allison stood up. "Now."

"What? Why?"

"Grab your things." Allison picked up her files and her handbag. "Charlie, now." She started toward the door with a quickened pace. Her hand grabbed the door handle when she heard Childers approach from the hall.

"Hey, where are you ladies off to? I thought you wanted..."

"Sorry, we forgot something back at the office." Charlie hustled to catch up to Allison as she was already halfway out the door.

When Allison reached the outside, Charlie pressed on. "Cripes, Alli. What the hell are you running for? Some of us don't have spider legs like you." Her short stride put her at a distinct disadvantage in a getaway situation.

Allison made it to the car and unlocked it. "Get inside, Charlie. Fast." She slipped onto the driver's seat and started the engine, waiting for Charlie to enter. "Come on, come on."

Charlie opened the door and stepped in.

"Close the door. Let's go." Allison shifted the car into drive and pulled away before Charlie closed the door.

"What in the world is going on, Alli? You're scaring the hell out of me." She patted down errant strands of hair. "And you made me mess up my do."

Allison kept her eyes focused on the rearview mirror. "Do you see that car?"

Charlie cast around her gaze. "What car? You mind slowing down so I can get a look?"

"I've seen that car before." Allison peered at Charlie with wild eyes. "I saw it when I was meeting with the parole officer."

"Are you sure? Who is it?"

"I don't know, and I didn't think much of it yesterday until I saw it driving slowly by just now when we were in the kitchen. It slowed down even more just in front of my car. I saw it yesterday and it just sat there. I thought it was someone waiting on someone else. But now."

"Okay, okay. So, who is it then?" Charlie pressed on.

"Like I said, I don't know. But I didn't want to stick around and find out. Someone's watching us, Charlie. Someone knew we'd be here this morning."

"Childers did leave the room to get the records. Do you think he made a call? Maybe he doesn't like us snooping around his books."

"We only asked for Logan's records, not his accounting records." Allison shifted her gaze between the rearview mirror and the side mirrors. "I think it's gone now anyway."

"Good, because my pits were starting to sweat." Charlie waved her hands at her underarms. "I don't know if or why Sam Childers would be worried about us looking into Logan's records. Or why he would bother having someone tail us if that was what happened." Charlie looked at Allison. "Which means we should get better acquainted with him and find out if he's working in Logan's best interest, or Detective Baylor's."

———

LOGAN ROLLED OFF THE OLD MATTRESS THAT LAY ON A broken bedframe in his trailer and rubbed his eyes. The sun burned through the single-pane window and heated up the tin shack quickly, which was what awakened him. Today was an important day. One that could free him or see him forever indebted to the Southside Runners. Meeting with Julius Hardin had been a risky decision. He was under surveillance by the cops and the FBI, probably the DEA too. They were all just sitting around, waiting for him to screw up and now he was about to. But how to turn down an invitation from a man who controlled nearly 80 percent of the cocaine distribution in the state? A man he had once tried to help convict, even if that effort failed.

Logan pulled on his jeans and hovered over the pedestal basin inside the dingy bathroom that had only a corner shower. His dark blonde hair hung in his face. His chest and shoulders were heavily tattooed, most of them added when he was on the inside. The rock-hard abs he'd worked on for five years were already beginning to soften. For a 23-year-old man, he felt middle-aged. Prison had seen him fend off abuse by the guards, sustain multiple injuries from prison yard scuffles and recover from drug and alcohol addiction. He'd lived a lifetime in those five years and held out hope for a new and better life. Otherwise, what was the point?

He splashed water on his face that appeared drawn out but carried youthful good looks. His wet hands pushed his hair back into place. A final examination in the mirror and in socked feet, Logan shuffled along the vinyl floor to the kitchenette. A jar of instant coffee granules sat on the counter, so he heated a mug of water in the microwave, dumped in a spoonful of the granules and swirled until it dissolved. He'd learned to live without cream and sugar.

The time was already 10 am. It was his one day off a week and he thought first of making a visit to the agency to see how Allison Hart was coming along. He wanted to believe she and the others could help. But maybe none of that mattered with Julius Hardin on the horizon. He was going to give that detective exactly what he wanted and all of the agency's work would have been meaningless. Still, Logan needed to tell them and made the call.

"ACL Investigative Services. How may I help you?" Lucy answered.

"Lucy Boyce?"

"Yes?"

"This is Logan Carr. Is Allison available?"

"She's out of the office at the moment. Can I help with anything?"

"Listen, can you tell her that I have a meeting later today and I was wondering if I should maybe, I don't know, maybe keep my phone on me and sort of have you guys on the line during this meeting."

"I don't know, Logan. Why would you do that? What kind of meeting are you going to?"

"Julius Hardin wants to meet me later today."

"I don't think that's a good idea. You're not supposed…"

"I know I'm not. Do you think I would be doing this if I had a choice?" He asked. "Please, Lucy. I need your help."

"Um, what time is the meeting supposed to take place?"

"Be ready for the call at about 3 pm."

"Okay. Sure. Logan, will you be safe? Should I inform the police?"

"The cops can't help me, Lucy. If this doesn't work, no one can help me. Not even you guys."

———

ALLISON CONSIDERED CHARLIE'S QUESTION AS SHE KEPT HER eyes on the road ahead. "I don't know if it's the cops following us or if it's the gang. What did Shane call them? The Southside Runners?"

"How would the gang even know about us?" Charlie asked.

"Exactly." Allison picked up her phone and pressed the contact. "I'm calling Shane."

"What's he going to do?"

Allison raised a finger and waited for the line to answer, placing the call on speaker. "Shane, it's Allison. Listen, I need a favor."

"What else is new?" he replied.

"I know. I'll owe you, okay? Hey, I've got you on speaker and I'm driving with Charlie. We just left the half-way house looking for records on Logan Carr."

"Any luck with that?"

"We had to tear out of there before we got the files," Charlie interjected. "Allison got a wild hair."

"It wasn't a wild hair. Shane, I saw a car that I'd seen yesterday at the parole office. Now before you get all excited, we're fine. Nothing's happened. But the reason I'm calling is that I need to know if it's the cops following us, or this gang Logan was associated with."

"Neither one makes me feel great about this," Shane replied.

"No. Me neither. What I need to do now is find out where this gang operates." Allison listened as Shane chuckled. "I'm being serious." She eyed Charlie.

"She's being serious. You should see her face right now. She's not smiling at all," Charlie replied.

"I'm not going to let anyone dictate how I run this investigation," Allison continued. "Be it Detective Baylor and the FBI or this gang of drug traffickers."

"What do you want to do, Allison?" Shane pressed on. "Because getting tangled up with Julius Hardin is a really bad idea. Like the worst you've ever had. You understand me?"

"I'm not looking to get on their radar if that's what you're asking. I might already be, I don't know. Can you give me an address of Julius Hardin?"

"I can give you what's in the system. Whether it's accurate, I couldn't say, but I wouldn't count on it. Detective Baylor has been looking for Hardin and no one seems to know where he is. What makes you think you can find him?"

Allison glanced at Charlie. "I just want to know if that car is there. I have no intention of confronting anyone, Shane," Allison said.

"If they are the ones following you, which I'm not sure is the case, you won't find the same car there. That much I know," Shane said.

"Don't let this go to your head, Shane, but I'm leaning toward your theory, so what do you suggest we do?" Charlie noticed Allison's stare. "Sorry, but I gotta go with Shane on this one."

"Can I record that?" He laughed. "Look, my suggestion is for you to go back to the office and keep working on Logan's profile and parole records. Don't screw around with this gang, Allison. I'm telling you; they aren't folks you want to mess with. And you just don't have enough to warrant a call like this. There has to be another solution."

"Maybe you're right," Allison conceded. "There's no reason the Southside Runners would know anything about us. I get that. But something tells me Sam Childers might not be as honest and forthcoming as he should be, at least where Logan is concerned. Maybe that's who we should be looking at." She peered at Charlie.

Charlie looked at her phone. "Hey, it's Lucy. I'm going to take this."

"Shane, we'll call you back," Allison ended the call.

"Hey, Lucy. What's going on?" Charlie began. "Alli's driving. I'm going to put you on speaker."

"Logan called. He was confronted late last night by members of the gang he used to be a part of. They told him he had to meet with Julius Hardin this afternoon."

"Had to? Sounds like they didn't give him a choice in the matter," Allison said.

"I don't think they did. Anyway, he called me and said he wants to keep me on the line once he's inside as sort of insurance in case something goes wrong."

"Where's he going and what time?" Charlie asked.

"He didn't tell me. Just said it was some place in St. Pete's and that it was supposed to happen around 3 pm today. What should I do?"

Allison checked the time. "It's still morning. Charlie and I can go to St. Pete's now. You know what, I think we'll call Logan from here and ask him about this. Besides, if he's meeting with Julius Hardin, the cops will be interested in knowing where. Everyone's been looking for him since the bust. I need to know where's he's going for his own safety. We'll call you back, okay?"

"Sure."

"Bye, Lucy." Charlie ended the call. "You want me to make the call?"

"Please."

The line rang and finally, Logan answered the call. "Hello?"

"Logan, it's Charlie. I'm here with Allison. We just got off the phone with Lucy. She told us what's happening later today."

"Hey, Logan, Allison here. Listen, we're headed to St. Pete's right now. We need to know where you plan on meeting Hardin later today."

Logan didn't answer and Allison looked at Charlie before breaking the silence. "Logan, we need to know what's going on here. With the history you and Hardin share, do you really think it's a good idea to meet with him? First of all, you'd be handing your head on a silver platter to the police. They've been waiting for you to screw up and they've been looking for Hardin. Two birds. And honestly, if only half of what you've told us about Hardin is true, you might not make it out of this meeting. I know you understand this."

"I'm supposed to meet him at a place called Stillwaters down by the port. 3 o'clock today."

"Thank you. And your idea of calling Lucy is dangerous. I'm not sure now is the right time to try to trap this guy if that's your intent. You have no leverage here."

"It was more of an insurance policy so she could send the cops if... Look, if I don't meet with him, he'll keep coming after me." The line was quiet for a moment. "This was a mistake. I should never have come to you. Julius Hardin is a dangerous man. I'm sorry." He ended the call.

"Logan?" Charlie asked. "He hung up."

"He's scared." Allison turned the wheel and pressed down on the gas.

"Where are you going?"

"He's going to meet with Julius Hardin whether we want him to or not. There could still be something we can do for him. Let's get to the Stillwaters restaurant."

"Alli, why would we go there?" Charlie asked.

Allison shot her a glance. "If he's going to do this, we can try to help him."

8

A request for a change of venue would ensure Allison and Charlie steered clear of any danger and it would keep the cops from swooping in to make an arrest, because that would all but guarantee an end to life as Logan knew it. However, Hardin was well-known for his paranoia and any change like that would spark concern about the meeting. Hardin was under enough scrutiny right now with the cartel and the last thing he would accept was a change in plans. It would be seen as a trap, no doubt.

Regret was an understatement as to how Logan felt about dragging in Allison Hart and her partner. He didn't think it would come to this. The prospect of seeing Hardin again after all these years. A small part of him believed he could put it behind him, but Hardin made clear that was nothing more than was a fantasy. Maybe Logan deserved it for what he'd done or tried to do to Hardin.

Now Allison and Charlie had insisted on driving to the restaurant in St. Petersburg. Logan knew the place well and had been there many times before. It was known in the criminal underground as a place where the Southside Runners could meet without fear of the cops or rival gangs. It was protected by the people who owned it and had a stake in keeping it off law enforcement's radar.

The mistake of getting the women involved couldn't be undone. But he could make sure they weren't put in harm's way from this point forward. He peered through his kitchen window at the view of the other derelict trailers. Everyone wanted him for different reasons. None of which would actually benefit him. Logan was going to have to see this meeting through and talk his way out of getting recruited again by Hardin, all while avoiding the likes of Detective Anton Baylor.

"Screw it." Logan turned away from the window and snatched his keys from the kitchen table. "They all think they know me. They all think they can bend me to their will. I ain't about to let that happen. Not again."

Logan pushed through the front door and jogged down the rotting wood steps, making his way outside to his truck. There was one place he could go where it was possible to find Julius Hardin. Maybe taking the pro-active approach would appeal to his former associate or maybe it would piss him off. Either way, Logan had to try to intervene before Allison and Charlie found themselves confronting the Southside Runners.

He jumped inside the truck and fired up the engine. It was almost noon. He still had time before the 3 pm meeting. The warehouse was where he suspected Hardin was holed up. The heat was on him big time with this massive cocaine bust and the place was as secure as the Pentagon. It was a good system and had worked for Hardin so far. Logan knew all about the warehouse and what went on there.

He pressed on the gas pedal and the engine of old pickup sputtered until clicking into gear. As he drove, the one question that lingered was why now? He'd been at the half-way house for six months and never heard a single word from or about Hardin. It wasn't until the drug bust that all of this broke loose. Was Hardin biding his time until Logan was freed of the half-way house and would be under much less scrutiny, or was this a case of Hardin believing Logan could have been the snitch that led to the bust? An impossibility to any sane person, but this was Julius Hardin, an irrational man.

It was a straight shot down the 75 toward the southeastern part of the city. The location of the warehouse was the perfect choice when the drug shipments came in. The front of the warehouse held machine parts. That was the legal side of the business. However, tucked away in a back corner of the facility was where Julius and the Southside Runners' drugs came in to be sifted through and distributed onto several smaller trucks and sent in all directions through southern Florida.

Logan's arrest had been due to the fact that he was driving one of those trucks and ended up in Tampa when he broke down. Stupid. He knew he should've left the shipment and fled on foot. Instead, a cop car pulled up behind him and offered help. It had been almost 2 in the morning. What the hell was that cop doing there anyway?

When Logan tried to tell him he had a buddy coming, the cop just wouldn't leave. Logan started to get nervous. The cop picked up on that and started asking questions. One thing led to another and he was opening up the back doors and what do you know? Cocaine.

That was it for Logan. Detective Boyce was assigned to the case and the rest, as they say, was history. Now here he was, five years later, out on parole. "Deja frickin' vu."

The warehouse appeared in the distance as Logan inhaled a

deep breath. He hadn't felt this nervous since he first went into the pen and it was his turn to take a shower. The time had just hit 12:30 and while Julius wouldn't normally be here at this time of day, he faced extenuating circumstances which forced him to lay low for a while. This was a pretty good place to keep hidden.

Logan had no idea who owned the warehouse, but somehow, Hardin or someone above him managed to keep it clean and off the radar of law enforcement.

Logan stopped the truck next to another building several yards away. He knew there were cameras all over this place, so he felt better coming in on foot. Like he was going to get the drop on Julius. That was never going to happen.

The heat from the sun felt good on his skin during an otherwise cool early January day. He wore a denim jacket with a t-shirt beneath and a pair of jeans he bought last week. A small token of his accomplishment for getting out of the half-way house and starting his brand-new life. "So much for that."

The heavy steel door was ten feet away. All Logan had to do now was knock. It was the back entrance, the one used when shipments came in. His pulse quickened and his palms grew clammy. "Calm the hell down." Logan closed his eyes for a moment to steady his nerves. He raised his fist and pounded on the door.

A camera was mounted above, and he gazed into it. They weren't going to open the door unless they knew who was standing there. If he'd had the balls, he would've smiled, but he used up the last of his nerve knocking on the door. Logan was at their mercy; if there was any mercy left inside.

The locks disengaged with a loud metallic thump. He stepped back and tried to swallow his fear. They would tear him apart if they smelled it coming off him. The door opened and a man he recognized appeared.

"What the? Dude!" He opened the door a little wider. "Logan? Is that you?"

"It's me." He smiled awkwardly to try to conceal the anxiety that had already reached catastrophic levels within him. "I have a meeting with Julius later today. I thought I'd try to catch him here, if he's here."

"I heard about that. This is some crazy shit, right? This bust and all. Dude, you thought he was paranoid before. Man, you should see him now, huh?" He offered a distant, mannish hug. "It's good to see you, bro. Come on in."

Logan peered behind him into the warehouse. He had to be cool, frosty. Not a care in the world. "Thanks, man. It's good to see you too, Mo."

Moses McDonald was Hardin's man on the south side. The skinny 34-year-old enjoyed a little too much of what he was selling. But Hardin cut him slack because he was the best spotter around. So long as the merch wasn't from his own stash, Hardin turned a blind eye.

"You're looking for the main man, himself, huh?"

"That's right," Logan began. "Like I said, I had a meeting scheduled for later but with as hot as this bust is, I figured I would try to help him keep out of sight so I took a shot he might be here."

Moses patted him on the back. "Well you are in luck, my compadre. Just like Julius always said about you—you had a nose for when shit was gonna go down bad. Come on, he's in the back."

———

ALLISON HANDED THE CASHIER A CREDIT CARD. "HERE you go."

He rang up the $250 charge and dropped the items in a bag. "And this is for you, ma'am. Here's your receipt."

She hated it when people called her ma'am, but on examination, the man before her wasn't older than 30. Allison took care of herself and always had, but time caught up with everyone eventually.

Charlie, however, wasn't as willing to accept their new station in life. "Ma'am?"

"Leave it," Allison said before turning back to the cashier. "Thank you." She headed toward the exit and pushed through the door outside. "This should work for us. Should we go?"

"Ready when you are, ma'am," Charlie replied.

"Don't push it, old lady." Allison smacked Charlie's shoulder. "That kid can get away with it, but not you."

"Yes, ma'am." Charlie laughed and hustled back to the car. "How much farther to the restaurant?"

Allison keyed the lock and opened the driver's side door. "A few minutes. Ten at most." She slipped inside and waited for Charlie to enter. "You mind reading up on how we use that stuff while I drive?"

"Didn't they teach you how to use listening devices in P.I. school?" Charlie opened the package.

"No. But I'll be sure and write to the school and tell them they should include it in the curriculum." Allison laughed and pulled out of the parking lot onto the road ahead.

Allison continued on the drive while Charlie ran through a quick read on how to surveil people. She was more worried about Logan now than ever. Maybe she had gotten into this situation without fully knowing the real dangers. Shane had encouraged her to take the case and she didn't question it. Not that he would ever put them in danger, but the deeper Allison dug into this, the uglier and more dangerous it appeared. Lines needed to be drawn, boundaries respected. But Allison didn't know what she didn't know. There were people who trusted her decisions. One of them sat in the seat next to her now. Allison still had a lot to learn about this business and recalled Tommy Boyce's words of warning at their first meeting. *"There's nothing glitzy about this job. It's dirty and reeks of human misery, and it's better if you understand that right off the bat."* She was starting to understand that now.

"Hey, Alli, isn't that the place right there?" Charlie pointed ahead at a restaurant in the distance."

"I believe you're right." Allison made her way to the parking lot and pulled into a spot, cutting the engine.

They both stared at the building. It was decent enough; overlooked the water. Just a typical seaside restaurant with an outdoor seating area. Neither said a word.

Allison finally looked at the time on her phone. "I'm going in. You coming?" She opened her door.

"We're partners, aren't we?" Charlie followed her out. "What's the game plan, my friend? The meeting isn't supposed to happen for another almost 2 hours."

"I want to go inside and see the layout."

"The layout?" Charlie hurried to catch up to her.

"First of all, I want to sit somewhere we can see cars arrive, preferably near an exit. I'd like to know if one of them might be the car we saw at the half-way house." Allison reached the front door and pulled it open. "Hi there. You're open for lunch, right?"

"Yes, ma'am. Two?" The hostess asked.

"Please." She glanced at Charlie and both smiled. Two ma'am's in one day and it was only mid-afternoon.

"Right this way." The young woman led them through the empty restaurant that had just opened. "Looks like you two can take your pick. Over there you'll get a great view of the water. Just sayin..."

Allison surveyed the open-floor layout and spotted an exit near the restrooms that would give her a clear shot to the front view. "How about over there?" She pointed in that direction.

"Oh, sure, yeah. If that's what you want. Follow me." She turned on her heel and started toward the restrooms.

"We're old," Charlie said to her. "We have to pee a lot. You'll understand one day."

The hostess laughed. "This is the perfect spot for you then."

Allison slid into the booth and Charlie entered the other side.

"Here are some menus for you and the day's specials are listed right here. Can I start you off with some drinks?"

"Iced-tea for me. Unsweetened," Allison said.

"Diet Coke. Thanks," Charlie added.

"I'll be right back with those."

Allison pulled down the menu to examine Charlie. "Good cover about the bathrooms."

"What cover?"

Allison surveyed the restaurant. "Why would someone like Julius Hardin choose to come here? It's so public. So out-in-the-open. Seems a huge risk."

"Maybe that's the way he wants it. He thinks he'd be protected," Charlie replied.

"I don't know. This place means something," Allison began. "I wonder who owns it?"

"How about I find out right now?" Charlie looked to the waiter who approached. "Hello, there. Where did the young lady go?"

"She works on the other side. I handle these tables. Is that okay?"

"Of course it is."

"Perfect. So, here are your drinks. Are you both ready to order?" The waiter asked.

"You know what," Charlie began. "I actually had a question. Can you tell me who owns this place?"

"Why? Is everything okay?" His face masked in concern.

"Oh yeah. No. Everything's fine. I was just wondering. You know, my husband and I are always looking for new places. We own a couple of diners to the north. Just curious," Charlie added.

"Oh, sure. You know, I don't actually know who owns it. I mean, it's a company, but I couldn't say."

"That's okay. No problem," Charlie said. "And, we'd like another minute or two to look over the menu."

"Of course."

"Thank you." Charlie pulled the menu in front of her face.

Allison grabbed it and pulled down. "He doesn't know?"

"Did you see the look on his face when I asked?" Charlie said. "He knows. He just didn't want to say."

Allison nodded. "That's what I thought. Might be a question for our client, don't you think?"

9

A makeshift bedroom had been set up in a 10 x 12 storage room of the warehouse. That was where Julius Hardin had called home for the time being. He stepped out of the room, buttoning up his jeans as though he'd only just gotten dressed.

"What the hell are you doing here?" Hardin began. "If I recall correctly, the boys said you and me were meeting at 3 o'clock at Stillwaters."

"It's good to see you, Julius." Logan offered his hand. "It's been a while."

Hardin eyed him before accepting the greeting. "For you, I'm sure it has. Five years in the joint must've seemed like a freakin' lifetime. Good to see you, brother." He paced the open area of the warehouse where tables were lined against the wall and men with guns under their shirts stood at the doors. "I guess I shouldn't be surprised you came here. As a matter of fact, you did me a favor."

"I thought the cops would be watching your every move right about now," Logan said.

"You got that right. Yours too, if they got any smarts, but my guess is they don't."

"Oh, they've been keeping a close eye, but no one saw me leave my place this morning. And I was careful to bob and weave my way here," Logan replied.

"Good to know. You want something to drink? I got pop, beer, whatever," Hardin said.

"Nah, man. I'm good. I'm here because you wanted to talk."

"Well that's exactly right, mi amigo." Hardin pulled out a chair and dropped onto it with all the breeziness of a man without a care. Instead of one who was hiding out from the law and the cartel. "You did time because of the Runners. Because of me. I get that. I also get that you weaseled your way into a pretty sweet deal to get less time."

"Julius, it's just..."

Hardin held up his hands. "Hey, I might've done the same thing if I was in your shoes. Oh, what am I saying?" He stood again. "Of course I wouldn't have. I would've kept my damn mouth shut and did my time like a man."

"I only gave them shit I knew would be useless anyway. They were never going to get enough on you," Logan replied. "Look, man. I'm sorry it went down like that. But no skin off your teeth, right?"

Hardin smiled though his eyes were somber. "Nah, man. So, the reason I wanted to talk was to see what you were thinking about now that you're on your own again. The past is the past. I'm willing to start fresh."

"I'll be honest with you, Julius. I'm looking to steer clear of all this. No offense, but I ain't going back to prison no matter what. I just want to do my job and go home to my shitty trailer and live out the rest of my days."

"Well don't that sound dandy?" Hardin laughed. "You know, sometimes we don't get a choice."

"I'm not talking to the cops, Julius. That's not what this is about. Not this time." Logan knew it was impossible to avoid the elephant in the room. Maybe clearing the air was the right move. But only if he could get out clean. Right now, that was looking like an impossible ask.

"I never took you for a snitch, Logan. I can't say I wasn't disappointed. Even if nothing came of what you said."

"That was by design," Logan interrupted.

Hardin inhaled a deep breath. "I guess that does leave us in a little bit of a lurch. I was counting on your support until all this blows over, which I assure you, it will."

"What support could I possibly offer?" Logan began. "I don't have the same contacts as back in the day. The cops are keeping me in their sights. I'd only bring more trouble for you, Julius."

"We'll have to agree to disagree. That said, there is something I will need from you and I'm afraid it ain't negotiable."

"What's that?" Logan swallowed down the fear that lodged in his throat.

"I need you to do one run. Just one. My people got too much heat on them. The cartel wants payback. They want fresh blood and that's you, my friend. You know how the game is played. It's how we make amends for them losing their merch. And believe me, they're plenty pissed about missing out on $80 million. They're ready to burn this shit down, you feel me?"

"Yeah, I feel you. I don't mean any offense, Julius, but what you're asking is a recipe for disaster. I have just as much heat on me as your boys do on them."

"Funny, cause you said you avoided the cops with relative ease today. How'd you manage that?"

Logan tried to find the words in his head, but he couldn't think of one argument that would work in his favor.

"I see. I guess you were just lucky." Hardin walked toward him and placed his hands on Logan's shoulders. "I'll tell you what. You got that kind of luck behind you, then you should have no problem getting lucky on this one last run." He patted hard with his hands. "Did I mention it was non-negotiable?"

———

THE RESTAURANT BEGAN TO FILL WITH LUNCHTIME PATRONS while Allison and Charlie sat alone near the restrooms.

"The food's good." Charlie took a sizeable chunk out of her burger. "It might look weird if we sit here for another hour."

"I agree. Once we're done here, we'll wait in the car for Logan to arrive. Once he's in, we'll make the call to Baylor and he can do what he needs to do. I just want to make sure he gets out of this safely."

"And then what? Why did we come in here in advance of the meeting?"

Allison unzipped her handbag and retrieved a device. "That's why we stopped for these. Once I spot the two of them at a table, I'll stroll casually nearby and drop this into one of the several fake plants near them. I'll return to the car and we'll wait for Baylor to turn up."

"Then come back inside and get the bugs." Charlie nodded. "I like it. I think it could work. Except, for two things."

"And they are?" Allison asked.

"You coming back in here and not getting spotted. And you coming back in to retrieve the bugs. The cops will be swarming this place after they arrest Hardin."

"I'm all ears if you have something better in mind." Allison noticed her phone ringing. "It's Lucy." She answered the call. "Hey, Lucy. Is everything all right?" She gazed at Charlie while Lucy spoke. "He did?" She shook her head. "Why didn't he call me?"

Charlie egged her on for a response, but Allison shooed her away, trying to listen. Charlie rolled her eyes and tsked before sipping on her Diet Coke.

"Okay. No, we're still here. I thought they would be coming, but I guess Logan decided to go his own way. Thanks for the call and I guess we'll be seeing you soon." Allison returned the phone to her purse. "So, looks like we won't have to worry about any of this. Logan decided to preempt the meeting. He went looking for Hardin on his own."

"What? Why would he do that and risk everything?"

"I'm sure it has something to do with our conversation earlier about him apologizing for getting us involved. Anyway, he's out there on his own."

"Do we know where?" Charlie asked.

"He didn't tell Lucy. Apparently, she just got a call from him. He said for us not to bother with the restaurant and that he had things under control. He told her he was sorry," Allison added.

"Damn. What do you want to do? No point in us staying here now."

"We'll head back to the office. I guess we won't find out if that car was going to turn up here. But we do know that there's something about this restaurant that made Hardin pick it in the first place. We should find out what that is."

———

As LOGAN DROVE BACK TO HIS TRAILER, HE EXPECTED A CALL from Allison. He hated bringing them into this and now regretted even more how this all played out. But what choice was there? Logan was going to be back in the game, and they couldn't find that out. There was nothing they could do about it. Whatever evidence they garnered to work in his favor didn't matter at all now. But he would pay them for their work. It was the least he could do. In fact, he'd pay them for the whole gig because it was a shitty thing for him to back out like this. He'd been a shitty person for a lot of years, and he wanted redemption.

Another pick up from a new location. A passage that was narrow and dangerous, but that was the Columbians' problem. Once there, it would be up to him to get it loaded and back to the warehouse. But who was he kidding? Did he really believe Hardin was going to set him free after that? Or maybe he was being handed over to the cartel as a sacrifice. Someone who didn't matter to Hardin in the first place and that would settle the score.

Logan slammed the steering wheel. "Damn it!" He picked up his phone. "Just make the call. Get it the hell over with." He dialed Allison's cell.

"Logan. I thought I might hear from you," Allison said. "Funny thing. Charlie and I went to that restaurant thinking you were going to be there later today. But it seems you had other plans."

Logan shook his head. "I know you're pissed off, Allison, and I'm sorry for that. Look, I'll come down to the office and settle my bill. All of it."

"We didn't finish the job," she said.

"I don't care. I owe you this. After all you've done, I go and drop this on you. Nah. I ain't doing that to Boyce's family or you guys."

"We're on our way back now. So as disappointed as I am, I

guess we'll see you there." Allison ended the call and peered at Charlie. "We just lost our first client."

"I can't believe it. I really thought he was sincere."

"I think he is. But I can tell you, a man like Julius Hardin doesn't just let you slide away free as a bird."

"What are you saying?" Charlie asked.

"I'm saying Logan's heading to the office now. We'll sit down and talk to him. He'll fess up to what's really happening."

"Look, Alli, I get you want to help this kid, but if he's lying to you, it's probably because he couldn't find a way out, like you said. We aren't the FBI or the DEA. I say we cut our losses."

Allison nodded as she gripped the steering wheel. "You're my partner, Charlie and you have a say. I understand where you're coming from. I really do. Let's just hear him out and if you feel the same, I'll side with you."

"Okay. Thank you."

"No need to thank me. This is your call too."

———

THE OFFICE BUILDING WHERE THE AGENCY WAS HOUSED ALSO included a psychologist's office and a CPA firm. Its narrow three-story design was nestled between other larger buildings that mostly encompassed medical offices. There were no short-ages of medical facilities in Tampa as it was a top choice for retirees.

Allison pulled into the parking lot and eyed Logan's truck. "He's already here."

Charlie opened the passenger door. "Let's go see what he has to say."

On their arrival, Allison spotted Logan sitting at Lucy's desk. The two seemed engaged in deep conversation.

Lucy noticed their return. "You're back. Good. Logan's here. But I'm sure you figured that out already."

"Hi, Logan. Thanks for coming by." Allison walked to her desk and set down her bag. "We've had an interesting morning. But it sounds like you did too?"

Logan stood. "Allison, Charlie. I'm really sorry to put you all through this. If I would've known it was going to turn out this way, I never would've come to you in the first place."

"But you did. And here we are." Charlie sat at her desk. "So, did you meet with him?"

"What did Hardin want from you?" Allison asked.

Logan cast a glance to Lucy and then turned his attention to Charlie and Allison who were only feet away. "You know, I thought it would be easy for me to just come here and settle up and move on. But looking at your faces. I can't lie to you. You've been so kind, and you believed me. That's not an easy ask from an ex-con. You deserve to know, but I will ask you this, no one else can know. Not the cops, not anyone. I won't make it out if that happens. I'll be free of him if I just do this one last thing."

"No good ever came out of the words 'one last thing,'" Charlie said. "What was the ask?"

"It's okay, Logan," Lucy said. "You can trust them."

Logan paced the room. "Okay, so Julius says he needs me for this next job."

Resigned, Allison closed her eyes.

"I know what you're thinking, Allison, but hear me out. He's in a bind because of the bust that went down last week. Everyone's on the lookout for him. He knows that. The cartel won't let what happened slide. As a peace offering, to smooth things over, he offered the next job at no charge. It was all he had to offer, and they accepted. He promised me that if I make one more run, I'll be out for good."

"And you believe him?" Allison asked.

"Julius Hardin isn't a man who excepts 'no' for an answer. The moment he sent his crew to arrange the meeting, I knew this was going to be the end result. It didn't matter how much evidence you gathered to present to the cops, I was going to have to do this no matter what."

"That's not true," Charlie said. "You can go to the cops. We have a friend..."

"No, I can't," Logan said. "Julius will know, and I'll be dead."

"You might not make it out of this alive anyway if the cartel is involved," Allison said. "This final run. Where and when?"

Logan eyed her with hesitation.

"I think we can help you, Logan. But you're going to need to tell us when this is supposed to happen," Allison replied.

"You can't help me." Logan walked to pick up his carrier bag. "I took out cash for the remaining balance of our contract." He laid it on Lucy's desk. "Thank you all for everything you've done. I should go now."

Allison caught up to him as he approached the door and placed her hand on his shoulder. "I know you don't think we can help, but I'm going to need you to trust me on this."

He spun around. "How? How can you possibly get me out of this?"

Allison examined Charlie and Lucy. "Give us this afternoon to figure it out. What you can do to help is tell us more about that restaurant where you were supposed to meet Hardin. It wasn't a random selection, was it?"

"No. He goes there all the time. We used to meet there a lot. All of us did. I guess they still do. I never thought much about it."

"We did," Allison added. "On the drive back, Charlie looked it up on her phone. She found the ownership information that was listed on the city's licensing website. A company called Seaside

Holdings, LLC is the registered owner. We don't know who the members are inside the company. Give us some time to look into this. It could be something, or it could be nothing, but we have to find out."

"Say it does mean something," Logan began. "What difference does it make for me and the run I'm supposed to make?"

"Honestly? I don't know," Allison said. "But it's all I have to go on right now."

10

In the first few weeks of January, Allison witnessed the opening of her agency and the arrival of the agency's first client. However, it wasn't the type of case she had expected to take. A mild longing for the simplicity of a covert affair or even a robbery of a precious heirloom took root inside Allison. Those were the types of investigations she had expected as a rookie private investigator.

But the moment Logan Carr walked into her office, simplicity wasn't going to be in the cards for ACL Investigative Services. The question remained; would they even be able to see it through? To protect their first and only client from the threats of a gang leader and possibly a Columbian drug lord?

These were the questions that haunted Allison as she drove to see the one man who might yet hold answers for her. She hadn't seen Milo Nash since the mayor's hearing. He knew she'd opened the agency and promised to check it out, but most of his time was being spent on ensuring the former mayor of Tampa remained behind bars for the foreseeable future. She needed him now. The multi-faceted Logan Carr case had grown far beyond anything Allison could have ever imagined.

Now it was time to bring Milo into the fold. The Seaside Holdings company was worth looking into and he could help Allison with that. In addition, Milo could offer guidance on coordination between the local police, aka Detective Baylor, and the FBI. The taskforce was already working on intelligence that would lead them to Julius Hardin and his connection to the cartel. The problem was, the inevitability that it would ensnare Logan Carr wasn't acceptable to Allison. If anyone could help her with that, it was the Special Attorney for the D.A.'s office. And his house was just ahead.

The historic district was one of several in Tampa and Milo's house was a beautifully restored Queen Anne revival which was somewhat rare in the area. The two-story, with intricate millwork and steep-pitched rooflines, was offset by the stunning deep burgundy and white color scheme. Allison could only imagine living in a home like this. Although, at first glance, it looked to be the quintessential haunted house.

She pulled alongside the curb that fronted the home and made her way to the stunning wrap-around porch and to the main door. The gold door knocker was so very Milo and she used it to announce her arrival.

The door opened to reveal her friend, Milo Nash. He stood roughly 5 feet 10 inches with a rotund appearance highlighted by his white Oxford button-down and navy blue suspenders. Milo was in a class of his own and his style reflected that.

"Allison." He stepped out, prepared to embrace her. "How are you? I've been meaning to get to your new office."

"I'm doing well, Milo." She returned the embrace and kissed his cheek. "I know how busy you've been. Don't worry about it. Besides, we're still unpacking. It's not ready for you just yet."

"You're here on another matter altogether though, aren't you?" Milo asked. "Please, come inside out of the cold."

"Thanks." Allison shed her sweater and hooked it over the coat rack. "I don't think I've been here since you painted the foyer. It looks stunning."

"I wish I could take the credit for it, but my designer deserves all the kudos." He started into the kitchen. "Can I get you a drink? It's after 5 o'clock, isn't it?"

"You're home, so it must be." Allison followed him. "I'll hold off for now, thanks. Just a water will do me fine."

"Suit yourself. You don't mind if I have myself a beer, do you?" Milo opened the refrigerator.

"Not at all. I'll be having one when I get home, I'm sure."

Milo handed Allison a bottle of water and twisted off the cap to his beer. "Based on our call earlier, it appears you're dealing with an investigation that could see you in a fair bit of peril. I don't mind saying I don't like that at all."

"Neither do I if I'm being honest. But I want to help this kid. He came looking for Tommy Boyce and found us. He almost abandoned us today, but I convinced him we could help."

Milo sipped on his beer before studying Allison. "And is that true?"

"I don't know. I'd like to think so, but there could be an element of danger to it."

"What else is new?" Milo asked.

Allison chuckled. "This kind of danger isn't exactly what I had in mind. But with your help, maybe you can steer this thing toward a safer solution."

"How can I help, Allison? Anything you need. I am at your disposal."

"I'm really glad to hear you say that, Milo. So here's the situation." Allison explained the entire ordeal up and until the point she convinced Logan to stick with them and let the agency help.

"You really like to go from the frying pan straight into the fire, my dear friend." Milo tossed back the rest of his beer.

"I can't disagree with you there. So what do you think? I could use your help."

"I'm intrigued by the idea there could be something to this restaurant you mentioned. What was the name of the owner?"

"An LLC called Seaside Holdings."

"That's something I can look into for you. Did you question Logan on how he managed to get early release for a drug trafficking charge meant to last seven years?"

"His parole officer said it was good behavior and I'll tell you, Milo, the people I've talked to all say he was a good kid who got involved with the wrong people."

"And by people you've talked to, you mean this Sam Childers who works for some private contractor that runs the half-way house, and the parole officer? Those are the ones you've already spoken to about Logan?"

"Shane also spoke to Tommy Boyce's old partner. He said the same thing."

Milo nodded. "I'd like to take a look at a few things and see what I can drum up. Logan made mention of a warehouse. I could use that address too. We're talking about three places or entities and I, for one, would like to know if they're connected in some way."

"What about Logan making this final run? Do you think it's possible we could get the taskforce involved without the gang or the cartel finding out? They would kill Logan, I'm certain," Allison said.

"You'd have to have the folks involved be at the right place at the right time. Meaning Julius Hardin will need to be spotted and tailed if necessary until it goes down. And don't even get me started on the Columbians. My recommendation would be to get Tampa's Drug Enforcement Taskforce in on that deal as soon as you think it's safe. Maybe sooner. They'll need to ready a team."

"I'm afraid Logan will pay the price if anyone finds out," Allison said.

"You'll have to decide if it's worth the risk."

She studied him. "Your eyes are telling me it's not."

Milo shook his head. "I honestly don't know the answer to that, Allison. But I can do my best to uncover a connection with regard to these places."

"Milo, I don't want this to turn into the same thing as what happened with the mayor. I just want to keep the kid safe and if it leads to the arrest of drug traffickers, then great. But he needs to stay safe."

"Then you just keep me posted on your progress and I'll do my part and get back with you just as soon as I have anything. Will that work?"

"I think that will work."

———

IN THE GREY MORNING LIGHT OF A NEW DAY THAT threatened a downpour, Milo drove through the industrial park where the warehouse was located. As it turned out, Seaside Holdings didn't appear to have a stake in the warehouse as they had in the restaurant. But something caught Milo's attention and that brought him to make a visit. According to the corporate filings, Seaside Holdings was a subsidiary of another company. However, when he researched that company, he came up with yet another name. That prompted him to check out the building and find out just what sort of place had multiple companies buried beneath multiple LLCs. That sort of business structure raised the hair on the back of his neck.

The building itself was near the back of the complex and was indistinguishable from the other buildings. He pulled to a stop in his pearl-white Lexus sedan along the curb fronting the warehouse parking lot. The lot had three cars in it, which for a weekday, seemed a light load and especially for a company supposedly shipping machine parts.

He continued around back. "No trucks." Milo turned the car around to the front of the complex once again. With his cell phone in hand, he made the call. "Hi there, it's Milo Nash with the D.A.'s office." He smiled while the other person spoke. "I'm doing very well, thank you. It has been a long time." With a nod, he pressed on. "I was wondering if you might do me a favor. I need to know the owner of the warehouse located at 689 S. Larkspur Avenue." He nodded. "Yes, that's in Tampa. I'd like to hold just a moment if you have the time to check now."

Milo waited on the line. The state issued business licenses including sales tax licenses. He needed to know what name appeared on those and if they might match any of the companies he'd uncovered so far. "Yes, I'm still here." He grabbed a scrap of paper from the center console and a pen. "Okay." He started to jot down a name. "This is wonderful. Thank you so much for your help. I do appreciate it. You have a good day as well." He ended the call and placed the phone down, peering at the scrap of paper. "Wilco Shipping, a partially-owned subsidiary of Marigold Enterprises, which is a partially-owned subsidiary of Seaside Holdings." He peered at the warehouse again. "Two out of three. Gotcha."

———

ALLISON SAT AT HER DESK AND HELD HER PHONE TO HER EAR. "Milo, this is great. No, yeah. I get it. There's still a lot of research to do, but what you've uncovered so far is fantastic. I just can't believe it. And you say Sam Childers is a member of at least one of the companies?" She smiled. "Perfect. Okay. Well, I'll let you keep looking. Thank you so much and I'll talk to you soon." Allison set down her phone and looked to Charlie. "How about you and I take a ride."

"Oh, does this have anything to do with your conversation with Milo?" Charlie asked.

"You are a keen observer, my friend. It absolutely does. I don't usually like to engage in speculation; however, I'm starting to think Sam Childers could be behind Hardin's sudden interest in Logan again. I want to know why."

"And how do we go about finding an answer to that?"

"We start with his finances," Allison began. "Banking, loans, properties his companies might own."

Lucy's interest was piqued as she pulled her attention from her computer screen. "Wait, what?"

"Yeah," Allison said. "Sam Childers apparently has his hand in a lot of things. He's an owner in the private contracting company, Galway Rehab, LLC. that runs the half-way house. Well, turns out they run several of them and, he's a member of another LLC that just so happens to have part-ownership in Wilco Shipping, the warehouse Logan visited. A company called Marigold Enterprises. This is all according to what Milo uncovered for us."

"Really?"

"But wait, there's more." Allison smiled. "Marigold Enterprises is connected to Seaside Holdings."

"The company that owns the restaurant," Charlie added. "Holy mother of pearl. Okay, so where do we go from here? You want to check out his finances. How do we go about doing that?"

"The best place for us to start is the public records department," Allison said.

"And then?" Charlie asked.

"Financial records won't be easily obtained, but according to Milo, there are some backdoors we can take to get a fuller picture of Childers' finances. One of those is to start with a search for any bankruptcies. Those are public. Then we can find out who held his loans, if any, through a records request, which Milo agreed to submit for us. In turn, he's working on tracing the full ownership trail of the warehouse and the restaurant Julius Hardin seems to be fond of in search for more partners."

Charlie nodded. "I like it. I'm ready when you are." She closed her laptop. "Lucy, you have enough to keep you going while we're out?"

"I do. But call me if there's anything you need," she replied. "Good luck."

"Fingers crossed." Allison grabbed her keys and coat and headed out the door.

Charlie followed and hopped in as they reached Allison's car. "How is he?"

Allison started the car and pulled out of the parking lot. "Milo? He's busy with the corruption and murder case on the mayor. But when I stopped by his house yesterday, he seemed well. He said he was more than happy to help us out. And he came through in spades." She made it onto the highway and headed into Downtown.

"Yes, he did. That's very good news," Charlie replied. "Have you said anything to Logan yet?"

"No. Not until we know more, and it isn't like he can do anything right now. I asked him to keep his head down and let us know when Hardin makes a move. We'll see what happens." She peered through the windshield. "This is it. Hillsborough County Clerk of the Circuit Court." Allison parked her car and looked at Charlie. "You ready to go in?"

"I was born ready, Alli." She opened the passenger door. A gusty wind blew through her hair even though Charlie treated it with every product known to man to keep it stiff as a board. "Hurry. My hair's moving." She jumped out and closed the door, rushing to the steps of the building for protection.

Allison joined her with sprigs of hair wildly springing out of her bun. "Come on, you look great. Let's go inside."

"You could use some help in the hair department, Alli. You know I have some great products."

Allison turned back to her. "Thanks. I'll pass. I like the wind-blown look."

"Sure. But that could be why you're single."

"What?" Allison shot back.

"I'm kidding! Because I can't explain why I'm single either. So, let's move on." She patted Allison's shoulder. "Where do we start?"

"Right through here." Allison pushed open the door and entered the Records department of the Clerk's office. "We'll start our search for foreclosure records. We can also pull criminal files here too. We'll start getting a clearer picture of Sam Childers' background. I think there could be more to him than we know."

"I agree," Charlie replied.

Allison approached the front desk. "Good afternoon. I'm Allison Hart. I'm the licensed operator of ACL Investigative Services." She held out her ID card. "My partner and I would like to access the public records files."

"Where's your ID, ma'am?" The man behind the desk peered at Charlie. "I need to see your card as well."

"Of course." Charlie retrieved the card from her wallet. "Here you go."

He examined the ID cards and handed them back. "Right through there, make a left. You'll find two workstations where you can look up file locations."

"Thank you." Allison replaced her card and waited for Charlie. "You ready?"

"Let's go." Charlie followed closely behind. "That's the first time I've used that card. Kind of cool."

"Well, they don't give us badges because they don't want us looking like cops, but we have to show them the ID cards listing our agency and my license number."

"It's the closest thing to a badge I'll ever use."

"You and me both." Allison made the left turn. "This looks like the place."

Charlie eyed the rows of files. "It's like a goldmine in here. I'll tell you; they make it easy to find just about anything on just about anyone. Come in here, check their computers and go to the numbered file. Boom! Job done." She approached the workstation and sat down. "Let's see where we can find him."

"Don't do anything wrong in the state of Florida." Allison stood behind her and peered over her shoulder.

"Hey, Alli?" Charlie cleared her throat. "A little space?"

"Oh, sorry." Allison stepped back. "I'll let you do your thing."

A moment later, Charlie found the file numbers and wrote them on a nearby scrap piece of paper. "Okay, here we go."

Allison retrieved a file and laid it on the table. "Looks like Seaside Holdings got foreclosed on for another restaurant owned a few years ago. That's interesting." She snapped a few photos before returning the file and retrieving another. "No bankruptcies from what I can see. But you know, what I'd like to see is lienholder information."

"That shouldn't be too hard to locate." Charlie returned to one of the workstations. "Let me see what I can find in the all-knowing machine." She typed in a few commands. "You already pulled trust information and foreclosures. Now we need to find property deeds. There will be lienholder details listed there." Charlie continued her search. "How do you think Logan is doing today? Have you talked to him?"

"Not yet. He's back at work, I believe." Allison retrieved another file. "I feel bad for this kid. On the one hand, you know, you can't let him off the hook completely. He was an adult and he made bad decisions. That's something we all have to deal with. But getting pulled back into something you want nothing to do with. It's just not fair."

"Since when is anything in this life fair, Alli?" Charlie studied the monitor. "Hey, I have a few more files to check. These are deeds." She jotted down the numbers and jumped up from the chair. "C2590 and C3677."

"Deeds to what?"

"That's what we're here to find out."

———

MILO WAS BARELY 50 AND HE CARRIED MORE WEIGHT THAN he should have. He didn't take care of himself as well as his wife had taken care of him. But he'd been divorced going on three years and in those three years, he had put on 30 pounds. He never was slim, but Milo knew it was time to look after himself. Maybe if he did that, he might find the energy to get out there and start dating again. Hell, he had a lot to offer any woman. A successful attorney with the D.A.'s office. He made a damn good living and had a great sense of humor, or so people told him.

Milo looked at Allison as an inspiration. She'd been divorced longer and had finished raising her children. She even started a new career. Yeah, he could take a page out of the Allison Hart manual and give it a try.

He headed to his office. "Hey there, Joyce, you mind holding my calls for about half an hour or so?"

"No problem, Milo." She returned a pleasant smile. "Did you have a nice lunch?"

He considered her question. "Yes. Yes, I did." He shed his coat and briefcase as he entered his office and closed the door. Milo returned to his desk and sat down, placing his reading glasses on and rubbing his hands together. "Time to unravel this corporate ball of yarn."

11

Allison removed her reading glasses as she hovered near Charlie inside the records office. "The bank that's the lienholder on the restaurant looks to be the same as the two other restaurants that Seaside Holdings owned as well." She peered at Charlie. "Makes me wonder if this bank also has ties to Marigold and Wilco."

Charlie considered the question. "You know, Childers admitted to serving time a while back. I thought it was pretty hard for an ex-con to get a job let alone a loan, or several loans."

"That does seem a little concerning. I'll ask Milo about the bank. Do you think it's worth a shot to talk to someone from this bank?"

"To what end?" Charlie asked.

"I don't think it's a coincidence that almost from the moment Logan is allowed to leave the half-way house that Julius Hardin comes knocking on his door, in a round-about way. And when we pay a visit to the half-way house run by a company Childers is a part of, he questions why we would want Logan's files. Logan was in his house for six months. I just don't buy it that all of a sudden, the moment Logan gets out on his own, trouble knocks on his door."

"It doesn't pass the smell test," Charlie replied.

"Exactly. And now we see there are other properties, other businesses including the half-way house. Milo needs to know what we found. There's more to this than what we're seeing right now. And I don't like where this could be going. Not for Logan."

"The more we find out about Sam Childers, the more likely it is he's the reason Logan Carr is being pulled back in with Julius Hardin," Charlie added.

"But why? Why him and why now?" Allison set down the files. "That's what we need to find out." She walked through the door of the filing room and made it back to the reception area with Charlie following behind. "Thank you so much." She signed the visitor's sheet once again.

"You ladies have a nice day," the man said.

As they walked outside into the brisk afternoon air, Allison stepped into her car and waited for Charlie to get inside. With her hand on the key in the ignition, she turned to Charlie. "You know what else might be interesting to learn?"

"If aliens exist." Charlie closed her passenger door.

Allison smiled. "Well, of course that, but also whether the bank has ever had any dealings with other partners in this coalition of LLCs. We don't know who they are, but we know they exist."

"And how do we go about finding that out?" Charlie asked.

"We have the name of the bank. Milo's trying to untangle the structure of these companies. We'll ask Shane if he can run a background on the bank. I know there's a rule that banks have to notify the government if an individual, or even companies, deposit large sums of cash. I think anything over ten grand. Something about money laundering. I don't know exactly, but I'll bet Shane knows or can find out."

Charlie nodded. "Okay. And what about lending practices? Is there something we can dig up on lending to felons? I thought places like the Small Business Administration didn't loan money to ex-cons. I don't know the rules exactly, but maybe we could look into that too? If Childers got these loans by lying on an application, he could have someone inside the bank helping him."

Allison nodded. "You're exactly right." She retrieved her phone. "You mind calling Shane and while I drive?"

Charlie retrieved her phone and pressed his contact. The line rang.

"Hey, Charlie," Shane answered.

"Shane. Listen, I'm with Allison. She's driving so I'm going to put you on speaker."

"Okay. What's going on?"

After Charlie put him on speaker, Allison began. "Shane, it's me. Charlie and I just left the County Clerk's office. We were doing some research on Sam Childers and an LLC he's a member of. Long story short, he's an owner of a private contracting firm called Galway Rehab that runs several half-way houses, including the one where Logan lived up until last week. He also appears to be connected in some form to the company that owns a restaurant in St. Petersburg. Apparently, it's a frequent hang out of the Southside Runners."

"What is it you need me to do, Allison?" Shane asked.

"Alli and I were hoping you could dig up some details on the bank Childers used to help him finance his business activities. We'd like to know if that bank has had any recent concerns about money laundering. Forgive my ignorance, but I understand there are forms they have to fill out when people deposit a lot of cash," Charlie added.

"Oh, you mean the form 8300 that banks have to file on cash deposits over $10,000."

"Yeah. Something like that," Charlie replied.

"Actually, we have people who can do that. I'll make a few calls and see what I can find. Can you give me the name of the bank?"

"Sure. I'll text it to you," Charlie said. "Hey, thanks, Shane. We appreciate it."

"What are you two doing now?" he asked.

"Heading back to the office," Allison said.

"Great. I'll give you a buzz or swing by later when I get a chance."

"Thanks, Shane." Charlie ended the call. "Well, we'll see where that gets us." She turned to Allison. "Say we get this information, what do you want to do with it? How can we use it to help Logan?"

They arrived at the office and stepped out of the car. Allison continued, "I think it could go a long way in our understanding that Sam Childers may be some sort of catalyst for Hardin to approach Logan again. I don't know what the connection there is, but we'll wait to see what Milo turns up. Once we get some solid information, Shane can take it to Detective Baylor."

"Why would we do that? He doesn't want to help us," Charlie replied.

"He knows Logan came to us asking for help. Offering up details that might help Baylor find Julius Hardin or understand that there could be a connection to the man who runs the half-way house could be what we need to get him off Logan's back."

Charlie pursed her lips. "I hope it's that easy."

The elevator doors parted, and they walked along the corridor until reaching their office.

Allison walked inside. "Hey, Lucy. We're back."

Lucy sat at her desk and pulled her gaze away from the computer. "How'd it go down at County Records?"

"It was eye-opening. Whether it moves us forward, I don't know. It'll be a waiting game," Allison replied.

———

Allison pulled onto her driveway and shifted her car into park. "Thanks, Charlie. I think we're on the right track and I'm glad you agree. Listen, I just got home so I'll see you in the morning?"

The speaker on her cell phone returned a slightly garbled response from Charlie. "Sounds good. Get some rest because I have a feeling we'll be up to our eyeballs in kingpins and gang lords and I ain't talking about Fortnite."

"Just another day at ACL. Goodnight." Allison ended the call and headed into the house. "Hey, I'm home. Nolan?" She'd seen his car in the driveway but not Micah's.

"Mom?" Nolan emerged from the hall. "Hey, Mom. Glad you're home." He kissed her cheek.

"Me too. Where's Micah?"

"Out with her friends, where else?" Nolan made his way into the living room. "I brought back some McDonald's if you're hungry. It's cold, but you can toss it into the microwave."

"Thanks, sweetheart. I just might do that." She walked into the kitchen and pulled out the burger still wrapped in paper and tossed it into the microwave. "How was your day? Any word back from the team?" She heard Nolan clear his throat and turned around to face him. "Oh my God!"

Nolan held up his team jersey and wore a wide smile.

"You're official! I can't believe it." Allison rushed around the kitchen island and pulled him into an embrace. "I am so proud of you."

"Thanks, Mom. I'm having a hard time believing it myself, but yeah, they're putting me in." He pulled back. "Dad made it happen."

"Don't you dare sell yourself short. You tried out. You made the team."

"I know. I know. But Dad found the manager and the manager sealed the deal."

"Regardless, there would've been no deal without you being a damn good ballplayer. Have you told your dad?"

"He knows," Nolan replied. "I mean, Spring training is a couple of months away, but it will give me time to get in better shape and be ready to showcase my talent."

The microwave dinged and Allison headed back to take out the warmed burger. "So what about school?"

"I might have to put it on hold for a while."

"Wait. That wasn't the deal." She dumped the burger onto a saucer. "The deal was, you could work around your classes."

"I don't think that's going to be a possibility, Mom. I mean, I suppose I can take classes at night. But when we travel, it just wouldn't work."

Allison felt deflated. She wanted to be excited for him and she was. But this was exactly how Leo did it. He quit college to join the triple-a team. Then he got hurt and was never good enough after that to reach the majors. Now she felt as though Nolan was going along that very same path.

Nolan raised his hands. "I already know what you're thinking, Mom, and it won't be like that. Dad got hurt. You can't control that. You can't predict it. If it happens to me, then I'll be out, and I'll finish school and then..."

"And then what? What will you do?" Allison asked.

"I don't know. I hope not to have to worry about that. And I'd appreciate it if you didn't focus on that either."

She nodded with her hands on her hips. "You know what? You're exactly right. You're an adult now and I can't tell you what you should do. If this is the path you want to take, then I'll support you one hundred percent."

"Good. I was hoping you'd say that. Listen, I'm going to meet some of the guys in a little bit to celebrate. But I didn't want to leave without telling you."

"I'm glad you waited. Go on. Go and have fun. You deserve to celebrate this." Allison watched as Nolan grabbed his things and slipped on his jacket. "Be careful."

"I always am." He walked out the door.

Allison grabbed her soggy reheated hamburger and walked into the living room to sit down. A notable sigh of relief escaped as she settled into her comfy spot to catch up on the news.

"*Our lead story tonight; a suspected drug trafficker arrested in last week's bust at Cove Harbor was found dead in his jail cell. He was awaiting trial for his part in bringing 6,000 pounds of cocaine in a narco-sub for the Columbian drug cartel. According to police, the cartel's network inside the city is extensive and it was likely someone ordered him to be murdered to prevent him from speaking out on the cartel's organization or its U.S. operations.*"

"That's one down."

Allison would do what was necessary to help Logan but drew the line at any interference in the taskforce's investigation into the cartel. Though her team was getting dangerously close to pulling away the layers of the Southside Runners. The connection to Sam Childers was tenuous but this was a man who saw Logan almost daily when he lived at the home. The question was, did he have anything to do with Julius Hardin's efforts to pull in Logan and if so, why?

Her attention was diverted when her phone buzzed on the side table. She answered the call. "Hi, Shane."

"Are you home?" he asked.

"I am. I got back a few minutes ago, actually. Are you at the station?"

"I just left. Listen, can I stop by?"

Allison picked up on the tension in his voice. "Sure. I wouldn't mind running a few things by you anyway. I asked Milo to look into a few things for us."

"Milo?" He replied.

"I stopped by to see him yesterday evening. Just come over and I'll explain everything."

"I'll see you in ten." Shane ended the call.

Allison assumed this was about the Columbian murdered in his cell. Detective Baylor and his people were probably scrambling to protect the others they captured with hopes of one of them offering the intel they needed. But this had nothing to do with her client, or so she tried to convince herself.

The knock on the door came sooner than she had expected. Allison pushed off the couch and wrapped her sweater around her, shuffling in socked feet to the door. "That was fast." She stepped aside. "Come in."

"Thanks. I hope it isn't too late for you." Shane walked inside.

"It's 8 o'clock. I think I'm okay."

"Well, I know how you get." He smiled and kissed her cheek. "Good to see you."

She closed the door. "You want a beer?"

"Sure."

"Me too." Allison walked into the kitchen and grabbed a couple of brews. "Did you catch the news?"

"I did. Interesting. Baylor and the taskforce have their hands full." Shane took the bottle from her. "This will hit the spot."

"Is that why you wanted to come over? To see how I was doing?" Allison twisted off the cap.

"No. You can take care of yourself. I learned that a long time ago. I'm here because I wanted to know how it went with Logan today."

"Not like I expected." She tossed back a long drink. "Look, I don't want to get into it too much because, frankly, there's a lot to it. But I will say that I asked Milo to step in and take care of a few things on his end."

"Like what?"

"He thinks it's a good thing what we're doing for Logan but there's an element of danger to it."

"Really? Then he and I are in agreement." He tossed back a swig of beer. "I'm pretty sure that's what I told you too. So what's the story and how can I help?"

Allison was about to explain when headlights shone in her kitchen window. "Is that Micah?" She approached the window and pulled open the shutters. "Yep. Let me go and open the door for her."

"Of course."

Allison walked to the front door and unlatched the deadbolt before pulling it open. "Well, hello there. I wasn't sure when you were coming home."

"Mom, it's like 8 o'clock. Seriously?" Micah walked inside. "Is that Shane's car outside?"

"He's in the kitchen."

"Guess I owe him an apology," Micah made her way into the kitchen.

Allison peered outside and was about to close the door when she saw another set of headlights flicker on. They came from a car parked along the curb down the road. She eyed the car as it pulled away. Her first thought was that it was the car from Sam Childers' house, but that wasn't it. Still, her hair stood on end and her instincts told her this was not her imagination. Allison noted the make and model of the car and managed to spot the plates before it sped away. "Gotcha this time. I'm not falling for that crap again." She closed the door and secured the lock.

Allison returned to the kitchen to see Micah issuing her apology to Shane.

"I shouldn't have said that and I'm really sorry," Micah said. "You've been a good friend to my mom."

"No need for an apology, Micah. It's kind of you, but totally unnecessary. Hey, I've been there. My folks split up when I was twelve. It sucked. Still does if I'm being honest. But it's a process that just takes time to overcome."

"Well, anyway." Micah offered a brief but friendly embrace. "Sorry." She pulled away and smoothed down her long dark hair, clearing her throat in awkward response. She turned and noticed Allison standing in the archway. "I'm gonna head to my room now."

"Sure, honey. I'll catch up with you in a little bit." Allison waited until Micah disappeared in the corridor. "So that was interesting."

"Her apology? It was sweet and not needed," Shane replied.

"No, I mean the car I just saw."

"What car?" He came to abrupt attention.

"After Micah walked inside, I was ready to close the door and I saw headlights turn on. It was a car down the road a little."

"Have you seen it before?" Shane asked.

"No. My first thought was that it was the same one from Sam

Childers' house and the parole office, but this was different. I don't know if I'm just being paranoid after what happened with the last case, but I went ahead and noted the make and model."

"Plate?"

"You bet your ass I got the plate." She walked to the pad of paper next to her phone and jotted down the information. "Since I have your attention, care to take a gander at who owns this car? Just to be on the safe side."

He took the slip of paper. "Just to be on the safe side."

12

The time had come for Allison to no longer dismiss the voice in her head. The gut feeling that something wasn't quite right. It was the essence of any good detective and that was what she was and had always been—a good detective. Whether it was her uncovering of Leo's affair, or getting a sense that a claimant was attempting to defraud the state, to this event now. Noticing a car parked near her home that happened to pull away the instant she took note of it; she was not overreacting. She was not paranoid. Allison was honing her instincts.

Shane had backed her up on the decision and the two returned to the stationhouse while the evening wore on. Amid the backdrop of the lively bullpen, Shane examined his computer again to confirm his initial findings. "It's police-issue." He looked at Allison who sat next to him at his desk. "Registered to Detective Anton Baylor."

"Why would he be sitting outside my home? I've done nothing wrong. My client has done nothing wrong."

"Your client is at the center of a potential sting operation intended to bring down the Southside Runners and along with them, the Columbian cartel. I think Baylor wants to know your next move."

"If only he knew that I had no moves. Besides, there are bigger fish for him to fry than going after a reformed man who has done nothing wrong," Allison replied.

"Be that as it may, now could be the time to bring Baylor into the mix so he understands what you've done for Logan and what you've gathered in his defense. Then explain to him Logan's being coerced into action by Julius Hardin."

Allison was reluctant and with good reason. "How do you think Hardin will react when he figures out Logan is being used against him? Because that's what Baylor intends to do. Shane, they'll kill him. I understand Baylor is working for the taskforce and their goal is to find Julius Hardin so they can build a solid case. But keeping tabs on me is where I have to draw the line. If this is how Baylor operates, I have no intention of handing over details to him about Logan. I think he'll find a way to twist it and use it to serve his own interests."

"Point taken," Shane replied. "But that doesn't change the fact that Baylor has set his sights on you. Hell, I wouldn't put it past him to start keeping tabs on me too."

"Then I'll need you to play interference." Allison held his gaze. "As I see it, the only way Logan gets out of this unharmed is for him to move forward with Hardin's plan and relay the details of it to me. I'll bring it to Baylor, and they can set up an operation to intercept the shipment. No one will be any the wiser. But if Logan takes that information directly to the cops, someone's going to find out. Me? No one knows me and I'd like to keep it that way."

"I wouldn't be too sure about that. If Sam Childers proves to be a valid connection to Hardin, and you start digging up dirt on him, he'll figure out who you are. So you had better be prepared for that."

———

WITHOUT REALIZING IT, ALLISON HAD INSERTED HERSELF into a dangerous game of Keep Away. Only the ball was Logan Carr and the person in the middle was Julius Hardin with her and the taskforce at opposite ends. Winning this game seemed an impossibility and concocting a strategy to do so kept her awake most of the night.

She arrived at the office the next morning to see Charlie and Lucy already hard at work.

"We were wondering when you'd show up." Charlie sipped on her mug of coffee.

"It's 8 am. I'm on time." Allison walked to her desk. "What brought you two in here so early."

"Well, Lucy here had a great idea." Charlie approached her. "Why don't you tell Alli what you came up with."

"I called you last night, but I didn't get an answer," Lucy began. "So I tried Charlie."

"I picked up." Charlie smiled.

"I was at the station with Shane. Sorry about that."

"That's okay. Anyway, I got thinking about our talk with Logan yesterday and how we're going to help him try to ambush Julius Hardin."

"I don't know if 'ambush' is the right word, maybe trap," Allison replied.

"You know how we were all worried that Logan would be found out and stuff," Lucy added. "Well, what if there was a way to know his exact location when Hardin takes him on a dry run for the drug pick up? Without any of us being there."

Allison sat down and swiveled her chair to her. "How do you mean?"

"I have a friend. He's super smart and went to school for computer science. Anyway, I remember a while back, he and I were talking about drones and stuff and how the FAA puts a lot of restrictions on them."

"Yeah." Allison glanced at Charlie. "I'm listening."

"He said there are drones that are virtually stealth. Undetectable. And the military has been using them for years. So has Russia and China, but that's another topic."

"Uh-huh." Allison folded her arms.

"So as we kept talking, he said he was getting ready to form a start-up. This start-up was for personal stealth drones. Not military grade, but they could avoid radar and they're for people who want to fly in restricted areas, like around national parks and such."

"Now before you say anything, Allison. I'll agree it does sound a little dubious, but hear her out," Charlie said.

"Yeah, I get that it does sound shady," Lucy continued. "But my point is, this technology exists. The product exists, even if it's just a prototype. Well, it could be beyond that stage now. I haven't talked to him in a while, but I could reach out again and get his thoughts on how far it has come."

"And you think we can use this technology to track Logan's location when Hardin readies him for the shipment?" Allison asked.

"Why not? I don't know the range of something like that, but we could position it as close as we can, and then have it fly out of sight and follow Logan and Hardin to the drop location. Logan stays safe and we get to know where the transaction will take place. We hand over the information to the taskforce and we're golden."

"I suppose we'd need to know the cost of using something like this," Allison began, "and if it's ready to use. But I think it could work, Lucy. We know Hardin's keeping a watchful eye on him. We'd all keep our hands clean, yet still get the needed results." She nodded. "Can you set up a meeting with your friend? The sooner the better."

"I'm on it," Lucy replied.

———

SHANE STOOD AT THE FOOT OF THE STAIRS INSIDE THE stationhouse and peered up. With some hesitation, he climbed the steps and approached the administration desk. "Hey Guerra, is Baylor here?"

"I think he's in a meeting, but you can wait for him at his desk. It's just ahead in the bullpen," Officer Guerra replied.

"Appreciate it." Shane walked toward the bullpen where several workstations crowded the open area.

Small cubicle walls surrounded each desk, not more than two feet tall, and were made from plexiglass. It offered a barrier against the noise of telephone calls or visitors but allowed for transparency.

He made his way to another detective's desk. "Morning. I'm Sully. I work downstairs. Can you tell me where I can find Detective Baylor?"

The detective was younger than Shane—and prettier, which was impressive enough. "He's in the conference room. That's his desk there. Have a seat if you want to wait."

"Thanks." Shane pulled out a chair and sat down.

"Hey," the detective said.

Shane turned around as though he had done something wrong. "Yeah?"

"Is there anything I can help you with?"

"Thanks, but no. I need to see Baylor." He turned his sights to the conference room enclosed with glass walls. Inside were four men, some of whom didn't look to be Tampa cops. Then he spotted Baylor and assumed that was the taskforce, or at least, part of the taskforce. Joint taskforces encompassed several officials from multiple intelligence and law enforcement entities. He wondered if one of them was the FBI man traveling with Baylor, an Agent Dave Reddick.

His wait was short-lived, and Shane stood when he spotted the men exiting the conference room. He locked eyes with Baylor and the look on Baylor's face was less than friendly. No surprise there as he'd already made no secret of how he felt about Shane. His reason for being here wasn't going to improve that outlook.

"Detective Baylor." Shane offered his hand.

"Detective Sullivan." He returned the greeting. "What are you doing up here with the big boys this morning?"

Shane was going to let the condescension slide—this time. "I was hoping we could talk—about Allison Hart and Logan Carr."

Baylor gestured for Shane to sit down and returned to his own chair. He leaned back and laced his fingers together over his paunchy stomach. "What would you like to discuss? I know you understand I'm working on a large-scale operation with the task-force that has the potential to involve young Logan Carr."

"Potential? Yes, I'm well aware." Shane resigned himself to the fact this was not going to be an amicable relationship, but he still had a job to do. "I'm also aware that you had a car sitting outside Allison Hart's home last night. Can I ask your reasoning for that?"

"See, the thing about that is, she's in direct contact with Logan Carr. I have no choice but to understand her role in this scenario. I'm not sure Ms. Hart has any idea the lengths to which the Southside Runners will go to ensure their relationship with the cartel remains intact. And I'm looking for evidence of that relationship. Ms. Hart could be jeopardizing my investigation and she could find herself in a whole lot of danger," Baylor replied.

"With respect, Detective, it seems as though you might believe Allison and her agency are attempting to undermine your operation, which I can assure you, is not the case."

"And what is your part in this, Sullivan? This isn't in your case. Hell, it isn't even your department. Why should you care what tactics I employ to keep Logan Carr and your friend safe from harm? I would think you would welcome it."

"Allison just wants to see to it that Logan Carr isn't going to be used for your benefit at his detriment. He hired her to do a job and that's exactly what she's doing. It doesn't interfere with your investigation. It is simply a way to exonerate Carr of any wrongdoing you or your taskforce might fabricate."

"Fabricate? That sounds an awful lot like you're calling me a liar." Baylor leaned into Shane. "I'll tell you what, Sullivan. You keep Hart out of my way, and I'll stay out of hers. If she wants to offer proof of Logan Carr's adherence to the terms of his parole, I'm all for it. But my job is to stop the flow of drugs coming into this state. And I intend to do that. So you can go back to your friend and tell her that if I feel the need to confirm her whereabouts for reasons of safety or otherwise, then that's well within my authority to do so." Baylor stood. "If there's nothing else."

Shane pushed off the chair. "Detective Baylor, everyone deserves a second chance. Allison is working hard to ensure Logan gets that second chance. I understand where you're coming from. I really do. But she's doing the job she was hired to do. Nothing more."

"Fair enough. Goodbye, Sully. Have a nice day." Baylor didn't offer his hand this time around.

Shane nodded and with derision in his tone, he added, "You too. I'm glad we could find a middle ground on this. After all, we're all on the same team."

13

Detective Anton Baylor had found himself on the defensive for most of his career with the Tampa police. What could he say? He had a chip on his shoulder. He knew it. Everyone knew it. Part of the reason was his own bias or what he perceived as bias from others, and part of it was just his nature. But by this point in his tenure, he'd hoped that chip would've fallen. Instead, it teetered precariously on his shoulder, and that was on him.

He couldn't help but reflect on what Sullivan had to say regarding Allison Hart. If he had been in Sullivan's shoes, it was entirely possible the outcome would have been the same. But for Hart to assume this was just another case for her was where the danger lay. He sat in front of her house the night before because he feared Hardin's men would come looking for her. Okay, maybe he had a little bit of hope that would happen, and he could be there to save the day, but Baylor wasn't the bad guy in this scenario. Nevertheless, he was starting to feel like he was.

The problem lay in his need for Logan Carr to propel the investigation that was growing stagnant. The taskforce had been chasing this gang for years and the bust last week was the closest they'd gotten in a long time. He had no delusions of grandeur they would actually bring down the Columbian cartel, but capturing a gang that helped them bring in the drugs would be a huge feather in his cap. It was necessary for Logan Carr to cozy up to Julius Hardin once again and then use him to catch the Southside Runners in action. If it just so happened to ensnare a few cartel members, then all the better for Baylor. It wasn't fair to the kid, but then, life wasn't fair.

FBI Agent Dave Reddick approached Baylor at his desk. His arms swung wide due to his oversized biceps and his neck almost disappeared into his shoulders. The disproportionate features made him appear almost cartoonish. "Baylor? We got a hit on the tracker we put on Logan Carr's truck."

"Oh yeah? What's the news?"

"Guess where he decided to visit yesterday?" Reddick dropped into a chair next to Baylor's desk.

"His mother's house?" Baylor replied.

"Hilarious, but no. You remember that warehouse we served a warrant on a few years back but got nothing?"

Baylor sat up with sudden interest. "Yeah."

Reddick tapped his nose with his index finger. "So, maybe it's time we take a second look at that warehouse and see if we can get another warrant to stick. If the Southside Runners are operating out of there, and that's where Hardin is holed up, this could be our shot."

Baylor nearly leaped out of his chair. "Let's go talk to the judge." He followed Reddick who had already started outside. "Don't suppose you happened to see who stopped by my desk after our meeting?"

"Sorry, must've missed that." Reddick picked up his pace.

"Sullivan from downstairs. Says he wanted to know why we were watching his friend, Allison Hart's, house last night."

"What did you tell him?" Reddick reached his car outside and pressed on the remote to unlock it.

"Exactly what we talked about. Sullivan has no clue how much danger that lady could be in because she's hanging around with Logan Carr."

"Good. Hopefully, he'll relay that information to her. We need her to back off before Julius Hardin figures out she's in the picture." He shook his head. "We sure as hell don't need any more fingers in this damn pie."

———

LUCY ARRIVED AT THE HARBORSIDE COFFEE SHOP AND ordered a drink before taking a seat at a table overlooking the bay. She peered through the window at the grey waters that reflected the dreary sky. So far, the new year was off to a good start. Lucy felt more like herself with each passing day, though she missed her father every waking second. Still, he would be proud of what she decided to do with her life. Well, maybe. She hadn't even finished her two-year degree from the community college. But following in his footsteps, she hoped, would have made him happy. Although ACL's first case, which resulted from a lead from her father's past, seemed an extreme example of what was to come. Lucy had hoped they could start off easy. But then, nothing in her life had been easy.

A man stopped at her table and caught her attention. She gazed up at him. "Oh, hey. I didn't see you come in."

"You looked deep in thought. I almost hated to disturb you." Kendall Murray leaned over for a brief embrace. "It's good to see you again, Lucy. I'm so sorry about your dad." He pulled out a chair opposite her and sat down.

"Thank you. It's good to see you too. Thanks for coming down."

"Yeah. No problem." Kendall wore a trimmed 5 o'clock shadow with wavy dark hair he kept short. The 22-year-old pushed up his glasses that had slid down his nose.

"Did you order anything? I can grab you a coffee," she said.

"I did, yeah." Kendall held her gaze. "So, I was surprised to hear from you, especially after what happened."

"Between us?" She smiled. "Well, sometimes things just don't work out. I still consider you my friend. That hasn't changed."

"Friend." He smiled and nodded. "Well, good. That's good. So listen, you wanted to talk about my business?"

A barista arrived and placed two coffees on the table. "Let me know if you need anything else."

"Thank you," Lucy replied. "Yeah. I was wondering, first of all, how it was coming along and second of all, if progress has been made, I'd like to discuss the use of the prototype."

Kendall sipped on his drink and studied Lucy. "Why would you be interested in my drone?"

"I think I mentioned, after my dad died, I sort of went into the family business. I went to work for another agency run by the woman who helped me get to the bottom of what happened to my dad. But we're all sort of partners if you know what I mean."

"Uh-huh. Go on," He said.

"We're working on something big right now and we could use that technology. It could potentially save lives."

"Saving lives. Can I ask in what way?" Kendall replied.

Lucy hesitated to bring him into the fold. The element of danger hung over their heads, though Allison and Charlie downplayed the risks. Perhaps they hadn't realized or accepted them. "Well, it's complicated."

"I see." Kendall nodded. "Lucy, this is my technology; my company. I can't let it be a part of something I have no idea about. You do understand that?"

"Yeah. No, I get it." She tucked her dark hair behind her ears. "Look, I know this sounds all clandestine, and I suppose it is, but I wasn't lying when I said it could save lives. We'd just need it for a few hours at a day and time that hasn't been determined but will come soon."

Kendall stirred his coffee with a wooden stir-stick and cast his eyes to the cup. Their deep brown hue reflected the concern and hesitation worn on his face. "So, if I do this, maybe you'll consider giving me a second chance?" His eyes darted up at her.

Lucy smiled. "You really want to ask that question? I remember it was you who wasn't interested in a second date. And not that I don't enjoy being blackmailed..."

"Blackmailed?" He laughed. "How about we call it a little quid pro quo? And maybe I was an idiot. Maybe I'd like a second chance."

"I'm all about second chances," Lucy began. "Fine. I'll agree to another date if you come and meet with my colleagues to talk about this. But Kendall, it's urgent."

"I'll clear my schedule."

———

LUCY RETURNED TO THE OFFICE TO FIND ALLISON AND Charlie at their desks.

"You're back. Great," Allison began. "How did it go?"

"Well," Lucy's full smile brought out her green eyes. "We have a meeting set up with the developer. He's coming here at 6 o'clock this evening if that's okay. I know it's late, but he said he couldn't leave his office until after 5."

"No. That's great. I'm happy to stay. Great work, Lucy," Allison said.

"Um, Alli, wasn't Micah supposed to leave for school in the morning?" Charlie began. "I thought you mentioned earlier you and Leo were taking the kids out for dinner tonight to say goodbye."

"Oh, that's right," Allison replied.

"That's okay," Lucy said. "I'm sure Charlie and I can handle things. Right, Charlie?"

"Of course. The boys are with their father tonight, so I'm free as a bird." Charlie walked to Allison's desk. "It's okay, Alli. We're perfectly capable of handling a meeting."

"I know you are. It's not that." Allison shook her head. "It's just that I'm angry with myself for forgetting. Micah and I are just now starting to get along better and I need to keep my priorities straight. I almost blew it."

"But you didn't," Charlie said. "I'll order some pizza and we'll make it a dinner meeting." She turned to Lucy. "Who is this guy, anyway?"

"His name is Kendall Murray. He's 22 years old. I went to school with him for about a year when he transferred to the University of Miami. He dropped out shortly thereafter to pursue the start-up. Backing initially came from a Kickstarter campaign but now he has a few angel investors. That's all I know right now."

"You've done your homework," Allison said. "How far along is he with his prototype?"

"He has three currently in working order. But only one has the stealth technology that seems to be working."

"Seems?" Charlie asked.

"I'm sure he'll tell us more when he gets here. But yeah, if it doesn't work the way it should, we might not be able to use it."

"Then let's keep in the back of our minds a Plan B," Allison said.

"What's our Plan B?" Charlie asked.

"When the time comes, if the drone isn't the solution, I'll follow him to the drop location."

Charlie nearly doubled over with a full belly laugh. "The hell you are. You're kidding right?"

"Charlie, I'm not kidding. I highly doubt Logan will be able to take a phone with him, otherwise, we could track his location. Julius Hardin wouldn't be the head of the Southside Runners if he wasn't smart. He already knows Logan doesn't want to do this and won't make it easy for anyone to find him. So, if this drone doesn't work out, I'll have no choice but to tail him and get as close as I can."

"On the night? No way, my friend," Charlie said.

"It won't be on the night of the actual pick up. I'm crazy, but not that crazy. No, I'm talking about on his dry run. We know Julius wants him to make a dry run for timing and checking the route. That's when I'll be following. But look, it's a last resort only. Okay? Let's keep our fingers crossed that the meeting with Kendall Murray goes well."

"We'll make sure it does," Charlie replied.

14

This agency meant everything to Allison. It had taken her years, but she finally found her place in this world. Succeeding at it would take more hard work than she imagined. And it wasn't arrogance that made her believe it wouldn't have been such a challenge. It was just that reality was always different than the fantasy. It wasn't unlike when she first became a mother. Allison imagined herself sitting on the sofa with a good book and a cup of tea while the baby rocked away quietly in the corner of the room, happy and cooing. In reality, it was nothing of the sort. Reading a book? Yeah, right. Like that ever happened again until the kids were at least in middle school. And having any peace and quiet? That didn't happen either, not for a long time.

So when she imagined herself running a private detective agency, she imagined herself diligently working from 9 to 5 and going home to enjoy what she had left of her family. Instead, the reality was, she brought her work home. It wasn't something she could turn off. And even though her partners were handling a meeting without her, it occupied her thoughts as she sat in the restaurant with her ex-husband, Leo, and their two adult children.

"Mom?" Micah said. "What do you think?"

Allison was pulled back to the moment. Muffled conversations became clearer, silverware and glasses clinked around her. She looked at Micah, who wore a mask of confusion. "Oh, sorry honey, what did you say?"

"I asked what you thought about me changing my major this year."

"Well, I suppose now's the time to do that since you'll be wrapping up your general requirements this year," Allison replied.

Leo peered at her. "Is everything all right, Allison? You seem distracted. Are we keeping you from something?"

The candle placed in the center of the table cast a shadow on Leo, making his plump, deeply lined face appear softer, younger. His thinning brown hair didn't look as thin. Allison felt as though she was gazing at the Leo from 10 years ago. Before the heartbreak, before the guilt of her failed marriage.

However, that didn't change the fact that Leo returned a look that proved irritating later in their marriage and was a sharp reminder of why they were divorced. It was a look that said *"You're the mother. You're supposed to be paying attention to your children."* Although, she didn't think he meant it quite as cruelly as it felt.

Leo had thus far been supportive of Allison's new career after initial reluctance. At least insomuch as he felt assured that she and their family were not in harm's way. They had reached an understanding that he was no longer in control of her future.

"I'm here. Sorry." Allison turned to Micah. "Yes, I think you should choose a major that suits you and I'll support whatever it is you want to study." She picked up her glass of Merlot and sipped on it. "So, you're meeting your friends first thing in the morning to drive back to school?"

"Yep. We're leaving early, 7am." Micah looked at Nolan. "We'll try not to wake you."

"You won't." Nolan stabbed at his cut piece of steak and shoved it in his mouth.

"Well, this is nice," Leo began. "All of us enjoying a family dinner to see Micah off to school. It's been really great having you home, Micah. Despite what you might think, we do actually miss you when you're away at school."

"I know. I miss you guys too." She looked at Allison. "I'm glad I came home."

"Nolan's got an exciting year ahead for him, don't you, son?" Leo asked. "Spring training and all that."

"Yeah, it should be great. I hope I can make you proud," Nolan replied.

"You would make us proud whether you made it to triple-a ball or not." Allison felt her phone buzz in her lap. She gazed down at the screen to see what it was. A text message had arrived from Charlie. *"Developer says drone is functioning. Wants to give us a test run before agreeing to put it to use."*

Allison smiled and returned her attention to the conversation.

"Who was that?" Leo asked.

"Charlie. She and Lucy had a meeting and it went well. They did great and didn't need me there at all."

"How is Lucy doing with everything?" Nolan swallowed down his steak.

"She's doing better. A lot better," Allison began. "I'm so glad she decided to do this with us. It's really made all the difference."

"Do you like her or something?" Micah asked him.

"No. I was just asking. She's been through a lot and now she's working with Mom. I think it's cool. She's tough."

"She is tough. And I wouldn't mind it so much if you had a soft spot for her." Allison revealed a sly grin. "You two are about the same age. You enjoy each other's company. How much better can you get?"

"First of all, Nolan needs to keep his focus on baseball. His performance in this league could mean he makes it to the majors. Something I was never able to do," Leo said.

"Okay, can we stop talking about me like I'm not here?" Nolan demanded. "Geez, you say one thing around here..."

Allison winked at Micah. "Oh, look. Our dinner has arrived."

———

NATURAL PRESERVATION AREAS WERE PREVALENT IN TAMPA and the surrounding areas. There was a lot of swamp to be found. It was determined that a location near East Tampa, which boasted several marshy areas and keys, was the best place to test the drone. Little to no air traffic and few people around.

Allison stood on the soft earth with the developer of the drone, Kendall Murray. Charlie stood on the other side of her while Lucy assisted Kendall with the preparations for the demonstration.

"How did your dinner go last night?" Charlie asked Allison.

"It went well. Micah was up and out the door early this morning."

"I know you'll miss her, and I'm really glad you two seem to be on the mend."

"I can't tell you how good it feels. It's still tentative, but we are making strides. So, what do you think about this? Last night's meeting went well."

"It did. You should've seen Lucy. She was amazing. We're really lucky to have her working with us," Charlie said. "My main concern is the cost and whether it truly is stealth."

"I agree. The last thing we need is for Julius Hardin to spot something flying over them while Logan's his captive audience."

"Well, we'll have to see how we do. Have you heard any news from Shane?"

"I haven't talked to him yet this morning. I'm not sure if he has gotten anywhere with the bank situation."

"Okay, everyone." Lucy walked back toward them. "Kendall's ready to operate the test flight."

He held a large tablet in his hands and made his way toward them. "We'll start by taking her out a mile and bringing her back."

"It'll go that far?" Charlie asked.

"Much farther, actually, but you'll see in a minute. I imagine a few miles will be well beyond your needs."

"It's hard to say at this point," Allison said. "But I'm excited to see what she can do."

"Then let's get started." Kendall used his index finger on the screen. Four blades, one on each corner of the drone, fired up and started to spin. "That's a good start." He gazed at his screen again and used his finger to press the commands. "She's off the ground."

Allison, Charlie, and Lucy watched as the drone ascended into the air. A small camera was mounted on the bottom and a live feed of the video broadcast to the tablet Kendall held in his hands.

He smiled. "And she's off."

They watched the drone disappear in the distance when Allison began, "how do you keep track of its location?"

"On here. The flight pattern, time, distance, all of it is centrally located on this command center application. And the video is live through this here." He positioned the tablet to show them the camera.

"Impressive," Allison said.

"That's the point of all this, right?" Kendall answered.

"So how do we confirm it can't be spotted on radar?" Charlie asked.

"Glad to see you're paying attention." He punched in a few more commands. "This screen here is the radar detector. As you can see in the split screen, the drone doesn't show up." He looked at Allison. "Your intended use of this is exactly the reason I created it. Not for those who want to skirt the law by flying in restricted airspace, but to assist law enforcement. I hope it will meet expectations."

"I'm sure it will. I just hope we can afford it," she replied.

"If this works, we'll talk about that because I want to present this to the authorities."

"You'd stand to make a killing if it succeeds," Charlie said.

"I won't lie and say that wouldn't be great, but I want it to help. We have a real problem in this state combating the influx of drugs. This could be something useful in the police's arsenal." He pressed on his tablet screen again. "Okay, let's bring her back home. She's reached the mile marker and I'm turning her around."

Allison viewed the radar and the streaming video feed. "This is incredible. I think this could work for us. It'll keep a lot of people safe."

"That's the goal, Allison," Kendall replied.

———

SHANE SULLIVAN'S PRIMARY JOB WAS AS A DETECTIVE IN Investigations and Support for the Tampa Police in downtown. He'd held this position after passing the detective test and was offered the DLIS, the District Latent Investigations Squad. These were the detectives who investigated property theft, auto theft, and even assaults. But Shane was generally assigned to the property thefts or counterfeit merchandise. Low-level break-ins, usually unarmed suspects. It was great and he was glad to be a part of the team. But he strived for the Major Crimes Unit. That was where the real bad guys were brought down. Murderers, drug distributors, human traffickers. He understood that these things took time and he was willing to put in that time.

So when Allison needed him to jump in on something, he was more than willing because, in the end, it could help him just as much as her. After what happened a few months ago, however, before Allison started her agency, things were scary for a while. Shane helped her and the detectives in the Major Crimes Unit bring down the city mayor and a few other bad guys. Two of whom tried to come after Allison. Now she had called on him again. This time, to look into the financial ties to a bank that companies connected to Sam Childers appeared to engage.

FinCEN, the Financial Crimes Enforcement Network, is a bureau of the Treasury Department tasked with fighting money laundering. The banks submit their BSA reports, the Bank Secrecy Act, which highlights suspected transactions. Shane made a request regarding the transactions of Seaside Holdings and the other LLCs that had Childers' name on them.

As it turned out, Childers wasn't the model reformed citizen he had portrayed himself to be. The printer room was near the back and after pulling off the reports, he marched straight into his Lieutenant's office.

"Hey, L.T., you have a minute?" Shane asked.

"Sure. Come on in, Sully. What's going on?" Lieutenant Loretta Cooper had been with the department for 15 years. She was fair but tough and exactly what Shane Sullivan needed in a mentor.

"This is outside of my usual scope of work, so I wanted to run it past you." He walked inside and sat down. "A friend of mine, a

P.I., came to me and asked me to run a bank inquiry on a company with ties to a man named Sam Childers."

"You'd better tell me there was a legitimate reason for doing so, Sully. You know the rules."

"I do. And yes, there was reason. It could involve that major drug bust last week."

"Baylor's case. I thought the purpose of our little sit-down with him was so you understood that you were not to get in his way," she replied.

"I know that and Lieutenant, I'm not getting in his way. Look, my P.I. friend."

"It's Allison Hart, right?"

Shane nodded.

"Just say Allison next time. I know you two are friends. Go on," she added.

"So anyway, I got the report back and it looks like Seaside Holdings, which Sam Childers is a member of, was flagged for suspected transactions by the bank's corporate office. The branch itself, however, doesn't appear to have been cited."

"I'm listening."

"I'm waiting to hear back from Milo Nash with the DA's office. He's also checking into the corporate structures of several LLCs that appear to include Sam Childers, but more importantly, this suggests a connection between Childers and Julius Hardin."

"Suspected leader of the Southside Runners. How so?"

"There's a known hang out of the gang. A restaurant called Stillwaters in St. Pete's. Sam Childers is part owner of this restaurant. Now I know that's not enough, but it's a start."

"So how many BSA reports have been filed?" She pressed on.

"In the past year, they have filed six BSAs on various companies including a few which name Childers as managing member."

The lieutenant nodded. "What would you like me to do to help you, Sully?"

"What if Hardin is using Childers' companies to launder some of the drug money he gets from the cartel? Suspicious cash deposits. A tangled web of legitimate-looking companies; assuming there's a connection, which appears to be the case."

"Appearances can be deceiving. Without anything to back up your claim..." she began.

"I think Nash will find the connection."

She nodded. "Okay, Sully. I can see you think you're on the right side of this. And you've been waiting for your big chance. Here it is. I'll let you see what you can dig up on Childers and work to tie him to Hardin. However, if you do." She leaned in to make her point clear. "You'll have to work with Baylor. You understand?"

"I understand. Thank you, Lieutenant." Shane stood up to leave.

"Just don't screw this up, Sully."

15

The confirmation Milo needed had just arrived. As he sat in his office, he peered at the computer screen and re-read the email just to be sure. He had friends in a lot of places. One of which was the Corporation Commission. He'd asked his friend to track down the members of Seaside Holdings. What came back was a trail of dummy corporations, of which Milo had discovered two already, but more importantly, was that he now had the names of those other members. Martin Hernandez, Sam Childers and a man named Miguel Cortez. Cortez was an attorney and not a direct member. He was just a signatory. This meant only one thing to Milo. "Cartel." And the origination of at least one other corporation tied to Seaside Holdings was in Bogota —Marigold Enterprises. The connection between Sam Childers and Julius Hardin was taking shape. The trail to the cartel was forming.

Milo pressed a button on his phone. "Hi there, Joyce. Do I have any free time today?"

"As a matter of fact, you don't have anything scheduled until 1 o'clock. Why?"

He checked the time. It was 10am. "I need to run out for a bit. I'll be back by 1." He released the button and stood to pull on his suit coat. "I told her I would stop by and see the office anyway. Might as well kill two birds."

———

THE TEST HAD BEEN A SUCCESS. THE DRONE RETURNED without fail and remained undetected the length of its journey. It was a good day, and as Allison prepared to step into her car, her phone rang. "Shane. What's going on?"

"Where are you guys? The office is closed."

"You're at our office? Sorry about that. Actually, we're all heading back now. Is everything okay?" Allison peered at Charlie who was about to step into the passenger seat.

"I got the information back from FinCEN you asked about. I thought you all might want to take a look at it."

"We do. Listen, we'll be about another 20 minutes. Why don't you grab a coffee or something and we'll catch up with you back at the office?"

"Yeah, okay. Where are you, anyway?" Shane pressed on.

Once Lucy stepped into the back seat, Allison looked at Charlie and pressed the mute button on her phone. "Shane wants to know where we're at."

"Tell him the truth," Charlie replied.

Allison nodded. "Of course, you're right." She returned to the conversation. "We're heading back from the east side."

"Why are you over there?"

"I'll explain when we get back. See you soon. Bye." She ended the call. "That's one way to handle it."

"Why don't you want to tell him?" Lucy asked as she buckled her seatbelt.

"I don't know. I'm not sure he would see the benefit to this solution and only present us with obstacles and reasons it won't work. Shane can be too cautious."

"That's because he cares about what happens to you—to us. He is a detective, after all, so he's sort of trained to sniff out problems," Charlie began. "Just explain when we get back. This was a good day, Alli. This situation just got a whole lot easier for us."

"I agree." Allison turned back to Lucy. "This was your doing, kiddo. Great job."

"I owe Kendall a date, but it's a small sacrifice."

"Sometimes you gotta take one for the team." Charlie laughed before turning back to Allison. "What did Shane want, anyway?"

"He got something back on the bank," Allison replied. "Whatever Shane dug up could prove useful to Detective Baylor and his team. They might see another way to handle Hardin that doesn't involve using Logan as bait," Allison said.

"You have a point," Charlie replied. "Speaking of, where is Logan?"

"Work." Allison reached for her phone. "Let's give him a call and let him know how things are progressing on our end." She handed Charlie the phone. "You mind?"

"Not at all." Charlie pressed his contact number and waited for the line to answer. "He must be working. He's not picking up." She returned the phone to the center console.

Allison nodded. "Okay. We'll tell him later."

———

THE ELEVATOR DOORS OPENED ON THE THIRD FLOOR AND Allison, Charlie and Lucy walked to the office.

Allison spotted Shane standing outside with a Starbucks in his hand and Milo next to him. "What, you didn't get one for all of us?" She continued her approach. "Milo. I wasn't expecting to see you today. I hope you two haven't been waiting long." She inserted the key to open the door.

"I went out, did some shopping, caught a movie, and then stopped at Starbucks before running into this guy." Shane thumbed to Milo. "But hey, you're here now and Milo and I were just catching up."

Charlie placed her hand on his shoulder. "Good to see you, Shane. You know, I think you've been hanging around me for too long. A snide comment like that deserves praise." She smiled. "And you, Milo. Long time no see. Glad you're both here."

"It's good to see you, Milo," Lucy said. "And you, Shane."

Allison walked inside and waited for the others to join her. "Okay, now that we're all here, I assume you two have juicy details to share. So we should get started. Milo? You and I met the other night and you were going to check out the paper trail behind Seaside Holdings. What did you find out?"

Milo surveyed the office and nodded. "First of all, I like what you've done with the place. It's starting to look like a P.I.'s office."

"That was the goal," Allison said. "Thank you."

"And with that, let's get down to business." Milo set down his briefcase on Allison's desk and opened it to retrieve a manila file folder. He laid it on her desk. "It took a little teeth-pulling, but what I discovered was that the part-owner of the restaurant, Seaside Holdings, is also, through a series of fronts, part-owner in the warehouse where young Mr. Carr visited his old crew."

"And Sam Childers is a member of Seaside Holdings?" Shane asked. "Because that company has had more than a few Bank Secrecy Act reports filed on them in the past several months."

"He is indeed and there is another member who is using a proxy named Cortez, so unfortunately, I can't identify him, but that member has a stake in Wilco Shipping. The warehouse."

"Well, who do you think this proxy member is?" Allison asked.

"My honest opinion is that we'll never know who it is. The individual is so deeply buried that there's little doubt in my mind whoever it is has a relationship with the cartel or is the cartel. That's how they do things. They pay their lawyers handsomely enough to conceal their identity in such a way that it'll probably never come to light. However, Sam Childers, on the other hand, we know he's entangled with these dummy corporations and so is a man by the name of Martin Hernandez. He's the other partner in Seaside Holdings. But I couldn't find his name among the other LLCs. So either he's buried in red tape, too, or maybe he's not the lead operator of this situation you got here." Milo flipped a few pages in his file. "Right here are the details behind the restaurant's history. Inspections, permits. They're all signed by Martin Hernandez and some are signed by the signatory for Seaside Holdings..."

"Sam Childers," Allison added.

"You got it, kid," Milo replied.

"So, what does this mean, or how does this tie into the fact that Sam Childers has received funding for these companies? Who's backing this guy and why?" Charlie asked.

Shane dropped onto the guest chair next to Allison's desk and opened his carrier bag. "That's my cue. What I have here are the BSA reports from the banks themselves. However, the reports were filed by the bank headquarters. That means there could be someone locally helping out Childers. And by using the LLCs, whoever it is could be helping to conceal from the banks that the ultimate beneficiary is Sam Childers and his partner, or partners."

"Interesting." Allison continued to read the documents. "Well, I'm not sure I understand this entirely, but what it does look like is that Sam Childers, Martin Hernandez, and some secret partner are connected through all these companies. And the money—gang or cartel—could be getting funneled through a bank to legitimize the businesses. Money laundering."

"You and I have the same understanding," Shane said.

"Someone inside the bank is responsible for helping Sam Childers and maybe the cartel. Is that the takeaway?" Charlie asked.

"That's the takeaway, along with the multitude of entities involved in this situation," Milo said. "There are a lot of things pointing to Sam Childers' involvement with the Southside Runners through the warehouse dealings and with Martin Hernandez, who is pretty clean from what I've seen, but who is also part owner of the restaurant with Childers. There could be more to him than meets the eye, but all these guys are heavily shielded from what I'm seeing right now."

"If we give this information to the taskforce, it would send them in a new direction and away from our client," Allison said. "Maybe all of this just goes away for Logan." She picked up her phone. "I think I need to let him know where we're at with all this. I tried him earlier but didn't get an answer." She held the phone to her ear. "Damn. He's still not answering." She ended the call. "Let me find the number of his restaurant. I'll see if he's working today."

"I'll get it." Lucy jumped up and hurried to the filing cabinet. "Here you go." She handed it to Allison.

"Thanks." Again, Allison tried the number and waited. "Yes, hello. I need to speak with Logan Carr. Can you tell me if he's working today?" She nodded while the others looked on. "I see. Okay, thank you so much." Her eyes searched the room.

"Was he there?" Charlie asked.

"No." Allison wore a stunned expression. "They said he quit this morning."

———

THE FIRST PLACE ALLISON WANTED TO GO WAS TO THE HALF-way house. In the darkening skies, Shane and Charlie accompanied her on the hunt for Logan while Lucy remained at the office in case he showed up there. Allison feared Logan fled, in part, because of her insistence he move forward with whatever it was Hardin wanted him to do. She didn't know Hardin, but Logan obviously did and was afraid of him. "If he misses his check-in with his parole officer, she'll come looking for him too." She turned back to Shane.

"He can't break the rules, or he could end up back in prison." Shane was in the backseat, peering through the windshield as Allison drove.

"Maybe that's what he wants," Charlie began. "Maybe he would feel safer back on the inside."

"I can't believe that would be true." Allison made the turn onto the street where they met Sam Childers, a man who appeared to be a ranking member of the people Logan feared. "Here we are." She pulled alongside the curb and stopped. "Should we go in? I don't see Logan's truck."

"None of us trusts this guy, right?" Charlie peered at them. "Sam Childers is working with the Southside Runners and Julius Hardin in some form or another. We just haven't figured that out yet. Do we really think Logan would turn to him?"

"Depends on how much he knows about Childers," Shane replied. "The kid's been in prison for five years. He might have no idea of how things have been operating in his absence. The problem I see with this is that if we raise the alarm that Logan has disappeared and we suspect Childers could be partnered with Hardin, we have to understand that word will get back to Hardin. And that might not be good for Logan."

"Then what?" Allison turned back to Shane. "What do we do? Logan's truck isn't here. Fine. Maybe he's not here. But what if he trusted Childers enough to go to him? What if Logan spilled his guts about everything and Childers decided he needed to do something about it?"

Shane appeared to consider Allison's argument as he gazed through the passenger window in the backseat. "What if we go to Baylor? Let him know what's happening. We already discussed bringing what evidence we have to the taskforce. And, hell, maybe he knows where Logan is. They've been keeping tabs on him since he came out of the half-way house."

Charlie nodded. "I don't care much for Baylor, but I think he knows how important Logan is to his own investigation into the Southside Runners."

"So you're saying you agree with Shane?" Allison asked.

"I think so, yeah." Charlie turned to him. "Don't get too cocky about it."

Shane smiled. "I'll try not to. We should meet up with Baylor and see how he wants to handle this. What we've uncovered just might be enough to put an end to all of this anyway." He picked up his phone while Allison pulled around the car and headed to the station. "Baylor, it's Sully." He peered at the road ahead. "We'd like to come and talk to you about Logan Carr if you have a few minutes. Are you at the station?"

"I am. And you need to get down here asap."

"Why?" Shane creased his brow. "What's going on?"

"Just get down here. Bring Hart with you."

He nodded. "Okay. We'll be there in about half an hour." Shane ended the call. "Something's going on. Baylor wants us there as soon as possible."

"He didn't say what it was?" Charlie asked.

"No. But it doesn't sound good."

"Oh no. Logan's gone and now this? Allison said.

"We've done what we can do for now, Alli. We've checked Logan's trailer, his work, and the half-way house. The kid is gone." Charlie shook her head. "Sort of makes all we've done up to this point an utter waste of time."

"Maybe not. Let's not jump to conclusions just yet. Logan's scared. He's young."

"He's not that young, Alli," Charlie said. "I know how you like to give everyone the benefit of the doubt but sometimes, people are just jerks. I'm not saying Logan is one of them, but he's already put us through the wringer and for what? Just for him to bail on us—again?"

Allison's phone buzzed in the center console. She peered at the screen. "You gotta be kidding me." She looked at Charlie. "It's Sam Childers."

"What do we do?" Charlie asked.

"Answer it," Shane interrupted. "Better yet." He reached for the phone and swiped. "Yeah?"

"Who's this?" Childers asked.

"I'm Detective Sullivan and you're Sam Childers. You called looking for Allison Hart?"

"Where is she?"

"Driving. What can I do for you?" Shane shot back.

"I know it was her who just drove away from the half-way house. I do have people who prefer to keep me informed. And I'm pretty sure I know why she was there. If you're with her, please tell her I'd like to meet up."

"Why?" Shane replied.

"Because I think she's looking for someone we both have concerns about. I might be able to help with that."

Shane peered at Charlie who hadn't taken her eyes off him. "Yeah, okay. When and where?"

"Tonight, 8 pm. She knows the place. She's been there before."

Shane heard the line drop. "Childers? Childers?" He looked at Charlie. "He hung up."

"What did he want?" Allison asked.

"Our schedule appears to be filling up. He wants to meet at a place he says you'll know. That you've been there before."

Allison turned to Charlie. "Stillwaters Restaurant. He knew we were there."

Shane double-checked the time. "It's only 5 now, let's keep to the plan. We'll meet with Baylor and once he hears what we have to say, it'll be up to him to relay it to his own people. But we need to find Logan and it sure as hell sounded like Childers knew where he was at."

The stationhouse appeared in the distance amid a line of patrol cars in front of the building.

"What the hell's going on out here?" Shane asked. "Allison, pull around back. I don't want to get tangled up in this mess."

"Yeah, okay." Allison pulled around to the rear parking lot and cut the engine. She stepped out of the car and waited for Charlie and Shane to join her before heading toward the back entrance.

Several officers milled outside on their approach. Shane opened the door to let Allison and Charlie inside. He turned back to one of the officers. "Any idea what's happened?"

"We got a big fish." The officer smiled.

Shane nodded but remained stone-faced. He followed them inside while they walked to the stairs and hurried to find out the reason for the chaos inside.

Detective Baylor stood at the top. "Good. You're here."

"What the hell's going on?" Shane asked while they jogged up the steps.

"You haven't heard?" Baylor started toward his desk but stopped and turned back. "Julius Hardin was found dead about an hour ago."

16

The words that spilled from Baylor's mouth still echoed in Allison's head. Logan was missing and now Julius Hardin, a man who had threatened Logan to do this one last job, was dead. Never mind the fact that he was the leader of the Southside Runners, a gang Detective Baylor and his taskforce had in their crosshairs.

"Where was he found?" Allison asked him.

"The very place he escaped our grasp. The passage where the drugs were supposed to be dropped and where the Coast Guard captured the vessel," Baylor replied. "Sort of puts things in perspective, don't you think?"

"How so?" Charlie asked.

"I told Sully the Southside Runners and the cartel were dangerous as hell. Now you see I wasn't spinning lies." He peered at Shane. "You said you all wanted to discuss Logan Carr. Your timing couldn't be better."

"Someone was sending a message to the gang, reminding them

of their screw-up." Shane followed Baylor to his desk while Allison and Charlie trailed behind.

"You're telling me. The very spot where Hardin's crew managed to flee before the Coast Guard reached them."

"How did you find him?" Allison caught up to Baylor.

"An anonymous tip. Now don't that raise an eyebrow?" Baylor stopped when he reached his desk. "So where is Logan Carr? Might be a good idea to put that kid in protective custody right about now."

"That's why we came here," Allison said. "We haven't been able to locate him. No one's heard from him since yesterday, and the restaurant said he quit."

"Well, how about that?" Baylor placed his hands on his full hips. "Hardin's dead. The kid's gone. I guess your client wasn't as innocent as you thought he was."

"Hardin was threatening him," Charlie spoke up. "And you guys wouldn't help. In fact, you wanted to egg them on. So, I see this as your doing."

"Look, there's no love lost for Julius Hardin," Baylor began. "The guy was a drug-dealing son of a bitch who killed anyone who got in his way. Now he's paid the price for his deeds. But what I see as the problem here is that Logan Carr is nowhere to be found. If he did this..." He held up his hands. "And I'm not saying he did. But the rest of the Southside Runners will undoubtedly assume that was the case. Then that kid is in far more danger than he ever would have been had he just come to me and my team for help. Instead, he went to you people. And where did it get him?"

"We can bicker about this all night," Shane began. "But the fact of the matter is, Logan is in real trouble now. Whether he did the crime won't matter. They'll be after him. Maybe the Columbians too. We need to find him."

"And prove he's innocent," Allison chimed in. "Logan didn't kill Hardin."

"Well, you must know something I don't, Ms. Hart," Baylor said. "If he didn't, then who do you think did?"

Allison glanced at Charlie for confirmation and after she nodded, Allison pulled out a file. "This is what we've uncovered so far. It's time to take a good hard look at Sam Childers, his associates and the multiple operations he's running." Allison peered at Baylor. "What you'll find in there should raise some serious concerns about who he is and who's helping him, including what appear to be some banking insiders."

"Sam Childers? The man who operates several of the half-way houses for the state. I've met him. You're sure you're not grasping at straws, Hart?"

"We discovered several fronts that are tied to Childers and a man named Martin Hernandez. There's another, but we can't seem to trace him back to anyone at the moment. One of the businesses Childers is tied into is Wilco Shipping. The warehouse."

"How do you know about that place?" Baylor appeared to understand the connection. "Never mind. Look, we've been there before. A couple of years ago. They were clean then, from what we could tell. Only recently, we gave it another shot because we discovered Logan Carr had taken a trip there."

"And how did you come across that little tidbit of information?" Charlie asked.

"It's my job to know," Baylor said. "Point being, we were in the process of obtaining another warrant, but the judge has been reluctant because of what happened last time."

"Well, what's in here just might give you what you need," Shane said. "In fact, if Logan was here, he would tell you that the restaurant Hardin had scheduled to meet him turned out to be owned, in part, by Sam Childers through a series of shell corporations a good friend of ours researched. You might know him. He's an attorney at the D.A.'s office. Milo Nash?" Shane appeared to want a reaction from Baylor but didn't get one.

"Logan was approached by Hardin for a meeting?" Baylor asked. "Why wasn't I told about this?"

"Shane didn't know until recently," Allison said. "Logan came to us. In fact, Logan wanted to sever ties with us because he felt things were getting too dangerous. He knew he wouldn't be able to back out of the meeting or anything that Hardin might request of him. But as it turned out, he preempted the restaurant meeting in what I can only assume was an effort to gain an upper hand. Logan decided to meet at the warehouse. That's how we know about it."

"Baylor, we're all working toward the same goal." Shane eyed the group. "Finding Logan Carr alive and keeping the Southside Runners from finding him first."

Allison looked at Baylor. "I'm pretty sure Childers knows Logan is missing. Just before we arrived, he called me and requested a meeting to discuss the situation. I think he wants to know what we know. And glean whether we have dirt on him."

"What did you tell him?" Baylor asked.

"We agreed to meet," Allison replied. "What was I going to do?"

Baylor rubbed his chin, appearing to consider her words. "I don't think I can let you do that, Hart."

Shane interrupted. "Look, Baylor, I realize Allison is a private investigator. As such, she has little in the way of legal authority. However, that could work to her advantage. If you and your team preempt this meeting or try to be a part of it, Sam Childers will understand that we know more about him than he thought we did."

"And he'll get spooked," Baylor replied. "Fine. Maybe Sullivan's right—this time. Where is this meeting supposed to take place?"

"At the Stillwaters restaurant," Allison replied.

"The place you say Logan was initially supposed to meet with Hardin?" Baylor asked.

"That's right."

Baylor nodded. "And you say Martin Hernandez is some partner in all this?"

"Yeah. You know him?" Shane asked.

"Oh yeah. If it's the same one, and I'm sure it is. I know him. Martin Hernandez is slippery. DEA has had him in their sights for some time but couldn't get anything to stick. Now you're telling me he's also an owner in this restaurant?"

"It looks that way, yes," Allison said.

"What else do you know about him?" Baylor asked.

"Nothing really. We've been focused on Sam Childers because we believe he led Julius Hardin to Logan. I think that's why this meeting is crucial. If he has been in contact with Logan, he might know where he is."

Baylor peered at Shane. "I don't like this. But if what's in that file gives us what we need to make an arrest, then I need to put my team on it asap." He sighed. "I would like to send someone out there with you. Just to keep an eye."

"Believe me, Detective Baylor," Charlie began. "When you read what's in there, you'll know the lengths to which Sam Childers has gone to protect himself and his interests. You can't think he won't be watching out for the cops."

"She's right, Baylor," Shane said. "I'll be with them. If Childers has any idea where Logan is, we need for him to tell us. He knows I'm a cop. But somehow, I don't think he's afraid of me. And that's a good thing. You and your people try to pounce on him, he'll bail."

Baylor relented. "Fine. But you best keep me posted. Sully, I'm trusting you to make sure nothing goes sideways."

"It won't."

————

THE RESTAURANT WAS IN SIGHT. ALLISON PULLED INTO THE lot and stopped the car. She looked at Charlie who appeared reluctant. "Everything's going to be all right."

"And if it isn't?" Charlie asked.

"It will be. Childers might know where Logan is. That's what we should focus on right now," Shane replied. "Besides, I'm not going to let anything happen to either of you. And you forget, I'm still a cop. Childers isn't that stupid."

Allison opened her car door. "Let's go."

Shane had reached the restaurant's entrance and opened the door for them. "The good news is, the place is packed. There's nothing to worry about. We have witnesses." He smiled.

"Now isn't the time, Shane." Charlie brushed past him and walked inside.

"Sorry." He let the door close behind him.

A small podium was at the entrance where a young man waited with a brimming white smile. "Evening. How many?" He placed his hands on the stack of menus in front of him.

"We're actually here to see someone," Shane began. "Sam Childers."

The man removed his hand from the menus and his face turned serious. "Wait right here please." He disappeared around the corner.

Only a moment later, the host returned wearing the familiar smile with which he had initially greeted them. "Mr. Childers is ready for you. Please follow me."

They followed the host through the restaurant where Allison and Charlie had been only days earlier. What they had failed to see then was the room to which they were now being led. A room near the back of the restaurant that looked like it was reserved for private parties. Except inside, there was only one man and that man was Sam Childers.

"Right through here." The host gestured for them to enter.

"Thanks." Shane started ahead of them and it seemed to be an intentional move.

Charlie cast a guarded look at Allison. "We could start running now. We'd only need to outrun Shane." A nervous smile played on her lips.

"I'll keep that in the back of my mind," Allison replied with a quiet titter.

Childers stood and tendered a greeting. "Hello again, Allison. You left the house so fast the other day I was worried I said something offensive. And then of course you stopped by earlier this evening but didn't make it inside. Please, have a seat." His gaunt features appeared even more so under the sickly amber lights hanging from the ceiling.

"I had forgotten something at the office. I apologize for being so rude." She didn't address the earlier arrival.

He offered his hand to Charlie. "Charlie. Good to see you too. Thanks for coming down. I know it's a bit of a drive." Childers peered at Shane. "I'm sorry. I don't think we've been introduced."

"Detective Shane Sullivan, TPD. Pleasure." Shane outstretched his hand.

"That's right. We spoke on the phone," Childers replied.

"Yes, sir. That was me. I work with Allison and Charlie when the need arises. We help each other out."

"That sounds like a good relationship." Childers returned to his seat. "First of all, I wanted to reach out to you, Allison, because

I got a call from the manager of the half-way house. You might remember him, Dale Meek? Anyway, he recognized your car from before and said you just took off like you did the other day. I was concerned. Was there a reason you came by?"

"We considered finishing our visit from earlier, actually. And to apologize for rushing out the way we did," Allison said.

"Why didn't you, then?" Childers added. "Come inside, I mean."

"Timing is everything, isn't it? Just as soon as we arrived, I got a call that once again pulled us away," she replied.

"I bet I know what that call was." He raised a brow. "I heard the news myself only a little while ago and I'm, frankly, pretty shocked. Julius Hardin, the leader of a dangerous gang found floating near Hell's Acre." He shook his head. "Karma gets you eventually, doesn't it?"

"It sure does. You knew Julius Hardin well, though, right?" Shane asked in his best interrogator voice.

"What makes you think I knew him? He was a drug-running gang leader."

"Well, you operate the half-way house," Allison interjected. "Logan Carr was a member of that gang before his arrest. And, of course, he lived in your house. It's not too hard to put two and two together."

"You have some funny math, Allison. Sure, I knew of Hardin. Most of the men that come to stay at the house had run-ins with Hardin's gang from time to time. But that was the extent of what I knew about him," Childers added.

Allison wanted to call him out and tell him they knew he was letting Hardin use this very restaurant to meet with his crew, including a meeting with Logan that never transpired. Instead, she would play along and see if he knew that Logan had been missing since this morning. "I don't suppose you happened to bring those files on Logan that we forgot since we left so quickly the other day. Was that the reason you asked to meet? I just assumed it was considering this place is so far out of the way and it's getting kind of late in the evening."

"Is it late?" He checked the time on his phone. "Oh, that's right. You have kids, don't you? You're a single mother, I believe?"

Shane shot a nervous look to her, but Allison didn't waver. "Well, my kids are grown now, but I was a single mom for a while, yes. Did I mention that to you?" She cast her gaze to the ceiling. "Huh, I didn't realize that." Allison knew at that moment Sam Childers was attempting to intimidate her. This restaurant, asking why she was watching his house and now this? He was trying to sow fear in her, but Allison wasn't about to be so easily intimidated.

Shane cleared his throat to garner Childers' attention. "You didn't happen to bring the files Allison was looking for?"

Childers turned to Shane. "You know what, I completely forgot. I had them sitting on my table and walked right out without them." He turned back to Allison. "Why don't we order some drinks? There are a couple of other things I'd like to talk about, assuming you're in no rush, Allison?"

"I have all the time in the world."

———

LOGAN WAS CURLED UP ON THE BENCH SEAT OF HIS OLD pickup truck that was parked in between two commercial buildings. The buildings had been abandoned and a narrow alleyway between them offered all the shelter he was going to get.

It was almost 9 pm and Logan had nowhere to go and no one to turn to. When word reached him about Julius Hardin's death, he knew they would come after him. The cops, the Feds, the Southside Runners, everyone. And he couldn't go to the agency. It would put them in more danger than he already believed they might be in, thanks to him. That was the last thing he wanted to do to Lucy Boyce, the daughter of the only man who stood up for him. Even if he had been the arresting officer the day he was hauled in for drug trafficking. Maybe there was another reason too, but she would never agree to go out with a man like him. Logan was an ex-con now and it was all he was ever going to be, should he survive this. Something that was still in doubt.

He called in to quit his job, threw whatever he could fit inside his duffle bag, and headed straight for the half-way house. It was the only place he could think to go. But even Dale said he needed to leave before anyone saw him there. Logan knew things were bad if Dale said he'd be better off someplace else. He only had a few bucks and the last time he ate was at 7 o'clock this morning. A bowl of Frosted Flakes. If he had realized that might be his last meal, he would've made the trip for McDonald's hotcakes.

Logan recalled a time when Julius Hardin and he were as tight as brothers. This was back in the day when he foolishly followed Hardin around like a puppy. Prison knocked that naiveté right out of him. The Stillwaters Restaurant was where they all used to go. They were protected there. Julius Hardin was like a god to him and he was Hardin's loyal disciple.

Logan's hair had been longer, he had fewer tattoos, and the fuzz on his face was only beginning to thicken.

"Another shot, brother?" Hardin looked at Logan with glassy eyes before he nodded to an approaching waitress. "Hey, yo. Another round for me and my partner."

The young waitress smiled. "Sure, Julius. I'll be right back."

Hardin leered at her as she walked away.

Logan noticed his stare. "Dude, you gonna hit that or what?"

"Already did, bro. Already did." Hardin turned to him and smiled. "You hear the news about Hernandez?"

"Martin?" Logan asked.

"Yeah, man. Martin. They're bringing him in from Sonora. Shit's getting serious over here now and they want his expertise."

The waitress returned with their shots. "You need anything else, Julius?"

"We're good, baby. We're good." He waited for her to leave before continuing. "I heard it from some of the boys inside. They think he'll start bringing in his own people."

"What's that gonna mean for us? For the Southside Runners?" Logan asked.

"I don't know, man," Hardin said. "But I have insurance against this sorta shit. I know what I gotta do to protect myself. To protect us."

Logan cocked his head. "Insurance? What kind?" He raised his shot glass to Hardin before they both threw back the drinks.

"The kind that'll give me a leg-up if I need it. I know you ain't gonna say nothin'."

"I'm not a snitch, Julius. We're brothers, you and me," Logan replied.

"Yeah, I know. Okay so, I got this place, this storage unit where I keep all kinds of shit. Shit that will get me out of tight spots if you know what I mean."

Logan leaned closer to him and whispered. "Like blackmail-type shit?"

Hardin smiled. "When you get to be in the position I'm in, that's the kinda shit you gotta think about. So, yeah. I protect myself. And those who are loyal to me."

Logan sat up in his truck. "The storage unit."

The Southside Runners would come for him now that Hardin was dead. What Logan couldn't shake, though, was the knowledge that Hardin had so much protection around him. Whoever killed him had to have been... "Someone on the inside?" He creased his brow, looking through the windshield at the gray buildings against the black, starless sky. "The cartel?" Logan knew the cartel had already come for their men operating the sub. Could they have come for Julius too? "To send a message."

But without their leader, how would the Southside Runners organize the next pick up; the one in which Julius insisted Logan participate? If it was the Columbians, then they might've shot themselves in the foot. No one in the city could touch the Southside Runners. Not in size or strength. If the cartel needed someone to distribute their shipment, it had to be Hardin's crew.

"So who killed him?" Logan's head hurt. His stomach rumbled and his body cried out for water. He was going to have to leave for provisions. But his old pickup truck was the problem now. Everyone was going to be looking for it.

Logan picked up his cell phone. "50 percent. That will barely get me through the night." He could charge up his phone when the truck was running, but not when it was just sitting here with the engine off. His fuel gauge was already at one-quarter of a tank. No point in wasting gas idling so he could charge up his phone.

He'd noticed several missed calls and text messages from Allison. She had believed in him because Tommy Boyce had believed in him. Maybe she could help and maybe there would be a way to keep them out of the line of fire. Especially Lucy. "You have to tell her. You can't sit here." Logan held the phone in his hands and pressed the screen. His index finger hovered over the contact button. "Allison won't answer. She'll be pissed I ran out on them again." Logan stared at the phone. "I have to try." Her number appeared, and he pressed the button.

———

ALLISON FELT HER PHONE VIBRATE IN HER PURSE. THE SOUND was loud enough to be heard by everyone in the room.

"Is that someone's phone?" Childers asked.

"It's mine. Sorry. It's nothing," Allison replied.

"Well, it must be something. Maybe it's one of your kids?"

Allison held his gaze. Childers knew far too much about her family and it scared her. "Possibly." She forced a smile.

"You should answer it. A mother should never ignore her kid," Sam replied.

Allison looked at Shane who sat across from her and then to Charlie. She had no choice but to pick up the phone. When she saw the name on the screen, her heart jumped into her throat. She answered. "Nolan, hey kiddo, is everything all right?"

"Allison? It's Logan. There's something I have to tell you."

"I can't talk now, son. I'm meeting with a prospective client. I'll have to call you back, okay? Love you. Bye." She ended the call. "You were right. It was just my son. Everything's fine."

"Okay then. We should probably get down to the reason I asked you to meet," Childers said.

Shane looked at him. "On the phone, you said something about Logan Carr."

Childers furrowed his brow. "I made no mention of Logan Carr. I understand, however, that Dale Meek, who runs one of my houses believes Logan might be headed for trouble."

"I think you said something to the effect that you knew Allison was looking for him," Shane added.

"I believe I said I thought Allison was looking for someone we were both interested in. But let's leave semantics out of it for the moment."

Allison picked up on the cue. "Whether you intended it to be Logan doesn't matter anymore. Logan cut ties with my agency. He paid off the balance of his contract and said thank you very much, and that was the end of that."

A flash of uncertainty appeared on Childers' face. He didn't know.

"I wasn't aware of that actually. So, you haven't seen him since, huh? Go figure. What I don't get then is why you came back to the house earlier today. If he cut bait, then there's no need for his files anymore, right?"

"True," Allison nodded. "But I wanted to finish the job in case he came back and decided it was best to keep working with us so that we could help him. And especially in light of Julius Hardin's apparent murder. I don't know about you, but I think the cops would be looking at Logan as a primary suspect. Getting that information is all the more important."

"I suppose so." Childers noticed the waiter. "Oh good. The drinks are here."

17

Something was wrong. Logan stared at his phone. "She called me Nolan." The night air crept inside the old pickup, so he pulled on his leather jacket, which offered little in the way of warmth. Layers, he recalled. He wore layers in prison to keep warm too. This almost felt like prison. He couldn't escape and he had nowhere to go.

Who had Allison been with when he called? The cops? As of right now, Logan had done nothing wrong. He hadn't violated the terms of his parole, at least not yet. Logan turned the ignition and aimed the vents toward his face and hands to let the warm air soothe him. He pulled the gearshift into drive and started in the direction of the nearest convenience store. He needed food and water, gas too. It was a waiting game now. Waiting for Allison to call him back. Waiting to find out who killed Hardin. But waiting to go back to prison wasn't an option. He would rather die.

———

Two drinks in and the conversation circled. Allison was getting nowhere fast with Sam Childers. They continued in the vein of assessing the situation of Logan Carr, but as the hour grew late, Allison wanted this to end. It was all just a game of chicken.

Childers plunked a French fry into his mouth. "You know what, I did hear something that maybe this Julius Hardin character might have been murdered by one of his own. Funny how Logan up and disappears at the same time." He looked at Shane. "That seems off to me. Doesn't it seem off to you, Detective?"

"To someone who didn't know Logan, sure," Shane replied.

"But you don't think there's any connection there?" Childers pressed him.

"Hard to say. You know, I don't work on murder cases. But I could put you in touch with the detective who does."

"Oh, that's not necessary. I don't have any information. I just find it curious is all." He turned to Allison. "Sort of like when people start getting into your business who don't have any reason to be doing so. Just sticking their noses where they don't belong. Nah, I don't want to be accused of doing that if I go talking to the cops about something I know nothing about."

And there is was; the reason for this meeting. He knew Allison and Charlie had discovered something. God only knew how, but he did. It was time to finish this. "Sam, you know it's about time I think we should be heading home. Long day of work ahead of us tomorrow."

"Yeah, of course. I'm really glad to have had this opportunity to talk with you all and try to help our mutual friend. And, Allison, if you're still in need of those files, please feel free to drop by tomorrow to pick them up. Like I said, they're sitting out." Childers stood. "By the way, how do you like my little restaurant?"

"This is your place?" Charlie asked, though she already knew this.

"I'm a partner, yes. But considering where I came from, I'm pretty proud of it," Childers replied.

Shane took a final sip of his gin and tonic and stood from the table. "It's a great accomplishment. That must be why you run the half-way house. To try to help other ex-cons see that there are ways to reach their goals after they get out."

"Ex-con is such an ugly term. I prefer formerly incarcerated people. But yes, absolutely. I'll show you all out." Childers led the way through the restaurant and to the main entrance. "Listen, if there's anything I can do. Anything at all. Please don't hesitate to call me, Allison." He captured her eyes with a deadly stare. "I mean that. Logan Carr is a good kid and I would really hate to see anything happen to him." He held open the door.

Allison nodded. "Yeah, me too. And I'll let you know if we need your help. Goodnight."

Shane was outside and Allison and Charlie caught up to him. They started into the parking lot toward Allison's car. When she opened the driver's side door, she peered back and spotted Childers watching them. A final smile back at him and she slipped onto the seat and closed the door.

Allison gripped the steering wheel with white knuckles as she waited for Charlie and Shane to get in. "It was Logan. The call I got; it was from Logan."

"I kind of figured it must have been. That's the good news. He's still alive," Charlie began. "Besides, Nolan wouldn't call. He would text."

"You played it off well, Allison," Shane said. "I don't think Childers caught on to it. I didn't."

"I'm not so sure about that. Did you guys pick up on what he said as we left? He made it pretty clear he knew what Charlie and I have been doing and that Logan would pay for whatever it was we learned about him." Allison pulled out of the parking lot. "I think Childers will come after Logan."

Charlie peered at her. "Right now, Allison, you need to call Logan back and find out where the hell that kid is. We need to get him someplace safe and fast."

———

IT HAD TO BE AT A PLACE NO ONE WOULD SUSPECT. AS THE hour approached midnight, Allison and the others reached the destination where they were to meet with Logan.

"I see him up ahead." Allison pointed toward the darkened alleyway where headlights flashed. "He's alone."

"Are you sure about that?" It appeared Charlie had grown cautious of the situation. "Someone could be watching him."

"I don't think so," Shane began. "Logan's in trouble and he knows it. I think the only person he turned to was Allision. Go ahead and pull up alongside him."

Allison nodded before flashing her lights in return. The destination was a place she knew well. The ballfields where Nolan had practiced and played for years. There were six fields, three restroom buildings, and the main concession stand. She pulled into the space between one of the restroom buildings and the large stand behind the field where trucks unloaded their deliveries. That was where Logan waited.

She stopped next to him and peered through her driver's side window. With a subtle nod, Allison opened her door.

Logan opened his.

They met in the middle under the dark skies and amid the brisk midnight air.

"What happened, Logan?" Allison zipped her fleece and tucked her hands into her pockets. "Did you do it?"

"No. I swear it." Logan examined the three of them as they stood next to each other, leaning against Allison's car.

"Who told you Hardin was dead?" Charlie raised the collar of her short peacoat to protect her neck from the cool air that funneled through the breezeway.

"I got the call from a friend. He listens to the police scanners and heard the call go out about a body near Hell's Acre. It didn't take long for word to come out that they suspected it was Julius Hardin. That was around noon or 1 o'clock. I was on my way to work when I got the call. I freaked out. I knew everyone would think it was me that did it."

"So you decided to call into work to quit?" Shane asked. "Why go through that step? Sorry, but it just screams guilt on your part."

"I know. But like I said, I was freaking out. I called in without really thinking about it. I just thought, I don't want to put the restaurant in a lurch and just not turn up." He snickered. "I was more concerned about my co-workers than myself."

"When you called me, we were meeting with Sam Childers at the restaurant you were slated to meet with Hardin the other day," Allison said. "He had heard about Hardin and knew you were missing. But he didn't seem to know where you were. That's a good thing."

"What am I going to do, Allison? We all know they'll come after me. The Southside Runners, the cops, DEA, FBI."

"Okay, okay. Calm down." Allison saw the fear in his eyes. His hands trembled. "Logan, we aren't going to let anyone get to you."

Shane shot her an uncertain look. "You're going to be the number one suspect, Logan. We need to let Detective Baylor know we found you so he can protect you."

"You can't do that. He's working for his own interests. Not

mine. You all saw that. He won't help me. He won't protect me. None of them will." Logan looked at Allison again. "If I run, I look guilty. If I hide, I look guilty. What can I do?"

"I have an idea," Shane began. "I know how you all feel about Detective Baylor. And I'll be the first to say he's not my favorite person. But his goal was to bring Julius Hardin to justice. Well, someone beat him to the punch. Allison and Charlie presented compelling evidence to suggest Sam Childers is or was connected to Hardin. Baylor is going to follow up with his taskforce to determine how best to prove that connection. We need to remember, the taskforce wants the Southside Runners and the cartel, not you."

"So what's the plan?" Charlie asked. "What about Logan?"

"As we discussed, Logan, you're going to have to go to Baylor. He'll put you in protective custody," Shane said.

Logan closed his eyes and shook his head. "For how long?"

"As long as it takes for them to get what they need to make an arrest," Allison interrupted. "The important part is that we make sure to keep you out of sight until they find who killed Hardin."

"Then it's settled. Let's go find Baylor." Shane returned to the car.

"Everything's going to be okay, Logan." Charlie offered a reassuring nod before heading to the car.

Allison turned to follow when Logan took hold of her arm.

"Allison, wait," he said. "I need to tell you something."

She turned to see Charlie getting into the car. Shane was already inside. "What is it?"

"I remembered something, and it could help us figure out who killed Julius." He stepped closer to her. "But it has to be you. I don't know what's in there. Hell, I don't even know if it's still there, but if it's the cops who go looking and other people find out..."

"What is it, Logan?"

"Julius protected himself. That protection might come in handy right about now."

———

DETECTIVE BAYLOR RESTED HIS ELBOWS ON THE BAR AND placed the bottle of beer to his lips. The television mounted on the wall above the backlit shelves lined with liquor aired ESPN. Since it was almost 1 o'clock in the morning, the sports commentators had nothing left to discuss except for European soccer, which Baylor detested.

"Hey, man. It's time to close up." The bartender wiped down the top in front of Baylor. "I'm going to need you to close out your tab."

"Yeah." Baylor reached for his wallet and retrieved a bank card, handing it to him.

The bartender walked toward the cash register where he swiped the card.

Baylor looked on and noticed there were only two other patrons inside the bar. This was his usual watering hole where a lot of his colleagues frequented, but it was well past the time any working Joe should be sitting and drinking in a bar. This time of night was reserved for the hardcore drinkers and the downtrodden. Baylor teetered between the two. However, tonight, there was a reason for him being here so late.

Hardin was dead. Baylor and Reddick searched for solid evidence based on leads provided by Allison Hart and her agency. It was all circumstantial, though they had people still working on it. But as of yet, they had found nothing to directly tie Childers to Julius Hardin, the cartel, or to the Southside Runners. The whole thing was looking like a losing battle; this drug war. Every time they made progress, another setback would force them to rethink their strategy. Of course, this had been going on since long before he became a cop. Hell, it started long before he even finished high school. And Florida had been the hub.

Baylor questioned himself almost daily as to whether he was actually making a dent in any of it. Now as he sat here, he wondered who the next Julius Hardin would be. And there was no mistaking that there would be another. There always was. But Baylor had to find a way to prove the Southside Runners were part and parcel of the cartel's Florida operations. That wasn't going to change because Hardin was dead. If anything, it would make the Southside Runners that much more indebted to the Columbians to keep doing business with them.

The Columbians were smart and grew smarter with each passing day, month and year. Their alliances had to be kept in check. New alliances had to be formed to stay a step ahead of the DEA, DHS and all the rest.

Baylor joined the taskforce as a way to be more involved in the protection of his city and the citizens who occupied it. But it had been three years and still—nothing.

He turned when he felt a tap on his shoulder. "You're cutting it close, Sully."

Shane Sullivan perched on the barstool next to him. "Thanks for sticking around. I'm sorry it's gotten to be so late."

"No problem. But it looks like you missed last call."

"My loss." Shane peered up at the T.V. "Soccer. I don't get the appeal of it. The entire world seems to love it. Me personally? Not my thing. Give me a good ol' baseball or basketball game any day of the week over that crap."

"We're in agreement on that," Baylor replied.

"Here you go." The bartender handed Baylor his card and

receipt. "Sorry, buddy, but we're getting ready to close." He looked at Shane.

"Do you think you could spare a glass of water?" Shane asked.

"Sure, man. No problem." The bartender filled a glass from the water sprayer near the beer taps and set it down in front of him. "Here you go."

"Appreciate it." Shane drank all of it in a single gulp.

"Agent Reddick and I scoured the information Allison Hart provided. It's good, but it's just not enough," Baylor said.

"Not enough for what? Bringing in Childers for questioning or not enough to move forward with opening an investigation into the idea that Childers might have been the one to kill Hardin?"

"Kill Hardin?" Baylor asked with a raised brow. "No, man, there's not nearly enough. Look, what they gave us is promising, but it's circumstantial. I can't question a guy because he owns some restaurant where Hardin liked to hang out. I can't question a guy because he's part owner of a warehouse."

"Where you suspect drugs are being run out of," Shane said.

"Be that as it may, we need hard evidence."

"What would that entail?"

Baylor scoffed. "Proof that these businesses are connected to either group. Proof that the partner, Martin Hernandez, also works for the cartel. So unless something good came out of that meeting you and your private investigator friends had with Sam Childers, I'm not sure how much help your people can be." Baylor signed his receipt and folded it before placing it in his wallet. "You're alive. So that's a win."

Shane turned to him. "Childers was looking to see if we knew where Logan was. He also knew Allison and her team have been doing their homework with regard to his business holdings. It was nothing more than a meeting for him to assert his power. The looming threat was crystal clear," Shane said. "Which brings me to why I wanted to see you. We have him."

Baylor shot him a look. His lips parted to say something, but no words came.

"First of all, I won't let you railroad that kid. He's done nothing wrong," Shane added.

"How the hell do you know? Have you been with him every day? You know who he's been meeting with?" Baylor asked.

"I do. And that person now happens to be dead. Look, Baylor, with Hardin dead, you're at a standstill. You've made it clear more needs to be gathered to pursue Childers. Let Allison and her partners do what they do best. Let them find that connection. They're a hell of a lot more resourceful than you know. That will free you up to get to the bottom of where the next drop is slated to take place. And possibly discover who killed Hardin in the process. We're pretty sure Logan was about to be taken to the next drop site before Hardin was found floating in the water. With Hardin dead, plans might change. The date or time or location. They'll tell the cartel about the risk and it'll all change. Then the gang, the cartel; they'll hunt Logan down to keep his mouth shut. You guys need to keep this kid safe, like we talked about. This is for Logan's safety."

"Fine. I can agree to that. You have the kid. Great. Where is he?"

Shane picked up his phone to text someone. A moment later, he turned when the door to the bar opened.

Logan walked inside and approached Baylor.

Shane eyed him. "Logan Carr, as requested."

18

When light spilled around the window shades in Allison's bedroom, the sense that another day had arrived was daunting. It was only minutes ago, she thought, that she had closed her eyes. But on glancing at the clock on her nightstand, the grim truth revealed itself. "7 o'clock." She was late and with Logan's future and his safety on the line, tardiness was unbecoming.

She pulled herself out of bed and into the shower, letting the steaming water cascade down her skin to soothe the tension. Upon stepping out, Allison wrapped a towel around her and tucked it into itself.

Her phone rested on the bathroom vanity and as it reached 7:30, she noticed a text message arrive. *"Where are you?"*

It was Charlie. She was supposed to meet her at the office. *"I'll be there in an hour."* Allison texted back.

"I'll pick up breakfast then swing by your house. We'll leave from there." Charlie sent her reply.

She continued to ready herself for the day, pulling her hair into a high-bun and sliding on a pair of snug jeans and an over-sized plaid shirt. A few swipes of shadow on her eyes and some color for her lips and Allison was ready.

Downstairs, she noticed Nolan sitting in the kitchen with a cup of coffee and a leftover donut. "Morning. Aren't you working out today?"

"Not for another hour," Nolan replied. "How are you? You look a little tired."

"A little, but I'm fine." She made her way to the coffee maker and poured herself a cup. "You want me to top you up?"

"No thanks." He peered at her. "This thing you're working on, it seems pretty important."

She joined him at the breakfast bar and sipped on her coffee. "It is. An old acquaintance of Lucy's father came to us. We're helping him."

"Is she still doing okay?" he added.

"She's doing well. I think she's a natural at all this."

"That's great, Mom. I'm glad to hear it." He carried his dishes to the sink and after placing them inside, he turned to Allison and folded his arms. "Mom, do you think maybe Lucy might like me a little?"

Allison cast her gaze toward the ceiling. "Well, I don't know. Maybe. Why? Are you interested in her?"

"Maybe." His cheeks flushed for a moment.

"You know, maybe when we're done working this case, I can put in a good word for you."

Nolan held up his hands. "Oh, God. No. Please don't do that."

"Why not?" she asked. "You said you liked her."

"Yeah, well, that doesn't mean I want my mommy to jump in and say what a good boy she has."

"Nolan."

"No. Mom. It's okay. I just wanted to know if she maybe felt the same way. I'll talk to her when I'm ready. Please don't say anything."

"Okay. Fine. I won't say anything." Allison heard a car pull onto the driveway and peered through the kitchen window. "Charlie's here. I have to go." She picked up her courier bag. "Listen, honey, I don't know when I'll be home."

"That's okay. This is your job now. I understand what it'll take for you to do it. I can get myself dinner if I have to. I'm a big boy now."

She leaned into him and kissed his cheek. "I know you are. Have a good day. Show them what you got, kiddo."

"I will, Mom. Love you."

"Love you, too." Allison made her way to the door and stepped outside. Her hand shielded her eyes from the glare of the sun.

Charlie rolled down her window wearing oversized sunglasses with her black hair perfectly in place. "Good morning, sunshine. Get in. We have a lot to do today."

Allison stepped into Charlie's silver Chevy crossover, a huge step up from her own crappy Honda. Maybe someday she would bite the bullet and get a new car, but with summer over, she already forgot about how the a/c didn't work. "Thanks for picking me up."

"I can't wait around for you all day." She shifted the gear into reverse and backed out of the driveway. "Where are we headed?"

Allison revealed a wide grin. "I thought we'd check out a place Logan told me about before we cut him loose and sent him to Baylor."

"Where's that?" Charlie asked.

"A storage unit."

Charlie glanced at her with a furrowed brow. "A storage unit? When did he mention that?"

"He pulled me aside before we left the ballfield. He said it was a last resort because he thought Hardin's crew might know about the place and thought they would go there and clear it out. But in the event that hadn't happened..."

"Okay. And what's supposed to be inside this storage unit?"

"It belonged to Julius Hardin. Logan wasn't sure Hardin still used it, but he thought he might have considering what he kept inside."

"Jimmy Hoffa's body?" Charlie replied.

Allison smiled. "If only. Logan said he kept things in there that would help him negotiate terms in his favor or maybe use against certain people. He thinks there might be something inside this unit that will help us uncover more about Sam Childers or his partner, Martin Hernandez, among others."

"We're going to a storage unit that holds what can only be classified as blackmail material. And the Southside Runners might know about it. So, how do you plan on getting us inside?"

"Logan gave me the code. Unless Hardin changed it, it should still work."

"Great. You know, we're due for some danger, Alli. We don't fear for our lives nearly enough."

Allison turned to her with a grin. "How right you are."

———

IT WAS APPROACHING 9 O'CLOCK IN THE MORNING AND THE storage unit was just ahead. Charlie turned into the compound and waited at the gate. "There are cameras everywhere." She peered at the camera stationed on the gate and then the other two nearby. "If Hardin's crew comes here, you know that'll be the first place they check; the cameras."

"For whatever reason, Julius Hardin considered Logan trustworthy, at least until the point of Logan's arrest years ago. And to be honest, if anyone else knew about this place, it was probably his killer and the unit will have been cleaned out." Allison looked at Charlie. "I guess what I'm saying is that if it's empty, then it's empty and someone else knew about it. If it isn't, I doubt anyone else knew other than Logan."

"I really hate it when you use perfectly logical arguments." Charlie pulled close enough to the gate to reach the entry keypad. "What's the code?"

Allison peered at the sticky note in her hand. "102309."

"Looks like a date. Does it mean something?"

"According to Logan, it was the date of Hardin's first murder," Allison replied flatly.

"Good God. I'm glad that stain's been wiped off the planet." Charlie entered the code. "Well, what do you know?" The wide wrought iron gate pulled back on its wheels and Charlie rolled inside.

"We're looking for unit number 34829." Allison narrowed her eyes as she peered at the numbers on the units. "Looks like it might be at the end, down a ways." She waited while Charlie continued driving slowly along the road between the buildings. "This is it. Right here."

Charlie stopped. "Okay. Let's be quick about this." She opened the door and stepped outside into the bright light of a sunny day. "I'll let you do the honors, Alli."

Allison entered the code on the keypad, the same one as before, and the latch unlocked. "So far so good." The two yanked up on the orange metal rolling door and she walked inside. Charlie trailed close behind.

"Where should we start? I don't like being in here," Charlie said.

"Neither do I. Let's just see what pops out at us." Allison headed to the back wall where three metal shelving units lined the space. "Oh good. Boxes with no labels. It going to be a crapshoot."

"There isn't as much stuff in here as I thought there would be. But whatever we find, Alli, we're going to have to notify Detective Baylor. Whatever is in here might help the taskforce put away some bad people, including Childers." Charlie studied the various items on the shelves against the other walls; boxes, machine parts. "Looks like Hardin was running his own chop shop too. Look at some of this stuff."

"Maybe. With the connection of Wilco Shipping to Seaside Holdings, anything is possible. Hardin's dead, so Sam Childers might be breathing a sigh of relief." Allison continued to search the boxes.

"Until he finds out about this place." Charlie raised the lid from one of the boxes and peered inside.

"Uh, Charlie? You need to see this."

"What is it?"

"Pictures." Allison shuffled through them. "It's Childers with another man and that man has a gun on his waist. There are several photos of Childers with him. He must be someone important. At least, important to Hardin."

"Take a picture of these with your phone and send one to Shane. He might know who that is, or he can find out," Charlie said.

"Good idea." Allison retrieved her phone and captured two of the images and texted them to Shane before dialing his number. "Hey, Shane. I just sent you some images. Do you happen to know who the man is with Sam Childers?"

"Let me take a look," Shane replied.

She waited on the line.

"Allison, where did you get these?" he asked.

"Charlie and I are at a storage unit. Logan told us about it."

"Why didn't you mention this to me? You're there alone? Just the two of you?"

"Shane, do you know who that is because we'd like to leave as soon as possible. And, to answer your question, it's just us. I didn't say anything because Logan wasn't sure the place was still in use. But it is, so here we are." Allison had grown increasingly wary and her nerves caught up to her. "Do you know who that is?"

"Everyone knows who that is, Allison," Shane said. "It's Enrique Esteban. "He's the suspected head of the cartel in Tampa. You two need to get out of there."

Allison looked at Charlie, her lungs suddenly out of air as though she'd been sucker-punched.

Charlie grabbed her arm. "He's right. Alli, we have to go."

"Yeah, okay. Shane, I'll have to call you back." She ended the call. "I'm sorry. I..."

"You were doing what you thought would help Logan. Let's just go." Charlie walked out of the unit and waited for Allison.

They pulled shut the rolling door and jumped back into Charlie's car.

Charlie keyed the ignition and made a beeline for the exit. "The head of the cartel. My God."

"Why would Julius Hardin keep pictures of Childers with this man, Esteban?" Allison pressed on.

"I don't know. Insurance, maybe," Charlie said. "Against what or who, I don't know, but Hardin captured those pictures for a reason."

"Maybe that's why he was killed." Allison pulled her seatbelt over her shoulder and pressed it into the lock. "Maybe Childers knew about the pictures."

"Let's not get ahead of ourselves. Besides, if he knew about them, why not destroy them?"

"You have a point. But you have to admit, it looks bad," Allison added. "Hardin is dead. Childers called that meeting to find out what we knew. What else could it be?"

"At this point, Alli, I'm not sure I want to find out."

———

LOGAN WAS HOLED UP IN A SHITTY MOTEL AT THE EDGE OF the city en route to Sarasota. The head of the taskforce, DHS Agent Erik Markham, arranged for the location and DEA Agent Pierce escorted him. It had been a long night without much sleep and now he sat on the edge of the bed, flipping through the broadcast channels in search of news.

Pierce knocked on the door before letting himself in. "I brought breakfast." He held a bag of food and two coffees in a drink holder. "I didn't know how you liked your coffee, so I just asked for cream and sugar on the side." He set down the items on the tiny round table pressed against the window. "How'd you sleep?"

"Okay." Logan peered at the food. "Thanks for bringing that." He walked toward the table and grabbed the coffee first, adding his cream and sugar. "So what happens now?"

"Well, you can get yourself cleaned up and then we'll head out," Pierce said, emptying a packet of sugar into his coffee.

"Where are we going?"

"You're going to show us the pick-up location," Pierce replied.

"I told you, I don't know where it's at. Julius didn't tell me before he..."

"Before he was killed? No, I'm sure he didn't."

"Then how am I supposed to tell you where to go?" Logan pressed on.

"We have someone on the inside, one of mine who's working with another gang. He also has contacts inside the Southside

Runners. He doesn't know the location of the pickup, but he does know the route where the next shipment is coming from. You're going to go in there and confirm it for us."

"Go in where?" Logan had been prepared for a bite when he pulled away the bagel from his mouth.

"The warehouse, and you can ask them yourself. Tell them you want to keep your promise to Hardin and do the deal."

Logan dropped back down onto the bed. "Are you serious? They think I killed Julius. I need to see Baylor. He knows the plan."

"Baylor isn't running this operation. I am. Don't worry. I have no intention of letting them harm you. You go in there standing up like a man and tell them you want to do what you promised Hardin. They won't question it. They never questioned him. Consider this an inside job. Look, you want the Southside Runners off your back, right? Help us get them. It's your best shot. This is our best shot—with you."

"What happens if I don't want to go?"

Pierce locked eyes with him. "Who knows if the Southside Runners will find you. But if you help us, we'll make sure they don't. Now go on, eat. I don't know when we'll get time to eat again."

19

Armed with new details about Sam Childers and photos of him with the apparent head of the Tampa cartel, Allison and Charlie arrived at the station to see Shane. Allison left unsaid how frightened she was as they drove away from the storage facility. She was sure Charlie picked up on it, but it seemed neither wanted to admit that they'd gotten lucky. Allison had promised herself she wouldn't be so careless, and while she didn't think this was going to be one of those times, it turned out that way. The only good to come from it was that there was physical proof that Sam Childers at least knows the head of the cartel in Tampa. Baylor would have to admit that was damning evidence.

As they walked toward the station, Charlie grasped Allison's shoulder to stop her. "Hey. Sometimes we need to do things that put ordinary people like us in extraordinary circumstances. I won't lie and pretend I wasn't scared. But you and me, we're tough old broads. I know I joke around a lot and make it seem like stuff just rolls off my back. This time, Alli—this time I was afraid. And I know you were too."

Allison listened while a rogue tear fell down her cheek.

Charlie offered a tender smile. "But this is who we are now, right? We're badass. I don't regret it because it could mean we put away some bad people. I don't want you to regret it either. You and me—we're in this together."

Allison wiped away the tear and nodded. "Thanks, Charlie."

"Now man up because we're going inside and we're going to get that SOB Childers and anyone else he's associated with."

Inside, Allison spotted Shane at his desk. They approached him.

"A storage unit with some serious evidence against Sam Childers," Shane began. "Nice work, ladies."

Allison set down her phone on Shane's desk. "There's probably a lot more in there, but we didn't want to stick around. This is what we have. What can we do about it?"

Shane picked up her phone. "Show me."

Allison opened the images. "These are the two that I sent to you. I got a few more just to add proof to the idea Childers was meeting with this man for reasons only Hardin might have known. This is big, Shane. This could be what Baylor and the taskforce need to end this."

Shane nodded. "So who were these intended for?" His question appeared more rhetorical than anything else. "Enrique Esteban. He's been untouchable for years."

"Maybe Hardin is dead because he planned on using this against Childers. I don't know how, but why else keep them? Allison asked.

"That's the question of the day," Shane said. "Baylor should be notified about this place and he can decide what to do about it. But for us and our concerns about keeping Logan out of the line of fire, I had a discussion with Baylor. It all goes back to the finances. He said what you two dug up was circumstantial at best. So, you'll hand over these, tell him about the storage unit. That'll be enough to keep them busy while we get to the bottom of where the money is coming from or who it's going to."

"You think that if we find evidence someone at the bank could be helping Childers, coupled with what we have to date, it could prove Childers killed Hardin?" Charlie asked.

"It could prove he had motive to kill him," he replied. "But it could also prove that Sam Childers is crucial to the taskforce's goal of dismantling the operation, both the cartel and the gang."

Allison nodded. "Charlie and I will handle the bank. That should be relatively safe. We'll let you take this to Baylor and let him and his people decide what to do about the storage unit. The more ammunition we gather against Childers, the easier we'll make it for Logan to get out from under the gang's thumb once and for all."

———

THERE WAS LITTLE TIME TO PULL TOGETHER A COHESIVE plan to approach the bank that was the lender used to fund operations of Seaside Holdings and Martin Hernandez.

Charlie pulled out of the station's parking lot. "Just a couple of things to point out here, Alli. First of all, what are the chances whoever we speak to at the bank will alert Childers that we're asking questions? Secondly, and probably more importantly, how will we know who to talk to?"

"We're going to use Martin Hernandez to get us in the door. We'll mention his name and say he referred us, and we'll see what reaction we get," Allison replied.

"So, we're winging it?" Charlie asked.

"A little."

"That's when I do my best work." Charlie continued into

downtown. "Did you manage to get any sleep last night? I don't mind saying you look a little worse for wear."

"Well, the possibility of being discovered by a drug cartel this morning took a little wind from my sails. But yes, eventually I found some rest last night. That was why I woke up late. Oh, by the way, Nolan confessed to having a little bit of a thing for Lucy."

"Ooh, do tell. I could use some flagrant gossip right about now."

"He asked me if she liked him too. I said I wasn't sure but thought maybe she did. Boy, you should've seen him when I offered to put in a good word."

"You didn't?" Charlie shot her a look. "Just what any young man wants. His mother to help him get a date."

"I said I'd keep my mouth shut. But that means you have to as well."

"If I must." Charlie squinted at the buildings ahead. "That's it there, isn't it?"

Allison nodded. "That's the one."

Charlie rolled into the parking garage and found a spot on the second floor. After cutting the engine, she began, "Okay. I know you don't like to do this, but you might have to try to be sexy."

Allison burst into laughter. "What? Why?"

"Come on, Allison. We've both been around the block a few times. We know how this works. Look at me. I can't do it. I look like an Oompa Loompa. You, on the other hand."

"Stop it. You're beautiful, Charlie. Inside and out."

"Yeah, yeah. This isn't a fishing expedition. I'm simply stating the obvious. Point is, you're going to have to use your feminine wiles, you understand?"

"Whatever. I don't think it'll be necessary, but we'll see. We're talking to a bank manager, not a strip club manager." Allison opened the door and stepped out. "Well? Let's go. The Lollipop Guild is waiting."

"You're hilarious." Charlie joined her. "All I'm saying is..."

"I know what you're saying. I'm not sure how this is going to work so I guess we'll both find out." Allison pressed the elevator button and when the doors opened, she stepped inside.

Charlie followed. "Lobby?" She creased her brow. "Do we even have an appointment?"

"Nope."

"What's the likelihood we'll get to speak to someone of any importance?" Charlie asked as the doors parted on the lobby floor.

"About as likely as me using my feminine wiles." She walked to the information desk. "Excuse me. Hi. We'd like to speak to someone regarding business loans."

"Of course. Our loan department is right through there. If you'll put your name on the list..."

"I'm sorry," Allison interrupted. "But we have some—extenuating circumstances. Would it be possible to speak to the bank manager about this? My name is Allison Foster, and this is my business partner, Charlie Weitzman. We'd just like a few minutes."

Charlie shot her a look.

The woman who appeared to be in her late twenties eyed them. "Well, I—I guess so. But I'm sure the loan dep..."

"The bank manager. Please," Charlie said.

"Okay. Let me see if she's available." The woman disappeared into the corridor.

"She?" Allison turned to Charlie. "Maybe I should rethink the whole sexy thing?"

"How about you rethink using better names for aliases?" Charlie shook her head. "At least I got one this time, but Weitzman? Really? I guess it's a good thing you can think fast on your feet. I couldn't have pulled those names out of my butt like that."

"Uh-huh." Allison kept her eyes glued on the hall, waiting for the woman's return. "This is starting to look like a longshot."

"Just hold tight. She's not even back yet," Charlie said.

"She's coming now." Allison pulled upright, adjusting her plaid shirt and wearing a broad smile.

"Okay, Julie Morris is our branch manager. She said she could spare a few minutes. I'll show you back."

Allison and Charlie followed her back until reaching the manager's office.

"Julie, this is Allison Foster and Charlie Weitzman. They'd like to talk about a business loan."

The woman offered her hand. "Of course. Please, come in. Welcome. I'm Julie Morris. You can call me Julie."

"Allison." She shook her hand. "Thank you for meeting with us. This is my partner, Charlie."

"Nice to meet you, Charlie. Have a seat." She returned to her desk. "So, I hear you're interested in applying for a business loan, but that you had some concerns." The woman wore a pleasant smile and clasped her hands together as she leaned in to listen. Her blonde hair skimmed her shoulders and her stocky build was concealed beneath a blazer and dress pants.

"I appreciate you seeing us, Julie, I suppose I should start with my main concern," Allison began. "And that is that I have a history that would come into question on an application. I suppose I'd like to know before jumping through the hoops if that would be an automatic disqualifier."

"Can I ask, are you saying that you have a foreclosure on your record or perhaps a bankruptcy?"

"Actually, I have a felony record. It was a long time ago, but as

I'm sure you know, it can be difficult for people like me to get a loan. I would like to know what your bank's policy is on that."

Julie eyed her as if she questioned the validity of Allison's statement. "Well, Allison, I have to start off by saying that a felony would disqualify you from a loan backed by the Small Business Administration."

"Of course. Is that the only loan I could apply for then?" Allison pressed on. "I thought I heard. And you'll forgive me if this comes out the wrong way, but I was under the impression there are other ways to achieve my..." She looked at Charlie. "Our goals."

"I'm not sure I understand your meaning."

Allison held her gaze, trying to read the woman, but all she saw was an unfortunate smile and unmoved eyes. "How do I put this... backchannels, I suppose you could say. It's just, well, I have some contacts who mentioned something like that." She turned to Charlie. "You know what, I think we've wasted enough of Julie's time." Allison stood and motioned Charlie to stand with her.

"I understand your hesitation. But, I'm sorry. Contacts?" Julie stood.

Allison returned her attention. "I was told Martin Hernandez has used your bank's services before. He said something to the effect that you are more forgiving than others where felons are concerned. But I see that we might have misunderstood. I do thank you for your time." Again, Allison started to leave.

"Wait." The woman caught up to her and reached for Allison's shoulder. "Allison, there might be something we can do." She handed over a business card. "You should contact this man here. He might have some suggestions for you."

Allison eyed the card and returned her sights to the bank manager. "This is great. Thank you so much for your help. We really appreciate it."

"Anytime. I wish you both the best of luck."

Allison nodded. "Thank you."

They walked back into the lobby, neither Allison nor Charlie speaking. Not until they reached the parking garage once again.

"A housewife, yeah sure. A MILF, of course. But a felon?" Charlie shook her head. "You look no more like a felon than Mary Poppins herself. But you pulled it out of your butt just like the names. You were right," Charlie said, unlocking her car. "You got her to give you a name and you were right. All that and you didn't even have to bat an eye." She stepped into the driver's seat, waiting for Allison to get inside.

Allison turned to her. "And she had no idea we used fake names."

"On that side note, Alli, maybe run it past me if you want to make up names for us. I've always wanted to be called Peggy. I look like a Peg, right? Just a thought."

Allison flipped the card between her thumb and forefinger. "This guy here. Allen Hayes. He might be the real thing."

————

CHARLIE DROVE TOWARD THE BUILDING LISTED ON THE business card the bank manager handed to Allison. "Looks like a regular old bank."

Allison peered through the windshield. "Yep. Sure does. I don't want to fly by the seat of our pants with this guy, though. I have a feeling he'll spot a fake a mile away."

"Well, you're stuck with the names. That Julie whoever could've called this guy already. So, we'd better play it off well."

Allison nodded. "You're right. But we might get lucky and get to him before she has a chance to give him a heads up. The longer we wait, the more likely he'll have had the time to look into us and figure out the truth."

"Alli, we need to be careful. If this man gives money to gangs and anyone associated with them, we'll be wading into dangerous waters."

"I know. But like you said earlier, we're badass. We can do this."

"I may have overstated our level of badass-ness." Charlie stepped out of the car.

Allison joined her. The late afternoon sun warmed her through the plaid shirt. "Gut check time. Are you feeling okay about this?"

"I am. Really. I'm good," Charlie replied. "We'll be fine."

Allison started ahead. "I was kind of hoping this job might get simpler. Not harder."

"It's all in how you look at it." Charlie patted her shoulder.

They made their way inside the bank building and Allison approached the lobby desk. "Good afternoon. We're here to see Allen Hayes."

"Do you have an appointment?"

"I'm sorry, no. We were referred to him earlier." Allison quickly figured out she would have to use the aliases even before getting a foot in the door. "I'm Allison Foster and this is Charlie Weitzman."

"Great. I'll let him know you're here and see if he has some free time." The receptionist reached for the phone and made the call.

Allison looked at Charlie with raised brows and a glimmer of a smile.

The receptionist hung up the phone. "He's on his way."

"Thank you." She stepped away from the desk and turned to Charlie. "Better put on our best face."

"Sorry to say, but this right here," Charlie motioned to her face. "This is as good as it gets."

The click-clack of men's dress shoes sounded on the marble floor. "Ms. Foster, Ms. Weitzman. Pleased to meet you. I'm Allen Hayes. Please, follow me back. We'll talk in my office."

They followed the short man with black hair dressed in a light blue button-down and navy dress pants. His shoes continued to click on the floor as he headed into the hall toward his office.

Allen Hayes sat at his desk arranging it in an almost compulsive manner. He wasn't what Allison had expected. She thought he would be cool and calm. Slick. Instead, he looked like a man who appeared jumpy, maybe even afraid. His mousy tone didn't lend him any confidence either. She was beginning to feel she and Charlie might have the upper hand in this scenario, fake names and all.

"Mr. Hayes," Allison began. "I was given your name by the branch manager downtown. She thought you might be able to guide us in the right direction."

"I can try. Why don't you tell me a little about your needs?"

"Well, through a series of acquaintances, it was suggested your bank is—how do I say this correctly—friendly to people like me.

"In what capacity?" he asked.

"Well, Mr. Hernandez. Uh, Martin Hernandez, according to a few people, has done business with..."

"I'm familiar with him." Hayes turned to his computer. "Let's see what we can do for you two."

"I should mention that I have a questionable background, which is the reason for our seeking out your institution. Because I thought it was—not allowed—loaning to people like me."

"You mean, felons?" He asked. "Well, for government-backed loans, that's true. However, we utilize other sources, other financial backers, that allow us to assist people like yourselves to get back on their feet and help them start their own businesses. The people I work with believe in second chances, Ms..."

"Foster."

"Ms. Allison Foster." Hayes eyed her for too long.

Allison felt her pulse rise. She needed to seize the moment before he had more time to think about this. "Good. So what do we have to do? My partner and I would like to start the process right away." She turned to Charlie. "Isn't that right?"

"That's right."

"Well, I will have to confirm your background..."

He knew. He knew she was lying about her name and now Allison needed a way out. It would only take a minute to put in her name and then he would ask for a social security number. She had to pull the plug. "I was made to understand, through our acquaintances, that the primary benefit of going this route was that there would be no hoops to jump. I honestly don't think we have the time to go through this just now, do we, Charlie?"

Charlie must've picked up on Hayes' change in tone and the look on his face. "No. I don't think we do." She stood. "I'm so sorry we wasted your..."

"Wait." Hayes held up his hands. "It is I who should apologize. You're absolutely right. Let's forego some of the finer details and just get some information as to what the purpose of your loan would be."

'Um, okay, yeah." Allison's mind spun in an effort to come up with something, anything that made sense. "We're interested in opening a restaurant. Which is how we crossed paths with Martin Hernandez and some of the partners he works with."

"Okay. A restaurant. Good." Hayes punched keys on his keyboard. "And how much were you planning on asking for?"

Allison swallowed down her nerves. "We think about $200,000 should get us off the ground."

His brow furrowed. "That might be a little light for a restaurant, depending on the size, of course. But let me see what I can do, and we'll go from there. It should take a day or two at the most. If you'd be so kind as to give me a contact number where I can reach you." He stood up to meet Charlie's gaze. "I wouldn't want Mr. Hernandez to think us unfair and especially to anyone to whom he is acquainted."

Allison jotted down a number that wasn't hers and handed it to him. "Well, thank you so much for your understanding, Mr. Hayes. It's very much appreciated." She turned to Charlie. "I suppose we have a lot do to and should let Mr. Hayes return to work." She looked at him again. "Thank you for taking the time to meet with us. And please don't hesitate to contact us with any questions." Allison offered her hand.

"Good day, Ms. Foster. And you Ms. Weitzman. I look forward to doing business with you both." Hayes opened the door for them. "You have yourselves a very good day."

"And you," Allison replied on her way out. Once they were out of earshot, Allison began, "That didn't go as I would've hoped."

"Not really." Charlie shook her head. "If Childers doesn't already know what we're up to, he will after this. And so will Martin Hernandez."

They hurried outside and reached Charlie's car.

"We'll track down Baylor and give him what we have so far. We have a bank and a name. It's going to have to be enough to prove money laundering."

"Money laundering?" Charlie started her car. "Did you just pull that out of your butt too, or is there a legitimate basis for your charge?"

"What else could it be? Financial backers? Childers and his partner or partners use that bank to clean either the cartel money, the gang's money, or both." Allison pressed on. "Hayes probably finds companies to finance and uses Childers' and his

partner's money to funnel through. It's a classic case of laundering. Didn't you ever watch Breaking Bad?" Allison peered
at her.

Charlie made it onto the highway and let loose a half-cocked
smile. "Your basis for all of this is a TV show?"

"Yeah, because I'm right. It's how Heisenberg cleaned his
money. He bought companies."

Charlie scoffed. "So, this is all just an episode of Breaking
Bad?"

"If you watched the show, you'd know it does sound like something Walter White would do."

Charlie stared through the windshield and gripped tightly on
the steering wheel. "Oh man are we in trouble."

"I think it might be a good idea to take a look at Tommy's files
on Logan's case again. We might get better insight as to the inner
workings of the Southside Runners. And to be honest, we weren't
looking at Sam Childers before, just Logan. His name might pop
up in those files. It could be worth a look," Allison said.

"Finally, a voice of reason." The office was just ahead, and
Charlie pulled into the parking lot and cut the engine. "Are we
going to be able to talk to Logan now that Baylor's people have
him?"

"I hope so. I don't know if he has his phone."

"What about through Shane?" Charlie added.

Allison opened her passenger door. "He should at least be
allowed to check up on him. We'll make a call and see what his
thoughts are." She started toward the elevators.

When the elevators parted on the third floor, the two walked
side-by-side to the office door. Allison opened it to find Lucy at her
desk.

"You guys are back. Good." Lucy eyed them. "How did it go?"

"We aren't sure just yet, but if you get a call from someone asking for Allison Foster and Charlie Weitzman, you'll know it didn't go well, and we were found out," Charlie said.

"Who?"

"Never mind. Alli over here thinks Sam Childers and Martin Hernandez are using this bank to clean gang and cartel money." Charlie walked to her desk and set down her bag. "Right now, all we know is that the bank appears to use less than legal ways to lend money. Now we just have to figure out how to make that information work for us." She turned to Lucy. "Hey, do you recall seeing the name, Sam Childers, in any of your dad's files we pulled on Logan Carr?"

Lucy appeared to search her thoughts for any recollection of the name. "Maybe." She headed straight for the boxes that still rested on a folding table and were labeled "Carr/Southside Runners." She pulled off the lid to one of the boxes.

Charlie joined her. "If it is there, I'll bet it's an old reference. I don't know if your dad knew Logan was released early and moved into the half-way house six months ago."

"It's possible," Allison said. "There could be something on his laptop. Where did we put all your dad's stuff the cops handed over to you, Lucy?"

"The computers are in storage, but his laptop, the one he kept at home, is at the house." Lucy eyed Allison. "You want me to run home and get it?"

"If you wouldn't mind. There could be information there. In the meantime, Charlie and I can keep going through these files and see if we spot Childers' name referenced anywhere."

Lucy grabbed her keys. "I'll be back in a flash."

———

THE AFTERNOON SUN SHONE DOWN ON AGENT PIERCE'S CAR, casting a wide shadow around its frame. He and Logan sat in it a few hundred feet away from the warehouse where Logan had been only days earlier.

While it was cold outside, and in the car, sweat still dripped down Logan's neckline. It was nerves. Showing up here a day after Hardin was found floating near Hell's Acre; it was a dangerous and brash move. But not for Pierce. He didn't appear overly concerned about Logan's well-being.

"I don't think this is the right way to go, Agent Pierce," Logan pleaded. "If they let me step one foot in the door without putting a bullet in my chest, I'd be surprised."

"They aren't going to gun you down," Pierce said. "Look, I understand you're nervous. But you won't be alone."

"What do you mean?"

"I mean I told you I have someone on the inside. He's embedded with a rival gang, but he keeps in contact with someone in there." Pierce tossed a glance toward the warehouse.

Logan scoffed. "How is that going to help me?"

"Let me finish. That person will be looking out for you and will get word if things start to go sideways. And I'm in direct contact with my agent. This will work and you'll be free of them soon. We just need this to build the case."

"Do I at least get to know who your contact is?" Logan asked.

Pierce studied him. "If you out him, I'll kill you myself. You understand?"

"I'm not whoever it is you think I am, Agent Pierce. I did my time and all I want to do is move on with my life. All this? This isn't me anymore."

Pierce nodded. "It's Mateo Figueroa."

"No. I don't believe it. He's been with Julius for years. Besides, if you have him, what the hell do you need me for?"

"Figueroa wants out as much as you, but if he starts asking questions to get us intel, the odds are, suspicions will be raised. He's just not that smart. I have an agent who I can't put at even greater risk because Figueroa screws up and lets something slip."

"Look, I know these men better than you do."

"A lot has changed in the five years since you've been away, Logan. This isn't the same group of men you worked with. With Hardin gone, someone will take the helm and whoever that is will want you by his side."

"You over-value my worth to them," Logan said.

"I don't agree." Pierce added. "Go on. The longer we sit here, the more likely someone will spot us."

Logan opened his door and turned back to the agent. "I hope you're right about this." He stepped out and closed the door behind him. With deliberate steps, Logan pressed on, feeling as though a gun was at his back and was about to be pointed at his front too.

He neared the main entrance and considered for a moment veering around to the back. However, he thought better of it and opted to stay in plain sight. Acting with an abundance of caution where these people were concerned was his best course of action. That meant staying in full view of the cameras. Logan arrived at the door and turned back to see Pierce drive away. "Looks like I'm on my own. Figures." He rang the bell.

The locks disengaged and the door opened. It wasn't Mo this time, just some henchman and the look on his face made Logan's blood turn cold.

"You got a lot of nerve showing up here." The man regarded him. "You carrying?"

"I'm not that stupid," Logan replied.

The beefy, well-armed man opened the door and stepped aside.

Logan forced his legs to move, to step over the threshold and await his fate. The door closed behind him. The sound of the thick steel slab clanked against its frame and echoed inside the near-empty warehouse.

"Wait here." The man headed to the back and disappeared.

Logan wanted to flee. The pounding of his heart against the wall of his chest felt like he was suffering a heart attack. But he knew it was nerves. The kind of nerves that would get him killed. Logan had no phone. His truck was someplace only the cops knew, and the only person who knew where he was seemed to be a self-serving DEA agent who only cared about getting his man.

"Logan Carr." Mateo Figueroa, with his wide-set brown eyes, a tall forehead and whose clothes hung off his too-slim frame, approached with a swagger. "You have some kind of death wish or something?" He eyed Logan. "What the hell are you doing here?"

Logan looked for any indication in Mateo's eyes that suggested he knew why Logan was there. But he was damn good at hiding it. A trait that would save his life because if the South-side Runners knew, Mateo wouldn't survive the day. "I didn't do it, Mateo. I swear to you. I didn't kill Julius. I was going to do some work with him. You know that. I came here to be upfront. To tell you that I'm still willing to be a part of this deal if you need me."

Mateo gave him a once-over. He reached out his arms and patted him. "You better not be wearing a wire."

"Come on man, you know me," Logan replied.

"You know this is bad, right? With Julius gone, the Columbians are freaking the hell out. I don't know what they're going to do if we don't fill the gap and prove to them the Southside Runners won't miss a beat now that Julius is dead."

"Are you stepping in?" Logan asked.

"Nah, man. Hernandez is. For now. It was agreed that it made the most sense." He folded his arms. "So what to do with you, Logan, old friend."

"Look, Julius didn't tell me much except that there was going to be another drop and the Columbians don't want to get screwed again. He said if this one goes down as bad as the last, no one's going to survive."

"That is a fact," Mateo said. "What are you bringing to the table?"

"Julius asked me to arrange the pick up for him. He trusted I would be the best man for the job."

Mateo shook his head. "I'm not so sure about that, old friend. Last time you made the run for us, you got your ass caught."

Logan noticed the shift in Mateo's expression and the nod to someone who stood out of his view.

A man grabbed Logan's arms and pulled back hard, forcing him to wince with pain. "You're making a mistake, Mateo. Julius wanted me to do to this for him—for the Southside Runners."

"Yeah, well. Julius ain't here no more. We'll let Hernandez deal with you."

———

LUCY RETURNED TO THE OFFICE WITH THE LAPTOP IN HER hand. "Here it is." She walked in and set it on the folding table. "I haven't looked at it yet."

"Well, let's see what Tommy thought about Sam Childers, if we get so lucky." Charlie made her way to the table. "Allison, you want to take a look?"

Allison pulled away from the table where she had been looking in the files and had her phone in her hand. "Yeah, sorry." She approached them.

"Is everything okay?" Charlie asked.

"I don't know, actually." She looked at her phone again. "I was trying to get hold of Shane. He didn't answer my call but sent a text saying he'd have to talk later and that something happened."

"He didn't say what happened?" Charlie asked.

"No." Allison looked away with growing concern. "Well, I'm sure he'll call when he can. We haven't found anything about Childers in your dad's files here, Lucy, so let's see if we have better luck on the laptop."

Lucy logged into the computer and retrieved the documents that were Tommy's old case files. "If Dad had any recent contact with Logan, he probably would've kept something in here."

"Would Logan have reached out to him to let him know he was out?" Charlie asked.

"I don't know how close they were. Logan seemed to trust Dad a lot. So, maybe they kept in touch. Although he didn't mention he'd talked to him since he has been out." Lucy continued to sort through the files.

"Logan must've trusted Sam Childers too," Allison began. "Why else stay at the half-way house he was operating?"

"Hey, take a look here." Lucy pointed to a file. "Dad's old partner, Benny Asher. There's a file here with his name on it."

"Asher was the one to tell Shane what he knew about Logan and the Southside Runners," Charlie said. "Let's take a look."

Lucy opened the file and it populated with several files and case numbers inside. "How are we supposed to know what these mean?"

Allison walked over to the boxes on the folding tables. "Well, we could start with this number here." She pointed to the number on one of the folders inside. "2013-578321."

Lucy searched for the number. "Here it is." She clicked to open the file. "There's a lot of stuff here."

Allison returned to her desk. "Send the files to each of us.

We'll split it into thirds and cross-reference them with what we have on the table. See if we get any hits."

———

SHANE STOOD NEXT TO DETECTIVE BAYLOR'S DESK. HIS ARMS were folded tight against his chest and his jaw clenched hard enough that he felt a headache starting in the back of his neck. "What'd he say?"

Baylor set down his phone. "Pierce says Logan Carr agreed to go inside with the understanding that his agent's contacts will ensure his safety. He expected Logan to come out of the warehouse and waited around the corner. It's been two hours and he's still inside. But the good news is that Pierce got word from his guy on the inside that Logan had turned up. That's all we know right now."

"For God's sake." Shane circled the area, unsure of what to do or where to go. "You really believe Logan would've put himself in that kind of danger?"

"Pierce said the kid bought into it," Baylor replied. "Logan seemed to think they'd come after him if he didn't follow through on the deal he made with Hardin. This was Pierce's best shot at moving the investigation forward."

"I don't buy it. No way. I was with the kid last night. He was terrified out of his mind. And I told you that when we met at the bar and handed him over to you. I told you that." Shane's voice raised.

"Hey. Calm down, man." Baylor noted the growing stares in his direction. "Sit down and let's figure this shit out, okay?"

"Where's your partner in this? Where's Reddick? He needs to know what the hell is going on."

Baylor reached for his cell phone again. "Yeah. I'll tell him to get down here ASAP."

Shane waited while Baylor made the call. He wanted to tell Allison, but right now, he knew nothing; whether Logan was alive or dead or where the hell he was at. It would only alarm her. "Well?"

Baylor returned his attention to Shane. "He's on his way. The taskforce is Agent Markham's to lead. The rest of us are just along for the ride. He and Agent Pierce hatched up this plan. We gotta give them a chance to see if it works."

"Sure. Let's just sit tight because we have all the time in the world, don't we? I mean, no one knows where Logan's at, and so, who cares, right?"

"That's not..."

Shane placed his hands on the edge of Baylor's desk and peered at him again. "Markham and Pierce screwed up. Maybe they really thought this was a good idea, but I think we can both see that it wasn't. The time's come to get into that warehouse and get Logan out."

"Even if the Southside Runners are holding him, it sure as shit wouldn't be at the warehouse. They know we're aware of the place now."

"What about that storage unit I told you about?" Shane asked.

"We're waiting on the warrant. You know that takes time," Baylor replied. "I don't know if we'll get in there before something happens to that kid."

"How much time do we have to pull something together?" Shane asked. "We're going to need a plan to get Logan back."

Reddick approached them. "What did you two screw up now?"

Baylor turned his attention to Shane again. "An hour, maybe

two. Any longer than that and we'll lose any leads we might have regarding Logan Carr's whereabouts."

"What's that you're saying about Carr?" Reddick asked.

Baylor snatched his keys. "I'll tell you on the way."

20

Without a warning, Tampa's finest and the FBI converged on ACL Investigative Services. The three partners, knee-deep in case files, peered up at the intrusion.

"Shane?" Allison pushed from her chair with haste. "What's going on? Who are these guys?"

"Sorry, Allison." He turned back to the others. "You know Detective Baylor. This one over here is his partner FBI Agent Dave Reddick. We're here because Logan's missing."

"What?" Charlie rushed toward them. "What do you mean he's missing?"

"We can get into the weeds in a minute." Shane peered at the three of them who stood shoulder to shoulder. "What do you know about Sam Childers?"

"There's the storage unit, for one," Allison replied.

"I'm working on a search warrant as we speak. You did good finding that place, but you put yourselves in a hell of a lot of danger by showing up there," Baylor replied.

Allison peered at her partners and brushed off the detective's comment. "We were just looking into what former Detective Tommy Boyce might've known about Childers." She started toward the table where the files and the laptop lay open. "Lucy brought in her dad's old files from Logan's case. That, along with the laptop he kept at the house."

"I just got it back from TPD," Lucy said.

"We've been looking for Childers' name referenced in any of these files that we might've missed the first time." Allison looked at Shane. "No luck so far, but we aren't finished yet. We've just started looking into files Tommy had on his partner, Benny Asher, to see what he knew."

"What about the banks? What do you know on that front?" Shane pressed on.

"We did some digging into how Sam Childers managed to get backing on his businesses. There's a restaurant, which I think you all know about already. And a partner named Martin Hernandez. Charlie and I discovered the name of the bank that lent the money for that restaurant. We were there earlier today."

"That's right," Charlie added. "And after some skillful maneuvering, Allison got the name of a man at another branch of this bank. Allen Hayes is his name."

"When we mentioned Hernandez, the guy sat at attention," Allison continued. "We think there's a chance Childers, his company Seaside Holdings, and the other businesses tied to Childers are running illegal funds through this bank. Which, based on the picture we found in that storage unit, could be tied to the cartel."

"I showed them the pictures," Shane said.

"It was our evidence to obtain the warrant," Baylor replied.

"Money laundering," Reddick folded his burly arms against

his square chest. "It's a long shot, but at this point, it's sure as hell looking like that's what we're dealing with."

Baylor nodded. "If nothing else, it gives us more ammunition. And then whatever we happen to find in the storage unit."

"What happens if the cartel finds out about the unit?" Charlie asked. "Don't you think they'll go in and clean it out?"

"Yes, they would," Reddick added. "But we already have a patrol set up to surveil the place and keep an eye out for anyone who goes in. We should have the warrant by tomorrow."

"Milo said the ownership details of these LLCs were so convoluted it was impossible to believe anyone else besides the cartel set them up," Allison said.

"This doesn't help up find Logan, though," Charlie added. "What are we going to do to find him before they kill him?"

————

LOGAN SAT ON THE CONCRETE FLOOR IN A SMALL ROOM THAT reminded him too much of the jail cell from which he had been freed only six months ago. He thought he was going to be safe. That the Feds would take care of him. But why? They wanted the Columbians and the Southside Runners, and they thought—Agent Pierce thought—he could get both by using Logan to set them up, regardless of the people they had on the inside. Now he was supposed to believe Mateo was going to be looking out for him. It didn't seem like that was the case based on his current situation.

"Logan, man. What the hell, bro? Martin's giving me one last attempt to get the truth from you before he comes to you himself." Mateo walked into the windowless room. "You gotta come clean if you want out of here."

"Come clean about what?" he asked, now even more confused about Mateo's allegiances.

"You're working with the Feds, bro. We all know that," Mateo continued.

"I'm not. I swear I'm not. I was going to help Julius because he asked."

"I find that tough to swallow, my man. Not that he came to you. I know he did. I told you about the meeting. But that you just ponied up and said, 'hell, yeah. When do we get started?'" Mateo shook his head. "I don't think that's the way it went down, brother. I think you were between a rock and a hard place. Hey, I don't fault you for that. I might've done the same thing if I were you. But the problem is, bro, you brought in the goddam Feds."

Logan shook his head. "I didn't. No one knows I'm here. I swear to you. I wanted to make things right."

"No, man. No more lies. Look, we got Martin coming. And he don't come for just anyone. He'll decide what to do with you." Mateo started on his way out but turned back. "Unless..."

"What?" Logan's tone turned desperate.

"Tell me where the Feds are looking. You tell me where they think the drop's going to be and I'll tell Martin. Have him go easy on you. And you might make it out of here alive."

Logan picked up on something. Mateo's eyes flashed. His lips pursed. He was asking these questions for Agent Pierce. Son of a bitch knew he was sitting in here and was about to let him take the hit. So long as he got what he wanted. Even though Logan didn't know anything right now.

Logan thought for a moment. He was going to play along. "I got no problem doing that. The Feds haven't done shit to help me. Why should I help them?"

"That's right, my man. And they never will." Mateo returned and squatted to meet Logan eye to eye. "So?"

Logan saw it now. Clear as day. Mateo was going to run to his contact and tell him every word from Logan's mouth and they would let him sit here and rot. "You know, maybe I should wait for Martin. I think I'll wait for him. I don't want any confusion."

Mateo smacked his lips before returning to full height. "Whatever, man. Just trying to do you a solid." He closed the door behind him.

———

It was sounding more and more likely the cartel had Sam Childers in their corner and with Logan Carr missing, it could be enough for Childers to be brought in for questioning.

"We have the photos. We have the possible money laundering situation, if we can prove it," Shane said to Reddick.

"I agree. We can bring in Childers," Reddick began. "But will that put Logan in greater jeopardy? I think we need to trust Markham and Pierce that the DEA is looking out for him. He's due back any time now." Reddick looked to Baylor. "We should go back and lay the groundwork for our operation."

"Then let's touch base in three hours and see where everyone's at." Baylor started toward the door but stopped and turned to Lucy. "Your dad was a fine detective. I didn't know him personally, but I can tell that much just by your actions."

"Thank you, Detective Baylor," Lucy replied.

———

Logan had lost all sense of time. He had no idea how long he'd been inside the room with no windows. All he knew was that he awaited Martin, a man he had met once, a long time ago. He was above Julius Hardin, that much he knew. But just how much higher on the food chain, Logan had no clue. There was an entire network, a web of people, who all did work for the cartels.

But it was the cartels that ran the state. The Southside Runners and those like them were sacrificial lambs.

The door opened and a sliver of light spilled inside, landing on his face, and cutting across his eye. Logan waited to see who was on the other side, though he suspected he already knew. As the door opened farther, the shadowy figure emerged. It wasn't Mateo. He was tall and slim. This figure was rounder, shorter.

"Logan Carr. It's been a long time, brother." Martin Hernandez walked inside turning on the light switch fixed outside the door.

The light burned Logan's eyes, but they soon adjusted, and he saw Martin. He looked much older than he remembered. Of course, in those days, he'd been drunk or high most of the time. "Martin."

"You shouldn't have come back, man. That was a stupid move."

"I wanted to keep my word to Julius," Logan replied.

"So you say. Why would I believe you, Logan?"

"I didn't do it. I told Mateo the same thing. I don't know who killed Julius or why. But you know the Southside Runners have more enemies than they can count."

"Truth." Martin continued inside, unfolding a chair he brought in with him. He sat down in front of Logan. "This puts me in a bad position. My guys are looking to me to settle the score. But maybe I'm not so convinced it was you that killed Julius."

"Then what can I do to prove my innocence?" Logan pressed on.

"The cartel wants retribution for the bust last week. I know you know that. They want the next job to be pro bono, if you catch my drift."

"Okay."

"But that's not going over too good with the Southside

Runners. They see the bust as the cost of doing business. Drugs were found when they were still on the sub, not dry land."

"Sounds to me like maybe the cartel took care of Julius, then," Logan said.

Martin nodded. "That could be. But what am I going to do about that, huh? Take out one of theirs? That ain't going to happen."

"What do you want from me, Martin? There are people out there who will be looking for me. Cops, other people."

Martin nodded. "I hear you, brother. Here's what we're going to do. I'm going to tell the Columbians that we have you and you won't be a problem. That we think you were the one to take out Julius and you'll pay for it, but not until after the pick up. We don't want any more heat on us than necessary. That'll smooth things over with them."

"And me?"

"When I find out who killed Julius, we'll talk again." Martin walked out with his chair and switched off the light.

21

So much of what had transpired during the course of this investigation had been out of Allison's control. The Drug Enforcement taskforce headed up by DHS Agent Markham had authority over everything as it related to Logan Carr. Allison's only job was to keep Logan out of their way and that had failed spectacularly. Logan was gone.

As far as ACL was concerned, they'd done all they could do. Photographic evidence suggesting Sam Childers was acquainted with Enrique Esteban, head of the cartel's Tampa operations. Possible evidence to suggest the bank Childers and his companies engaged had been nothing more than a source for laundering money. They were at a standstill while Detective Baylor and his people attempted to find Logan Carr and build on the evidence Allison and her team had gathered.

The women sat at their desks in virtual silence as if frozen in place. It wasn't until Lucy stood up that she broke the quiet.

"I need to run out. I have an idea and I'd like to follow through on it if it's all right with you guys."

"Do you need any help?" Charlie asked.

"No. You two should stay and wait to hear from Shane. I can take care of this."

"Okay. Go for it," Charlie began. "If anything breaks loose, we'll call you."

"Thanks. I'll be back soon." Lucy grabbed her keys and started out the door. There was someone who she thought could paint a clearer picture of Sam Childers, Julius Hardin, and the Southside Runners. Her dad wasn't around anymore, but there was another. That someone was hanging on by a thread and she couldn't guarantee his memory would be altogether there. But she had to take a shot at it.

The hospice center was about five miles away and while she had never met former detective, Benny Asher, she felt as though she knew him.

Lucy thought the man had more to offer on the topic of the Southside Runners and while the others were forced to sit idle, she could act.

The center was just ahead, and Lucy pulled into the parking lot in her dad's black classic 1985 Chevy Monte Carlo SS. He had restored the wreck years ago and refused to sell it. Now that he was gone, it was hers, although it didn't quite seem like a car a young woman of 19 would be driving. Then again, Lucy never fit into any mold. She was her father's daughter.

Inside, the building had the familiar odor she recalled when her mother was in a place like this. She had died of brain cancer. It wasn't one of the better-known cancers. Not like the ones with the 5k runs and the ribbon awareness campaigns. It had been a secret killer. An inoperable tumor no amount of money-raising could've helped. But the smell was the same; sickness and death.

"Hi." Lucy approached the front desk. "I was wondering if Mr. Archer might be accepting visitors today?"

The red-haired woman donning scrubs sat behind the counter and peered over her reading glasses. "And you are?"

"My name is Lucy Boyce. I don't know if he ever mentioned my dad..."

"Tommy Boyce?" The woman nodded. "You're Tommy's daughter, huh?"

"I am, yes."

"I'm sorry about what happened to him. Benny mentioned it here recently. Your dad had a real impact on Benny's life."

"Thank you. Do you think he might want to see me?"

"That depends. You're Tommy's daughter. Does that mean you're a cop too?"

"No, ma'am. I do work for a detective agency, like the kind my dad owned after he retired from the force. I just wanted to ask Mr. Archer a couple of questions about an old case."

"I see." She nodded. "Same as that other fella who popped by last week. "A Detective Sullivan." She pushed back her chair and grabbed a visitor badge from the desk behind her. "Put this on. I'll take you to his room."

Lucy clipped the badge to her blouse and waited for the red-haired lady to show her the way. "How's he feeling?"

"Oh, you know, about the same, which for this place, is pretty good." She stopped. "But you do know Benny's terminal, right? That's the type of folks we get here."

"I'm familiar."

"Okay then." She started again. "It's just, well, you look pretty young and I just wanted to be sure you knew what you were getting yourself into."

"Yes, ma'am. My mother was in a place like this before she died. She had cancer."

"Oh, I am sorry to hear that." The woman knocked gently on

the door before pushing it open. "Benny? You got yourself a visitor. It's Tommy Boyce's daughter."

"Lucy?" He pushed up a little and coughed. "Lucy Boyce?"

She nodded for Lucy to walk inside. "Yes, sir. She's come to chat with you for a minute."

"Well, all right. Come on in." His voice wheezed and another, deeper cough, surfaced.

Lucy offered a closed-lip smile on her approach. "Mr. Archer. I'm Lucy Boyce, Tommy's daughter. I hope you don't mind the intrusion, but I was hoping to talk to you about something."

"Have a seat, kid." Benny turned to the nurse. "I'll take it from here, Maggie."

"All right, Benny." She closed the door.

"So, you here about the same thing that detective was here for the other day? Something about the cartels and the Southside Runners."

"Yes, sir. I was wondering if you might know anything about a man named Sam Childers."

Benny nodded. "Oh. I was wondering when you folks would get to him."

"So, you know who he is?"

"Oh, yeah. That man has a lot of powerful people looking after him. I'm not sure you want to dig too deep on that one, Lucy."

"The people I work for, the agency, we've been trying to help Logan Carr."

"Yes, I know him too. Kid got the shaft if you ask me. What a shame."

"We think so too, which is why I'm here. Mr. Archer..."

"Call me Benny. Your dad did and you can too."

"Benny. Logan Carr disappeared. We think he was taken by the Southside Runners. We're afraid once they get whatever it is they want from him, they'll kill him."

"I have no doubt about that," he replied. "What is it you think I can do to help you?"

"My dad didn't have anything on Sam Childers. I was hoping you might recall something about him that could shed light for us."

"Well, I do know, back in the day when we were working the Southside Runners case, that a couple of our informants mentioned Childers. Said he was coming up in the ranks. Course, he ended up serving time, if I recall."

"Yes. We did discover he served and about a year of that time overlapped with Logan Carr."

"That's right. Like I said, the informants didn't give us much, but we passed it along after Logan was sent to prison and old Julius Hardin got off free as a bird."

"Do you remember, besides Childers coming up in the ranks, what else those informants might've said?"

"Well, I'll tell you, Lucy, my mind isn't what it used to be, I'm afraid. And this damn cancer's made it even worse. But I do have files, much as I suspect your dad did too. I have a book on that case. You take a look inside there and you'll find whatever it was I discovered about Sam Childers."

"Where is this book?"

"In storage. None of my family wanted my things. Not my case files anyway, so I put them away. And it's a good thing I did, by all accounts."

Lucy smiled. "Yes, sir. A very good thing."

"Why don't you give me a piece of paper and I'll give you the address and the code to get inside. You'll find the files in numerical order, based on year..."

"Like my dad's."

"Probably so," Benny replied. "But I do this on one condition."

"What's that?" Lucy asked.

"You better come back and tell me you put Sam Childers back

inside and that he'll stay there. And, of course, I'd like to know how young Logan is doing. Should you find him."

"We'll find him. Thank you so much, Mr. Archer—Benny. I'll be in touch." She stood.

"Lucy? Your dad. He was a good man. One hell of a detective. I miss him, even though we didn't work together but a few years. In my opinion, he was the best cop I ever knew. I'm real sorry he's gone. But I do know this. He'd be proud of you."

"Thank you, Benny." Lucy touched his hand and turned to leave. She didn't get what she wanted but might still and held out hope. Benny Asher was in pretty bad shape. He didn't look like he had too many days left in him. Lucy hoped she would return in time to give him the good news that they put away Childers and found Logan.

———

LUCY STOOD INSIDE THE STORAGE ROOM. SHE KNEW EX-COPS never really put aside their unsolved cases. She found the book Benny Asher mentioned and recalled her dad having some of those types of books lying around too. Once a cop, always a cop.

Inside was even more interesting than she thought it would be. Her dad kept his notes on Logan Carr in the case file, but what she found here was much more comprehensive with regard to the Southside Runners. She suspected, because Benny had been a cop after her dad retired, that he continued to file away pieces of information hoping it might be useful one day. And Lucy thought that day was today.

She tucked the book under her arm and walked out, closing the door behind her. She entered the code to lock the door and waited until she heard the click.

On her way to the car, she grabbed her phone. "Allison, hey, where are you guys?"

"Heading to see Agent Reddick at the FBI's field office downtown. Where are you?"

"I paid a visit to my dad's old partner, Benny Asher. Allison, he told me where I could find his case book on the Southside Runners. I need to show you guys what's in here. Can I meet you there?"

"Absolutely. See you soon."

Lucy ended the call and jumped into the black beast of a car, turning the engine as its stock 5-liter V8 rumbled. She looked like a child inside this car. Lucy was a respectable 5 feet 6 inches, but in here, she looked like a shrimp.

Lucy hustled, breaking the speed limit a few times, but staying cautious and she arrived after 25 minutes. She parked the SS and jumped out, almost forgetting the binder.

The FBI field office was sophisticated, almost elegant with modern designed glass and metal. And it had a lot more security than the downtown Tampa police station. Lucy had never been inside a place like this before. Metal detectors, a conveyor, like at airports, and plenty of men and women standing around in suits and wearing serious faces. She stood inside the entrance, looking lost when she noticed Allison and Charlie heading her way.

"What did you find?" Allison asked on approach.

Lucy walked toward a coffee table in the lobby and opened the book, parking her backside on the sofa. Charlie and Allison joined her. "This is the book Benny Asher kept regarding the Southside Runners." She flipped through some of the pages. "Right here. Sam Childers."

Allison leaned in and Charlie too. Both reading the page before Allison began, "This says the detective believed Sam Childers was working with the cartel and acted as a liaison between them and the Southside Runners, run by Julius Hardin." She looked at Lucy. "Is there proof of that in here?"

Lucy smiled and flipped to another page. "This is a transcript from what appears to be a phone conversation. It's between Childers and a man named Martin Hernandez."

Allison and Charlie traded knowing glances.

"Hernandez appears to be a member of the Columbian cartel or at least has close ties to them, and the call discusses Childers recruiting the ex-cons from his half-way house to use as the gang saw fit.

"How old is this conversation?" Allison looked for a date on the transcript. "It's from a year and a half ago. Why didn't Archer say anything when it happened?"

"I don't know unless I ask him, but I would think..."

"He might have obtained the transcript illegally," Charlie said. "I'll bet Archer couldn't use it."

"What does that mean? This is proof Childers was, at least then, working with the cartel and his partner, Hernandez," Allison said.

"Yeah, but if Archer couldn't do anything with it, what makes you think we can?" Charlie asked.

Lucy eyed them. "Maybe we can't. But we can show the task-force and let them decide."

22

The formation of government taskforces seemed a hollow gesture at times. It gave the appearance that something was being done to stop a particular problem. Tampa's Organized Crime Drug Enforcement Taskforce had the potential to take on the cartels and drug traffickers in the city. Instead, it seemed each agency involved had their own agendas. And as Allison always said, everyone had their own agendas.

So when DEA Agent Pierce and DHS Agent Markham made the decision to put Logan Carr's life on the line without consulting other members of the taskforce, the move was seen as self-serving. Pierce left him hanging in the wind; his life, hanging in the balance.

Lucy held former Detective Asher's case book in her hands as she trailed Allison and Charlie. They reached the second floor of Reddick's FBI Field office to disclose what Lucy had uncovered.

Allison was aware the team had been meeting in one of the conference rooms. "Excuse me," she asked the man at the front desk. "Can you tell me where I can find Agent Reddick?"

The man gestured to a corridor. "He's in a taskforce meeting right down there. Conference Room B. Is he expecting you?"

"Yes." Allison started ahead without waiting for permission, nodding to Charlie and Lucy to follow. "This is it." She pushed inside and before they had a chance to acknowledge them, she began, "I apologize for the interruption, but Lucy found something you all should take a look at."

Lucy appeared out of her depth but was determined to press on and set down the binder on the table, opening it up to the transcript. "This is from a retired detective with TPD. He was my dad's partner. It's a transcript of a conversation between Martin Hernandez and Sam Childers."

Markham, who sat at the table, pulled the binder toward him. "How long have you had this?"

"About an hour. I met with the former detective. He's in hospice care. He offered this to me in hopes we might find something to help us."

Allison stood next to Lucy like a protective mother. Her hands firmly planted on her hips and stone-faced. "No one's heard from Logan and we have to assume that when Pierce dropped him off at the warehouse, the Southside Runners took him somewhere else and are holding him captive," Allison said.

"He's under our protection," Pierce said. "He's in no danger."

"God, I hope you're right," Allison replied.

"And to put your mind at ease," Pierce began. "My agent just made contact with me. Logan is safe and is being held at a shipyard."

"Then what are we waiting for?" Allison pressed on.

"I wish it were as simple as going in after him but doing that now will jeopardize his life and several others. They won't hurt him, Allison. You're going to have to trust us on this," Pierce added.

"Just like I trusted Baylor to protect Logan in the first place?" She eyed him and all he could do was shy away from her stare.

"Let's get back to this new evidence," Shane began. "Based on what you three have discovered with the connections through the bank, the pictures Hardin had in the storage unit and now this. Isn't this enough to hold Childers, not just question him? Maybe we can use him as a bargaining chip to secure Logan's release."

"Yes," Baylor said, and he looked to Reddick for agreement. "Now is the time."

"There's one other person you're forgetting about here," Allison began. "Sam Childers' partner, Martin Hernandez. He must also know what the Southside Runners are doing."

"So, you're saying if we bring in Childers, he might give up Hernandez?" Shane asked.

"But how does that get us any closer to getting Logan out of this shipyard where you say he's being held?" Charlie asked. "There's only one person here who matters to me. And that's my client. ACL's client, Logan Carr." She looked at Baylor. "You people are the experts here. We have the evidence. You need to extract Logan before the Southside Runners kill him."

Reddick turned to Baylor. "How close are we to getting that warrant on the storage unit?"

"Should be any time now. I've got people pushing the judge. So far, my team who has been patrolling the area hasn't seen any signs of others looking to get in there. That's good news for us. It means it's possible no one else knows about it."

Allison turned to Shane. "Look, we've done all we can do. Sam Childers is ripe for the picking. We're looking to you guys to get Logan out. It's time to make a move. Please."

"Agreed." Shane turned his attention to Markham. "You have enough to bring in the heavy-hitters. Allison's right. I understand Pierce's concerns about his people on the inside. But he chose to use Logan believing he could coerce someone inside the gang to reveal when and where the next shipment was coming in. The insistence that your DEA agent on the inside could protect him is all well and good. But at this point, we need to pull the plug. You all can put an end to this. I get that this is your call, but there's a kid in there who has done nothing to get himself in this situation. You gotta bring him home."

Markham grabbed his things. "Baylor, you and Reddick will track down Sam Childers and drag his ass in here. Pierce and I will do what we can to get Logan out."

"What about the upcoming drop?" Reddick asked. "We're so close. We can't let this opportunity slip through our fingers."

"Then we'll grill Childers. If he wants a deal, he'll give us what we need. When he does, we'll have a team ready." Markham turned to Shane. "So, you want in on this too, or what?"

———

EVIDENCE HAD MOUNTED AGAINST SAM CHILDERS BUT WHAT Detective Baylor had pinned his hopes on was the storage unit. According to Allison, it could be a treasure-trove of damning evidence against the cartel, the higher-ups in the Southside Runners, and anyone else Julius Hardin deemed a threat. The warrant had been issued and a team was ready to go.

While that was underway, Baylor and Reddick were on the hunt for the man himself, Sam Childers. He was their only remaining lead to the Southside Runners. A tenuous connection at best, but one that couldn't be ignored.

"I have no idea if he's here. He suspected Allison and her team were digging up dirt on him so he might already be taking precautions." Baylor pulled the car up to the half-way house oper-ated by Childers and looked to Reddick. "He wasn't at the address listed as his home. For him to be here is definitely a shot in the dark. If he is, though, should we be prepared by calling for backup?"

"No way. If he is here, he'll bolt at the sight of patrol cars racing down this street. He must know the walls are closing in especially if he knows the Runners have Logan Carr."

"What are the odds he doesn't know about Carr?" Baylor asked.

"As sure as I'm sitting here, Childers knows everything," Reddick replied. "You and I are going in alone—now." He opened the door and stepped outside, adjusting his suit jacket. Clouds hung in the air and blocked the sun, but he squinted nonetheless from the brightness of the day.

Baylor joined him and the two walked along the short pathway to the front door. "Should I do the honors?" Baylor asked.

"Be my guest."

Baylor knocked on the door. A few moments passed and he knocked again. "Tampa Police."

A man opened the door. "Yeah?"

"We're here to see Sam Childers," Baylor said.

"He ain't here. I'm the only one in the house."

Baylor furrowed his brow and cast a glance to Reddick. The man answered the question as if he already knew why they were there. "I'm Detective Baylor with TPD and this is Special Agent Reddick. Do you know where Sam is?"

"Nope." Dale Meek stood at the door, half in and half out. He scratched at his scraggly beard. "Can I help you with something?"

"Yeah, you can tell us where Childers is," Reddick replied. "You should think twice about your previous answer."

"Hey man, Sam doesn't tell me his schedule. You want to find him, maybe you should try calling his cell." Dale closed the door.

Baylor stood speechless with the door inches from his face.

"Son of a bitch." He turned to Reddick. "He's going to make us put out a BOLO on him."

"No way are we doing that. That call goes out and everyone associated with Childers will vanish."

Baylor started back toward the car and Reddick followed. "Then what do we do?"

"We check his other operations. If we strike out, then let's meet up with Markham."

Baylor opened his driver's side door.

A car's engine roared and then a vehicle tore away from the curb a few feet ahead. Baylor whipped around to see. "That's him. Get in!" Baylor fired up the engine and waited for Reddick to step inside.

"Why is he running?' Reddick gripped the handle above the passenger door. "He has no idea why we'd be here."

"I wouldn't count on that." Baylor hammered on the gas pedal and followed. "Call it in. We need backup now!"

———

THE DOOR OPENED AND THE LIGHT BURNED LOGAN'S EYES. HE squinted to see who stood in the doorway. "Who's there?"

"It's time to go, man. Come on." Mateo walked inside and pulled up Logan by the arm.

"Where are we going? Where's Martin?"

"It's time to roll. Tonight's the night."

Logan gathered what was happening. The pick up must have been scheduled for tonight. But why was he going along? The agreement to make the run had been made with a dead man. He hadn't prepped for it and didn't know the route. "What am I supposed to do, man? No one's told me Jack. I don't even know where the drugs are coming in."

"You'll be told everything in a minute. Now let's go. We're behind schedule already." Mateo continued to drag Logan along at a quick pace.

They reached the doors to what appeared to be another warehouse, though the smell of the sea wafted around him. He was near water, and on walking outside, the odor validated his suspicions.

"How much? When? Where is this going down?" Logan pleaded with Mateo.

"Shut up and you'll find out soon enough. Get in." He pushed Logan into the back of a moving truck and slammed the large metal doors.

A thick rod secured them shut and Logan heard the lock click into place. He was in darkness again. Where were they taking him this time? It was still daylight, at least mid-afternoon. They wouldn't be foolish enough to attempt a run in the light of day. No. They would wait until nightfall. After midnight, certainly. The roads would be quiet. But these were concerns that weren't his to ponder. Right now, all he wanted to do was make it out of this alive.

23

Allison sat at her desk with her head in her hands. The call from Shane that Childers had fled doused all hope of bringing the man to justice. The odds of finding him were slim thanks to the man's powerful friends.

Childers had danced around the question at their meeting, testing Allison as to whether she knew where Logan was. It was only by luck she received that call from Logan, reaching out for help. Now Logan was in the hands of the Southside Runners. Would it take only a single call from Childers to end Logan's life? That depended on how much Childers knew about what evidence the taskforce had collected against him.

"He's gone," Allison said. "That was Shane. Detective Baylor and Agent Reddick are attempting to track down Childers. Apparently, he took off from the half-way house on their arrival."

Charlie pushed up from the side chair at Allison's desk and paced the room. "What are we supposed to do? Alli, we can't just sit here and do nothing."

"We've done what we can do, Charlie. I don't know what else

there is. I mean, we've handed these guys everything on a silver platter. We've gathered more evidence for them to use than they've been able to gather themselves in years. Doesn't that seem odd to you?"

The office door opened and captured their attention. A dark-haired, stout man wearing faded jeans and an untucked Oxford shirt walked inside.

"Hello. I hope I'm in the right place."

Allison stood from her chair on nervous legs. "Well, I don't know. Are you looking for ACL Investigative Services?"

"Then I am in the right place." He approached her with an outstretched hand. "My name is Martin Hernandez. I believe you know my partner."

Allison forced a smile, though every bone in her body froze in fear. She eyed Lucy, then Charlie. She recognized this man. They all did. "Um, possibly. My name is Allison Hart. It's nice to meet you."

Hernandez gazed around the office with an approving nod. "Nice place you got here. And who are these lovely ladies?" He turned to Charlie.

Allison walked out from behind her desk. "This is my partner, Charlie Wells and this is Lucy Boyce."

Hernandez offered his hand once again to Charlie first and then Lucy. "Nice to meet you both."

Allison smoothed down her shirt and cleared her throat. "How can we help you, Mr. Hernandez?"

"Please, call me Martin." His brow creased as he peered at the credenza. "I don't suppose there's any water in that fridge. I'm parched."

Lucy retrieved a bottle for him. "Here you go, sir."

"Thank you, Lucy." Hernandez opened the bottle and tossed back a long swig. "Ah, much better." He walked to Allison's desk. "I have to say that you look a lot different than I expected."

Allison did her best to conceal her alarm. "Is that so? I'm sorry, were you referred to our office?"

"Something like that." He gave her a once-over. "You don't look like a private investigator. And my partner said nothing of just how attractive you are." He placed his hand over his heart. "I'm sorry. That probably sounded extremely sexist."

"It's okay. I'm not easily offended, Mr. Hernandez—Martin." Allison pushed back a few loose strands of hair and sat back down at her desk. "So, how can we help you, Martin?"

Charlie stood at Lucy's desk as if protecting her. They both peered at the phone, apparently thinking the same thing. However, neither acted on the impulse to make a call.

Hernandez sat down in the chair across from Allison's desk. "I think you probably know why I'm here. But I'll remind you just in case. You've taken an interest in my partner, Sam Childers."

"As a matter of fact, I have," Allison replied.

"Yeah, I heard something to that effect from Allen Hayes." He cocked his head and pointed at her. "You know him too, right?"

Allison's mouth dried and her lips stuck to her teeth. He knew about the bank. Hayes must've grown suspicious and alerted him. Maybe he wasn't here about Sam, but about the bank and what she and Charlie figured out. Allison was a quick thinker, seldom at a loss for words. Now, however, she could only think of one thing, that they were in danger and a dangerous man sat before her. "Yes, I believe I have met him."

"Yeah, I thought so." He held her gaze with growing intensity. "You know, Allison, I'm sure you have much more important things to do than to sit here with me. And so do I. But there are a few things I'd like to ask you about if you can spare the time."

"Of course," she replied.

"You and your cohorts here have put me in a unique situation. I think, and please correct me if I'm wrong, but I think we'd both like to know where we can find Sam Childers."

Allison narrowed her eyes just for a moment, recognizing that this may not be what it seemed. "I haven't spoken to Mr. Childers in a few days. We did meet him to discuss our client."

"Logan Carr," he replied.

"Yes."

Hernandez leaned back. "Here's the thing, Allison. I'm aware of what you and your team here have been doing. Allen Hayes is a very loyal man. He had concerns about you asking questions. He thought they were strange, to say the least, and as you mentioned my name, he thought it best to reach out to me. Between that and the brief conversation I had with Sam, who also mentioned a blonde who came to visit him, it was fairly easy to put two and two together. Which brings me to why I'm here now. I can help you find Logan Carr."

"Oh. Is he missing?" Allison asked.

Hernandez raised a corner of his mouth in a crooked smile. "You got some guts, Allison. I'll give you that."

Charlie cleared her throat for attention. "What do you want in return?"

"Ah, I see Charlie is the one who gets down to brass tacks. Good. I like that." Hernandez pressed on. "Sam Childers is being hunted down by the authorities as we speak. Looks like you guys have put together some pretty compelling evidence against him. All I would like to ask, as it seems you're in direct contact with those searching for him, is that you inform me when he's found. You do that and I'll give you Logan."

He was asking her to hand over Sam Childers. To let the cartel or the gang do whatever it was they saw fit to silence Childers. If Allison agreed, she might as well pull the trigger on Childers herself. But maybe there was another solution. A deal that could be worked out. "If we do that, you have to agree to turn over Logan before we give up Childers."

"Alli," Charlie said flatly.

Allison raised her hand to stop her. "Logan can't be involved in whatever your people have going on and I don't know when or if they'll find Childers. I can't risk waiting for them to find him."

"How would I know to trust you'll keep your word?" Hernandez asked.

"You don't. But I have nothing else to offer. And you have a lot to lose."

He laughed. "You drive a hard bargain, Allison. I can see why you and Charlie work together. Okay. I know where Logan is now. I'll see to it he's released. But if you don't hold up your end of the bargain, I'm afraid I can't guarantee your safety. Any of you."

Allison stood. "Have Logan dropped off outside the TPD downtown stationhouse in an hour."

"Two." Martin stood. "That's the best I can do." He offered his hand. "Pleasure doing business with you, Allison. You and your partners. I'll be in touch."

Allison reached for his hand. The lump in her throat was hard to choke down, but she shook the devil's hand anyway.

———

Sam Childers had yet to be located. The taskforce, along with Shane had returned to the downtown stationhouse after getting the call from Allison about the surprise visit from Martin Hernandez.

DEA Agent Pierce had awaited a call from his agent on the inside to confirm Logan was still at the shipyard. They'd gathered a team to extract him, but he refused without confirmation. He claimed it was too risky.

"Even Reddick's people can't find him. Every place Childers was associated with has been searched. Nothing." Baylor said as he sat at the conference table upstairs. "I think our window might've just closed on finding Sam Childers."

Shane spotted Allison and the others approach. "They're here." He waved at them from inside the room. At her arrival, Shane began, "Allison. You have to tell us everything that went on in that meeting."

"They're bringing him here," Allison began.

"Who?" Pierce asked.

"Logan. Martin Hernandez agreed to have him brought here to the police station." Allison looked at the time. "In an hour and a half."

"How the hell did you manage to get him to agree to that? The fact he didn't kill you surprises the hell out of me," Markham said. "Do you have any idea what kind of danger you've all put yourselves in by dealing with that man directly?"

"I'm not sure we had a choice in the matter, Agent Markham," Charlie said. "He showed up at our door. He found us. Not the other way around."

"I hate to state the obvious, Charlie, but the way you all went after Childers, you sort of asked for this," Pierce replied.

"We handed you everything you needed to arrest Sam Childers," Allison began. "And you let him slip through your fingers. We were doing our jobs, Agent Pierce. We were looking to protect Logan Carr while all you wanted was to hook him on your line and dangle him in front of a dangerous gang."

"Okay, I think we're getting off-topic here." Shane looked at Allison. "You're right. You were doing your jobs. Unfortunately, when you're dealing with drug traffickers and cartels, this is the kind of shit that goes down."

"We got Logan freed," Lucy said. "What are you guys going to do to end this?"

———

THE MOVING TRUCK HAD BEEN STOPPED FOR AT LEAST 30 minutes, as far as Logan could tell. No one had come in. He could hear nothing and inside, the sheet metal surroundings held in the cold. They were either at the distribution center where the drugs would be split up, or they were near the retrieval site. Neither location mattered to Logan because at this point, he didn't believe he would make it home. They were going to use him and leave him to the cartel. Why else drag him here?

The door opened and now he could see the scant light on the horizon. Dusk. He peered at the man who had forced him inside this tin can. A man he knew was working with the DEA but could say nothing about it. "I need to take a leak. I've been in here for hours."

"Come on, bro. It's time to get out," Mateo said.

Logan pushed off the steel floor of the trailer. His legs were stiff, and his butt was numb, but he was up and walking. He reached the doors where Mateo waited on the ground and lowered himself out, jumping onto the asphalt. Logan surveyed his surroundings. He stood in an empty parking lot. "Where are we?"

"You said you had to take a piss, so go on, take a piss." Mateo pointed toward a tree planted in the parking lot.

Logan eyed the tree. As he walked toward it, he noticed a building in the background. It didn't look like a warehouse. It looked more like an old grocery store. He didn't recognize it. In fact, he didn't recognize anything around him. "Where the hell am

I?" Logan approached the lone tree with a thin trunk and did his business.

"Let's go," Mateo shouted.

Logan shook twice then zipped up his pants and started back. If only there was a way to get the hell out of this mess. As far as he knew, the man in front of him was the only other person out here. But he had no idea if there was anyone inside that building. And, as he let his eyes rake over Mateo, he spotted the gun not so subtly hidden in his waistband at the front of his jeans. So, maybe taking off into some unknown direction wasn't the brightest idea he'd had today.

"Today's your lucky day, bro," Mateo said.

"Why is that?" Logan asked.

"'Cause you get to live."

24

Time had crept along so slowly, Allison wanted to scream at the wall clock inside the police station lobby. Anything could go wrong when a deal was struck with a drug-running, money laundering criminal. They weren't the most trustworthy of people.

Shane checked the time. "It's been an hour. Do you really think he'll keep his end of the bargain?"

"You're asking me if I understand the mind of a drug trafficker," Allison began. "I do know that he would have more to lose by keeping Logan than by letting him go. And I don't think he believes Logan killed Julius Hardin. If he did, I'm pretty sure Logan would be dead already."

DEA Agent Pierce appeared from the corridor. "That was the call we've been waiting for. It's going down tonight. And yes, the instructions were to release Logan Carr." He peered at Allison. "That was a crazy, bold-ass deal you made. But it worked."

"Then we can move forward with putting a team in place," Markham replied.

"How quickly can you assemble them?" Detective Baylor asked him. "Once this thing starts, we'll have to move fast or risk losing Childers and his partner, Hernandez."

"You're assuming Childers will be there, but I'm not so sure. I have them on standby," Pierce replied. "One call and they'll be ready." He looked at Allison. "I'm going to need the three of you to sit tight once we get the ball rolling." He raised his hands. "I know you're going to say it was your idea. However, the truth of the matter is, none of you are law enforcement. I'm sorry, it's just the way it has to be. But don't think for one minute your support hasn't mattered."

"You won't get any pushback from me, Agent Pierce," Allison said. "My job was to make sure Logan was safe and proven innocent. We've accomplished one of those goals. I'll leave it up to you to accomplish the other. Like I said, if Hernandez thought for one minute Logan killed Hardin, he'd be gone. I think the reason he wants his partner found is that he believes it was Childers who killed Hardin. And that probably has him more concerned than anything because that means Childers has gone out on his own." She turned to Charlie. "Which could explain the pictures we found of him with Enrique Esteban." Allison turned back to Pierce. "We'll go back to the office after they give us Logan and wait it out there."

"No. I can't let you do that," Shane said. "I think it's best if all of you stick around here, including Logan. You'll be safer here. Until we get both these men into custody, I think that's the best solution."

"I agree." Reddick returned from a call. "You will be safe here."

Allison's face masked in sudden recognition. "I can't believe I didn't think of this before. Lucy, what about your developer-friend?"

She appeared confused for a moment. "You mean Kendall?"

"Yes. We could use his drone to trail the vehicle that drops off Logan."

"Wait. Hold up," Shane began. "What are you talking about? What drone?"

"It's a long story, but we met a man through Lucy. He has this prototype of a stealth drone," Allison replied.

"That's right," Charlie added. "That's a great idea."

"A stealth drone?" Markham asked. "We have drones, Allison. And while I like where your head's at, in this instance, I don't think that will work. DHS, DEA, and the FBI use what we call a Predator B drone for surveillance. The problem with that drone is that it has a wingspan of 66 feet. It's huge and would be easily spotted."

"DEA has employed the Insitu ScanEagle drone for surveillance," Agent Pierce began. "That could be a possibility."

"Again, it's still a large craft," Markham insisted. "It's too risky. If these people realize we're following, that's it, game over. They'll divert and we won't know anything."

"This one is different. We've seen it in action," Lucy began. "It's small, undetectable by radar."

"Like the Hummingbird," Agent Reddick added. "I recently attended a training seminar with the Bureau that talked about it. It's stealth and has something like a 7-inch wingspan."

"Do you have access to that because I don't," Pierce said. "It's untested for distance. I heard its flight time is something like 15 minutes. That won't do us any good."

"Please. Just hear me out," Lucy interjected. "I realize I'm the youngest person here. And I'm not in law enforcement like the rest of you, but I'm telling you, Kendall is smart. He's tested his prototype. It will do what we need it to do."

"Look, I've met this kid. He gave us a demonstration when we were looking to use it..." Allison seemed to realize no one else knew they had considered using this drone before. "Never mind. My point is, this drone is undetectable. What if we get him down here, get it set up, and have his drone follow whoever drops off Logan?" Allison looked at the others. "I know it's a risk, but if you put a tail on that car, you'll be discovered, and Hernandez will know what's up. This way, no one knows anything. That car will lead us somewhere important. Somewhere that might lead you to Childers or to where the drugs are coming in. Either way, you'll have a substantial lead and maybe a place to send your team."

Pierce held her gaze and inhaled a deep breath, making his broad chest expand even more. "Fine. I'll agree to it. But I'm getting my expert down here first. He'll assist your friend to ensure we have no snags in this operation. Agreed?"

"I've heard worse ideas," Markham said. "Make the call."

———

THEY HAD LESS THAN TWENTY MINUTES BEFORE THE TWO-hour timeframe expired. Lucy made the call and Kendall Murray had just arrived.

"I can't tell you how grateful we are that you're willing to do this for us," Lucy said. "I told you you'd be saving lives."

"Hey, that's why I developed this. I want to help law enforcement," Kendall replied. "I heard someone from DEA is going to monitor me?"

"Yes. It was the only way they would agree to use your drone. He's like an expert in drones or something."

"I don't have a problem with that," he replied. "I'm happy to let them observe all they want."

Reddick approached them. "Not that I don't appreciate you coming here, Mr. Murray, but this is a one-time deal. We could get in a lot of trouble with privacy laws alone. The ACLU will be up my ass if word gets out."

"I understand your concerns, Agent Reddick, and I'm more than willing to speak to the Bureau if anyone is interested in looking into my research. I'm not looking to make an enemy out of our intelligence services. I am sincere when I say that I want to use this to assist law enforcement and what better way than to track down a drug deal?"

Agent Pierce and his DEA drone expert approached the others. "Good. You're here. Why don't you show us know how you plan on executing this?" Pierce said.

The agents, along with Allison and her team, gathered around the back of the stationhouse while Kendall set up his equipment.

"After one of you gives the 'all clear' and you have your man, I'll fly her up and tail the car as far as I can go. I haven't tested her beyond 10 miles, so I'm afraid I can't guarantee results, but if nothing else, you'll have a direction to head, should she get too far out of range. But I don't think so. I think she'll push through."

Shane looked at Allison. "You three should go up front and wait. Two of our officers will be standing at the entrance with you. Whoever is bringing him might have orders to only release him to you two. Once you have Logan and the vehicle starts to leave, be sure to get a plate and note the make and model. We may need it for backup. When you tell my guys we're good, they'll radio me back here and we'll be off and running."

Allison nodded. "Got it."

———

THE SUN HAD DIPPED BELOW THE HORIZON AND THE AIR chilled. Allison and Charlie waited at the front of the stationhouse with two armed officers flanking them.

"I hope we made the right call," Allison said. "If Hernandez suspects we're setting him up, I'm not sure any of us will be safe."

"Believe me, Alli, he'll take precautions after they drop off Logan. I'm sure he didn't get into the position he's in by being careless. His people will watch for tails, which is why using this drone will be perfect. This was the right call. I wasn't sure at first, but I believe it will work." Charlie eyed her. "I need you to believe it too."

Allison revealed a smile when headlights caught her attention. "Hey." She tossed a glance at the road ahead. "This could be it. Officers, this could be our guy."

"Got it," one of them replied.

The car drew nearer. Allison didn't recognize it as the one she saw at Sam Childers' house the other day. She wondered if the officers might stop the car and try to detain the driver. If they did that, there was no telling what Martin Hernandez would do in retaliation. It wasn't part of the plan, but the temptation must have been there.

The car slowed. It was an older model Chrysler 300, black with dark tinted windows. It looked like it belonged to some rock star or pop artist. Much too flashy for someone who should be concerned with keeping a low profile. It rolled to a stop in front of the station where Allison, Charlie, and the officers waited. The rear passenger door opened, and Logan rolled out. His hands were tied behind his back, but he appeared uninjured.

"Logan." Allison rushed to his side, but the officers beat her to it. She noted the plate number as it squealed away. "Now." She looked to them. "Call Sully now."

Logan tried to stand but could only perch on his knees. He eyed Allison. "I'm okay. I'm not hurt." He moaned a little while the officers pulled him to his feet. "Can I get some water? And maybe get these zip ties off my wrists?"

"Of course." Allison looked at the officer. "I'd like to take him inside if that's okay."

"Yeah. The call's been made." The officer grabbed a pocket knife and cut off Logan's ties.

"Come on. Let's get you inside." Allison lifted Logan's arm over her shoulder and the officer took the other side. "You're sure you're okay?"

"I'm okay. Just thirsty. Could probably use a shower too." He offered a half-smile.

Charlie waited for the car to disappear, then cast her gaze to the sky. "I don't see it."

"It's dark. I hope they don't see it either," Allison said as she helped Logan in.

Charlie followed and when the officers felt they were in the clear, they made their way inside too.

"Should I go around back and make sure everything went as planned?" Charlie asked Allison.

"Please. I'll get him some water." Allison helped Logan to a chair and lowered him down.

Charlie made her way through to the back of the station and outside where the equipment had been set. "Well? They're gone. Please tell me the drone is following them." She eyed Kendall.

"She's doing her job," he replied. "How's your friend?"

"He seems okay. Allison's getting him some water. He looks tired and a little dirty, but otherwise unharmed."

"Thank God." Lucy turned to Kendall. "Will you know before it gets out of range?"

"Yes. The screen will beep, and I'll be notified of the last location before it quits. So far, so good, though. Fingers crossed."

"Did you guys get the car details?" Shane asked Charlie.

"We did. Black Chrysler 300. Alli got the plates."

"Don't hold your breath that'll do anything for us," Reddick replied. "These guys don't drive around vehicles registered to themselves."

"I'll need warning if your drone starts to crap out," Agent Pierce said. "I have air support on standby if we need to take over."

Kendall nodded. "So far, so good. Here, take a look." He pointed to the screen. "It's following the car south on Palmetto. They've traveled almost 3 miles and she's still going strong."

"I think we should get our people ready now," Markham said. "Pierce, once you get the call from your undercover agent, we'll have the location of the drop, regardless of where that car is headed. If we aren't prepared, we'll miss it and that'll be it. We won't get a third chance."

———

WITH JULIUS HARDIN DEAD, IT WAS UP TO HERNANDEZ TO run the operation. Yeah, Sam Childers was missing, but he wasn't involved in the day-to-day like Hernandez was. This shipment was too important to trust anyone farther down on the food chain and especially after what happened last time. Hardin had a snitch working for him and didn't know until it was too late. That snitch was dead, and so was Hardin. Hernandez still didn't know who killed him, but with Childers in the wind, it was starting to look like he had made a call that wasn't his to make. Now Hernandez was left to clean up the mess.

He sat in the all-terrain vehicle, camouflaged in a jungle net to obscure it from view of Coast Guard planes or boats that might be searching the coves. Right now, the only thing on Hernandez's mind was to ensure a successful transition. Get the drugs off the boats and onto the trucks, which sat nearby and were also camouflaged.

Hernandez pulled upright at the flicker of light in the water. He picked up the radio. "Did you see that?"

Static sounded and then a voice. "Saw it. Could be them."

Hernandez peered around. "Is everyone in place?"

"In place and ready to go," the voice replied. "Anyone see the CG?"

"No," Hernandez said. "Get the boats on the water. Now."

———

LOGAN FINISHED THE ENTIRE BOTTLE OF WATER BEFORE HE began, "I think I know where they're going."

Allison stood at attention. "They told you?"

"No, but I overheard something when I was inside the truck. A radio call came in and Mateo answered. Allison, the man who freed me, Mateo Figueroa, was working with Pierce's undercover agent. I didn't say anything though. I was careful so he wouldn't be found out."

"Good. You did great, Logan," Allison said. "Go on."

I was cuffed but I could crawl, and I did, toward the front of the truck. I overheard parts of their conversation."

"Where? Where are they going?" Markham approached him with hurried steps. "And when is it going down?"

"I don't know the time," Logan replied. "But I think it's going to be near Midnight Pass."

"Christ, that's south of Sarasota," Reddick began, "Hell, it's south of Siesta Key. That's a long way to go just to drive it back up to Tampa. Are you sure about this?"

"Pretty sure," Logan said. "I heard them say Midnight Pass. It's secluded. It's near a reserve. Very little residential. It's a good location."

Reddick looked to Pierce. "Well? It's your people on the inside. You think this is credible or can you find out?"

"I can't risk making contact again. He said he would reach out when he knew," Pierce said.

"Fair enough," Reddick continued. "How long would it take our people to get down there?"

"We figured it would be a south-end location. Not that far south but let me make a call." Pierce turned to Allison. "You better go out back and have a chat with your buddy. If that drone makes it that far, I'd be surprised as hell."

"What do you want me to say?" Allison asked. "Should we keep the tail?"

"Yes. Just let him know where we think the drop will take place. That car they're in, I doubt it will make it in that terrain. Marshy stuff out that far. So, I say keep an eye on the Chrysler and see where it goes. I'll work the situation on my end," Pierce added.

"I'll go with." Charlie followed Allison as she started outside. "Lucy's still out there, right?"

"She is." Allison continued through the halls of the station and arrived at the rear exit door. She pushed through and headed to the folding table where the laptop and other tracking equipment was set up. "How's it going so far?"

"We're still tracking the car," Lucy replied. "It's gone farther than the ten miles he had as a test module."

"That's good news. Listen, Logan thinks the drop will take place at Midnight Pass," Allison continued.

"Where's that?" Kendall asked.

"South of Sarasota, about fifteen miles south," Charlie replied. "Do you think your toy can handle that?"

"It's not a toy," he replied.

"I'm sorry. You're right. I should restate my question. Do you think the drone will make it that far?"

He gazed at his laptop, which tracked the drone's GPS location, and then turned back to the others. "I'd like to say with certainty that yes, it will. But I don't think so. I think she'll run out of battery before making that far, even if she could make it that far."

"What's the answer?" Lucy asked.

"Pierce doesn't think the Chrysler will do well in the terrain. He thinks it'll divert somewhere else. That's where I think we'll be one-up on this plan. Let's stay on it as far as it goes. Wherever they stop will be somewhere significant," Allison said.

"Got it. We'll keep on it," Kendall replied.

"How's Logan doing?" Lucy asked.

"He's tired, thirsty. But he seems all right," Allison said. "My concern is Sam Childers. If we let Childers out of our reach, I don't know what will happen when this drop is over. Hernandez will have kept his end of the bargain and we won't have kept ours."

Kendall jumped to attention. "It stopped. The car stopped."

Allison rushed to the screen where Lucy was already looking. "Where is it?"

"GPS coordinates are..."

"No, just give me a street, a town, anything," Allison interrupted.

"North Sarasota," he began. "It's a recycling plant. Tidewater Recyclables." He peered at Allison. "That's not that far away."

"And not that far north from where the drop is slated. It's a distribution center. Has to be." Allison turned to Charlie. "We need to tell Pierce. They have to get down there, now."

25

The shuttered recycling plant was the perfect location and had taken weeks to scout. Sam Childers was good at his job which was why the Columbians wanted him in charge. They had lost faith in Julius Hardin and Childers had convinced them he could run the operation better than Martin Hernandez.

The Feds were after Childers, but Enrique Esteban promised there would be no evidence found to use against him. The cartel could get to anyone, anywhere, and if there was evidence, it would disappear before the Feds even knew it.

The arrangement had been made. Once the drugs arrived on shore, the plan was for Hernandez to follow it to safety. A growing faction inside the gang and the cartel had turned sour on Hernandez and Childers used that to his advantage, turning several of them against him. Now, Hernandez only knew what Childers wanted him to know and he had Esteban's blessing.

Enrique Esteban was the cartel's operations officer for Tampa and had arrived at the plant only minutes ago. "When is the shipment due to reach us?" The high-ranking member of the cartel lived in Tampa and had ensured operations ran smoothly. With the exception of Julius Hardin and the bust almost two weeks ago, they had. Esteban had to ensure there would be no snags this time around and had already taken care of those who screwed it up the last time.

"If everything remains on schedule, it should be two hours." Childers approached him as he spoke. "Hernandez will trail the shipment."

"He's still unaware of our deal?"

"To my knowledge. I haven't spoken to him since yesterday. He might already know the Feds came after me this morning. I don't know. But he would do nothing to jeopardize the operation. He's not that stupid. Once the shipment arrives here, I'll handle the rest," Childers said.

"You appear to have everything under control. Good." Esteban moved closer to him and stood just inches from his face. His black hair was thick and stood tall with a face covered in a heavy beard. But it was his eyes that sent fear through anyone who dared look. "If there are any fuckups this time around, it will be the end of you, too."

Childers felt the fear rise in his throat, but any sign of that would show his weakness. Men like Esteban didn't like weakness. "Nothing will go wrong. You have my word."

———

ALLISON AND CHARLIE WAITED FOR SHANE'S RESPONSE AS they hovered over his desk.

"The taskforce's team is already on their way to the suspected drop site. They could finish this before it begins, just like the previous bust," Shane said.

"Come on, Shane. We know there are people waiting at the recycling plant. Why can't you go there and make arrests?" Allison asked.

"First of all, we'd have to coordinate with Sarasota PD. It's out of our jurisdiction."

"Hey, it would be a huge collar for anyone," Charlie began. "They'll be behind you on this, Shane. There's no time to sit here and contemplate protocol. We're wasting time."

Lucy approached with Kendall in tow. "Charlie's right. Kendall said the car is still there. Whoever drove it is part of the plan and they're just waiting."

Shane stood up. "Let me run this past the lieutenant." He walked to her office. "Lieutenant Cooper, can I talk to you about something?"

She peered up from the stack of papers on her desk. "If this is about the impending raid, there is protocol. The taskforce doesn't need permission from me, but you do. What's your plan, Sully?"

"Sarasota PD will need to be brought into this. We have a location of where we believe the drugs will be taken to and distributed from," he said.

"And the taskforce? If they make the bust before the drugs leave the drop site?"

"Then this conversation won't matter, except to say that we know there are members of the Southside Runners there ready and waiting. If nothing else, we can put a dent in their operation."

"And charge them with what?" she asked. "No drugs, no crime. Unless I'm missing something."

"It depends on who else is there."

She studied him. "What do you mean? Who do you think will be there?"

"There's a chance Sam Childers could be there. I don't think he would run out on the cartel when the operation is going down. He would want to be sure to take the credit for the success of the mission possibly to prove he's ready to take on more responsibility," Shane said. "I can't say this with any certainty, but he might be looking to oust Hernandez. Some of the evidence Hart and her people uncovered could prove that's the case."

The lieutenant nodded. "I'll call Sarasota PD and get it set up. You head down there, and you assist them. Do you hear me, Sully? You assist them."

"You want me to give up the collar?"

"I'm saying this is well outside our jurisdiction. You know that. Give them your intel. I have no doubt you will be credited for the work you've put into this already. Go. It sounds like you don't have a lot of time to make this happen. And keep in contact with Baylor." She picked up the phone but turned to him. "Oh, and the P.I.s, they can't go with you."

"I understand," Shane said.

"Make sure *they* understand too."

Shane nodded and left her office, returning to his desk where the partners of ACL waited alongside the developer of the drone that brought them this far. "The lieutenant is coordinating this with Sarasota PD. I'll be heading down there now to work with them on raiding the recycling facility."

"And us?" Allison began. "What are we supposed to do?"

"You'll have to wait. I'm sorry, but you know I can't bring you with me. It's against the rules. I'm sorry, Allison. I know how hard you all have worked to make this happen."

Allison nodded with pursed lips. "No. It's okay. We get it. We're not cops." She peered at him. "Just do me a favor, don't let Childers off the hook. Not in some shootout. Bring him in. He needs to see justice."

"It's out of my hands, Allison." Shane gathered his things and checked his weapon. "I'll be in touch if I can. Remember, I'd prefer you to sit tight here where I know you'll be safe."

Allison watched as he walked away. "Well, I guess we did our part."

Charlie eyed her. "We're not staying here, are we?"

Allison peered at her colleagues. "We'll stay here, but there is something we can do." She approached Logan who was still in the waiting area with his eyes closed. "Logan. Wake up."

"Huh?" He pulled upright on the chair. "What's wrong?"

"Nothing's wrong. The cops are doing their jobs and now it's time for us to do ours."

———

THE DOORS TO THE TRUCKS SLAMMED SHUT AND HERNANDEZ secured the locks. The skiffs that had met the narco-sub before it reached the shoreline and loaded the much smaller shipment of cocaine had returned. The sub had been scuttled and its crew joined the drivers. The deal had gone down without a hitch. Hernandez had succeeded in redeeming the Southside Runners in the eyes of the Columbian cartel.

The final leg of the journey would see Hernandez trailing the moving trucks to their destination—a recycling plant on the outskirts of Sarasota. From there, the drugs would be distributed to other vehicles and, like tentacles, would extend out to other parts of the state, including Tampa.

"Let's move out." Hernandez hit the side of the truck and returned to his own vehicle. It would be dawn in a few hours and by the time the sun arose, the shipment would have been disbursed and order restored. The only variable was Sam Childers. He was usually in contact with Esteban and Esteban wasn't talking; a potential problem as Hernandez saw it.

He keyed the ignition and waited for the trucks to move out on the marshy road that would be better suited for all terrain vehicles. The trucks were equipped with all-wheel drive and Hernandez kept his fingers crossed for safe passage.

As he rolled along, his tires lost their grip and slid the SUV sideways, but soon regained traction. "Come on. Just another mile." He peered into the dark passage with only the red taillights of the truck ahead. Another car led the way in front and so the truck was wedged between two vehicles.

However, even if trouble arose, there was no place to go. Not for a while longer, then they would reach a paved road. Hernandez felt his body tense as his grip on the steering wheel tightened.

The radio in his car buzzed to life. "Everyone doing okay back there?"

It was the lead driver, Mateo Figueroa, and Hernandez picked up the receiver. "All good here."

The driver of the truck replied, "Good here. Just get us the hell off this road."

"Copy that," Figueroa replied.

It took several minutes to cross the treacherous swampy grounds and when the roadway was in sight, Figueroa made the announcement. "This is it, boys. We made it."

Hernandez listened with a sigh of relief. They'd evaded the Coast Guard, the DEA and had now made it to the roadway where it would be smooth sailing until they reached the plant. "Good job, boys," He replied.

———

FIGUEROA FELT HIS TIRES HIT THE PAVEMENT AND HIS

shoulders sank. He picked up his radio. "This is it, boys. We made it."

They missed it. He'd given the undercover agent the coordinates and his people didn't get there in time. It was Figueroa's only way out. The deal was to catch them in the act, arrest all of them, then give Figueroa a new identity and set him up in Witness Protection until the trial. He'd wanted to tell Logan, but the risk was too great. He didn't know how Logan managed to negotiate his own release, but it made things easier knowing he was out of the way.

Now, however, he would have to keep up the charade. The Feds missed their golden opportunity and Figueroa was right back where he started.

———

THE ROADWAYS WERE QUIET IN THE MOSTLY SUBURBAN AND resort areas that led to the recycling plant only a few miles away now. Timing was critical and the shipments needed to be disbursed before daylight. The trucks needed the cover of darkness to assist them.

When the plant was in view, Hernandez could breathe again. The worst was over. He had feared the DEA and the other authorities, but he feared the Columbians even more. This was his do or die moment and so far, he had done his job. "Let's bring it in," He radioed.

Figueroa led the convoy around the back of the plant to the loading docks. Hernandez parked his SUV behind them and stepped out into the chilly early morning air. With about an hour until sunrise, time was still on his side. He made his way to the door of the building and pressed the button. He eyed the driver inside the truck who waited to back up the trailer to be unloaded.

Figueroa was already on his way to the rolling doors and finally, the back door opened.

"You made it. I didn't think you would." Sam Childers stood beyond the door with a dubious smile.

"What the hell?" Hernandez took a step back. "Now you decide to show up after everything is done? You know you have the Feds on you, right?"

"Get inside." Childers held a gun in his right hand and aimed it at Hernandez. He held it low and out of sight of the others. "We have a lot to discuss."

Hernandez eyed the weapon. "You're out of your mind. We have less than an hour to get this shipment onto the other trucks and out of here. Esteban won't be happy about this."

"Let me worry about Esteban. In fact, he and I have already had a discussion about this very thing. Now get inside, or I'll gun you down where you stand."

Hernandez surrendered to Childers' demands. "If this goes sideways, it'll be on you. Not me. I did the hard part."

Childers kept his gun trained on Hernandez. "Keep walking. There's an office up ahead. We'll have ourselves a little sit-down and hash this out."

"I brought you into this and this is how you repay me?" Hernandez said, keeping his back to Childers. "I built the relationship with Esteban, not you."

"This is it. Just get inside." He pushed the gun into Hernandez's back and forced him into the small office. He turned on the light and closed the door. "Tell the men to unload the shipment and get everything inside and on the distribution tables."

Hernandez grabbed his radio. "Bring everything in and put it on the tables ready to be sorted. Now."

"Copy that," a voice chimed in.

"Looks like some of them still listen to you." Childers walked around to the desk and sat down. "Please, have a seat. We have a few things to discuss."

DEA AGENT DOMINIC PIERCE POUNDED ON HIS STEERING wheel as he peered out onto the grounds known as Midnight Pass. "Damn it! We're too late."

Markham sat next to him with Detective Baylor and FBI Agent Reddick in the back seat.

Baylor pulled up toward the front. "How can you be sure? No one's out here."

Pierce jumped out of his SUV and landed on the soft earth. His shoes sunk into the roadway. "Tracks." He leaned into the opened door. "That's how I know. There are fresh tracks everywhere. Son of a bitch." He slammed the door.

Baylor and Reddick joined him and scanned the area. Baylor began, "They must've used a boat to reach the shoreline. No way one of those cartel subs could get that close. It's like soup out there. They loaded up the drugs out in the distance and brought them in."

Pierce turned to him. "Yeah, I can see that. Point is, we missed the whole goddam thing."

Reddick turned to them. "Not entirely. We still have the distribution center. We make the call to the teams and redirect them. But we better make the call fast. They hit these roads and half of them might not make it out."

Pierce seemed to consider the new plan. "Fine." He picked up his phone. "Change of plans, boys. I'll text the address. The drugs are headed there." He turned back to the others. "Let's roll."

ALLISON STUDIED THE SCREEN. "WHEN DID THE DRONE TAKE these pictures?" she asked Kendall.

"Just before I set it down. I circled a final time and got a few aerial shots thinking it could be handy for the police to have."

"That's the car I saw when Charlie and I were at Sam Childers' halfway house." She turned to Charlie. "It's the same one I saw at the parole office too."

"What are you saying?" Lucy asked. "Who does it belong to?"

"I can't be sure, but I'll bet it belongs to someone who works for Childers. Which could mean..."

"He's there," Charlie said. "He's at the plant waiting for the drugs. Why would he go there and not get the hell out of town knowing the taskforce is looking for him?"

"The deal was made," Allison said. "The drugs were coming whether Childers had the cops after him or not. What choice did he have but to follow through? We already suspect he was making unilateral deals with Enrique Esteban. And in all honesty, what we found is circumstantial. The pictures, the banks. Unless we go through the accounting for the half-way house, the restaurant, and all the others, we can't prove there was money laundering happening. So maybe Esteban has a way of cleaning things up before the government can make a case. Either way, Charlie, I think Childers is at that plant."

"Logan, what are you doing?" Lucy said as he started away.

He stopped and turned back. "I'm sorry. I can't stay here." He turned away again.

"Wait. Logan. Where are you going?" Allison pulled open the door and followed him. "This is over. We won."

"They'll never let me be free, Allison. The cartel or the Southside Runners. Regardless of what happens tonight. No one escapes them. Ever. You just suggested that exact thing. Assuming Esteban and the cartel will clean up things for Sam, so he'll get away clean too. Their reach is too deep." Logan held her gaze for a moment. "I'm sorry." He walked away.

"What in the..." Charlie's face masked in shock. "Why did he do that? Where is he going to go?"

Allison turned to her, dumbstruck. "I don't know. Maybe he's right, Charlie. No matter what we prove, the cops might not go after Logan, but the gang or the cartel will."

"No. No, that's not true." Charlie shook her head wildly. "If they had wanted him dead, Logan would be dead. Hernandez let him go, Alli. Come on, we have to go after him. We'll convince him to stick this out."

Allison grabbed her arm. "I don't think we will. We need to go back now, Charlie. The information we have could mean the cops will be ready for Childers when they arrive. And they might still stand a chance at capturing him tonight."

———

ALLISON HELD THE PHONE TO HER EAR AS SHE STOOD INSIDE the lobby of the station. "What was I going to do, Shane? Keep him at gunpoint? He's done nothing wrong. He wasn't under arrest. He's a free man."

"He'll have broken the terms of his parole. They'll come after him, Allison," Shane replied over the phone.

"Where are you anyway?" She pressed on, ignoring his words about Logan.

"With Sarasota police. We're getting ready to head out to the recycling plant. Baylor called me and said they missed the pickup but that they were headed to the plant in hopes of catching the drugs getting ready to be distributed."

"Did you tell them we saw that car? Shane, there's a damn good chance Childers will be there."

"I agree. And yes, I'm going to get the word out. Look, you three just sit tight until you hear from me. I'll be heading to the plant with these guys and I'll keep you posted when I can."

"Thanks, Shane." Allison ended the call. "He's going to the plant. He says the taskforce is headed there as well."

Charlie nodded. "Sounds like it's showtime. If only I had popcorn."

———

PIERCE ROLLED SLOWLY ALONG THE STREET THAT FRONTED the recycling plant and killed his headlights. "I don't see any cars."

"They must be around the back," Baylor replied. "But this is the place we got from the drone operator. They're here."

Markham picked up his cell phone. "ETA?"

"Two minutes. Right behind you, Agent Markham," the voice on the other end of the line replied.

"Kill your lights, coast in," Markham added. "It looks like the vehicles are in the back. No movement up front. We'll drive around."

"Copy that."

Markham set down his phone. "Once we confirm this is the spot, Baylor, I'll need you to get on the horn with Sullivan and tell him to give Sarasota PD the thumbs up."

"You got it," Baylor replied.

Pierce started around to the rear of the building. With his lights off and engine at near idle, he made the move as quietly as possible.

Detective Baylor kept his eyes peeled in search of any movement outside. Snipers on top of the building, or in surrounding bushes. When it came to the cartel and the gangs inside this city, he took nothing for granted. Not one of those groups would hesitate to take out any officer of the law or federal authority. Because to them, answering to the cartel was much worse than answering to the US government. "I see something." He pointed ahead. "That's the Chrysler 300. It's still going down."

"Baylor, get on the phone now. Call Sully and have him get those guys down here like yesterday. I know they're close." Markham picked up his cell to notify his first-in-command. "Get into position. We're moving in."

Baylor made the call. "Sully, it's going down. Get those boys here now." He dropped his phone in his pocket and moved to the rear passenger door, ready to jump out when Pierce gave the word. "I think I see them."

"Who?" Reddick surveyed the area. "Yep. That's our team."

"So far, so good," Markham said. "Now let's get the local boys down here and we'll have ourselves a party."

"Ask and ye shall receive." Baylor pointed at the rear windshield. "I think that's the boys in blue rolling in now."

Markham picked up his cell again. "We're in the back. Ready to roll when you're in position. Just like we talked about."

One of the patrol cars pulled alongside Pierce's SUV. The passenger window rolled down.

"It's a beautiful morning for a drug bust, boys." Shane offered a thumbs-up. "Are we doing this now or what?"

"Follow me." Pierce pulled ahead and trailed his own team until they were in position. "Get out. We're doing this now."

The doors opened and the agents spilled out. Baylor approached a Sarasota officer.

"Which one of you is running the show?" The officer asked.

"That'd be me." Pierce raised a hand. "They're here. We get in, secure the exits and make sure we get Sam Childers and Martin Hernandez alive."

"Just to confirm," the officer began. "We should get everyone alive, right?"

"Whatever it takes to get the job done. Don't let these drugs leave. The people either." Markham eyed the team. "It's now or never."

The team headed into their positions, each stationed at an entrance and around the front and back. The building was surrounded. Shane tailed his Sarasota counterpart and worked his way to the front entrance.

"Seven. I see seven men inside." Shane peered through a small window and retrieved his weapon. It was the first time he'd ever brandished his gun. He thought about Allison and what she'd been through to get Logan Carr to safety and prove his innocence. She was braver than he imagined. And now it was his turn to do his job. This was what he wanted. This was the big leagues.

"Now!" Markham shouted over the radio.

The doors burst open. Front, back, every exit in the building. Markham's team and the cops, ten in total, rushed inside with guns at the ready.

"Stay where you are, boys," Markham shouted. "My guys won't hesitate to take you out."

Five men stood around the multiple tables as they prepared the shipments for distribution. Their eyes widened and hands went up.

Markham eyed Reddick. "Go find Childers and Hernandez. I know they're here. Take Baylor with you."

Reddick nodded to Baylor who quickly joined him. "They have to be in the back."

"Then what are we waiting for?" Baylor walked beside him as they started ahead. "They would've heard us come in. Be prepared for anything."

Reddick nodded at the door, silently suggesting they go inside. "Ready?" he mouthed.

Baylor held up his fingers, signaling, one, two..." He raised his leg and kicked at the door. The frame splintered, but the door remained fixed.

Reddick used his brawny shoulder and rammed into it hard enough to finish the job. "FBI! Don't move."

Sam Childers held a gun to Hernandez's head. "I thought I heard someone. Come on in."

"Put down your weapon, Childers," Baylor said.

"I can't let you arrest me, Detective. If I did that, I'd be killed the second you put me in jail."

"It doesn't have to be that way and you know it," Reddick said. "Put down the gun. It's over. Whatever relationship you had with the cartel is over too. Both of you are going away for a long time. Unless of course, you have something valuable to offer."

Sam laughed. "You guys are in way over your heads if you think you can win this."

"It's been a long night," Reddick said. "We're done here."

Sam raised his gun to Hernandez's temple. "Yeah, I think we are." He cocked the gun.

Baylor took aim. "Don't do..." But before he could finish the sentence, Reddick pulled his trigger and a bullet flew past him.

Hernandez collapsed to the ground. Childers' face was splattered with blood and he looked at Reddick with wide eyes. "What the?"

Baylor's mouth dropped. "What the hell did you just do?"

26

Light from a rising sun shone inside the stationhouse. Allison was curled up in a chair while Charlie sat upright next to her. Meanwhile, Lucy had stretched across a short bench in the lobby. All awaited word of the raid on the recycling plant and as the hours passed with no reply, Allison grew increasingly concerned.

"We should've heard from Shane by now," Allison said to Charlie.

"There's nothing you can do for him, Alli. We just have to hold out hope that all went to plan. He's not there alone. He has a lot of firepower behind him and a lot of experienced law enforcement. I'm sure he's fine."

The lieutenant in charge of Shane's department appeared from her office and approached them. "Allison?"

She whipped around and pushed off the chair. "Yes? Have you heard from Detective Sullivan?"

"Sully's fine. However, there was an incident. Martin Hernandez was shot and killed by FBI Agent Reddick."

"Hernandez?" Charlie joined Allison and stood shoulder to shoulder with her. "What about Sam Childers?"

"Apparently, there was an altercation between Childers and Hernandez and Childers was unharmed. Detective Baylor and Agent Reddick placed Childers under arrest. They're bringing him to the FBI field office now," the lieutenant continued. "And according to Baylor, they got into the storage unit and discovered valuable information to use against Sam Childers and the cartel. Allison, we will need you and your partner to make a statement, and if this goes to trial, and I suspect it will, you will likely be called to testify."

"Sam Childers should be put away for life," Allison said.

"You won't get an argument from me." The lieutenant peered around. "You all should go home and get some rest. The paperwork alone on this will take Sully hours and he informed me that they only just left the scene. Sarasota PD will remain on site until the taskforce finishes collecting the evidence. The good news is, the drugs will remain off the streets. We all have your friend with the drone to thank for that."

Allison looked at Lucy who had just opened her eyes. "I'll be sure to let my partner know how much it helped. Thank you, Lieutenant." She nodded to Charlie and the two walked toward Lucy. "Hey, kiddo."

"I heard a little bit. Shane is okay?" Lucy sat up.

"He is. Hernandez was killed and Childers was taken into FBI custody," Allison said. "You made this possible. You and your friend Kendall. He's a smart man who stands to make a killing on that drone."

"He went home a while ago, but I'll tell him." Lucy stood. "Thank you, Allison, for trusting me to bring him in."

"We trust you with our lives," Charlie said. "We're lucky to have you on the team."

"There may be some concerns with a trial and statements and things like that, but we did what was right," Allison said. "Childers will get what he deserves."

Charlie peered at her. "What about Logan? Alli, we'll need him to back us up. Especially with Hernandez out of the picture. Childers will do what it takes to stay out of prison, even if it means blaming Logan. The cartel will do what they have to do as well. The kid's an ex-con. He'll be an easy target."

"Let's just get through this first. The trial, if there is one, won't happen for a long time," Allison replied.

"Okay. But that doesn't mean the cartel will forget about Logan. And we've already seen how long their reach is."

Allison nodded. "I understand." She checked the time. "It's 6 o'clock in the morning. Let's all go home, like the lieutenant said, and just get a few hours' sleep. Shane's going to be tied up for a while. Then, we'll regroup and figure all this out."

———

ALLISON RETURNED HOME AFTER DROPPING OFF THE OTHERS and slogged to the front door. Nolan opened it as she prepared to insert her key into the lock. "Oh, hey, hon. What are you doing awake?"

"I couldn't sleep until I knew you were okay." Nolan stepped aside and closed the door behind her.

"Nolan, honey, I texted you and said I was at the police station. It was the safest place for me to be. Look, you're going to have to get used to me being gone odd hours." She started into the kitchen. "It isn't that I don't appreciate your concern. I do. But I think this is just the way it's going to be sometimes. I'll always keep in touch with you. You know that." She poured a cup of coffee that had already brewed. "Thanks for putting on some coffee though."

"You should probably go straight to bed and skip the coffee so you can sleep," Nolan replied.

"Probably." She sipped on the coffee anyway. "No school today?"

"I told you I was going to skip this semester, Mom. The team starts practicing in a week and then there's spring training. I can't do school right now. We talked about this."

"No. You're right. Of course we did." Allison set down her cup. "I forgot, that's all."

"You still don't think it's a good idea, do you?" Nolan sat on the stool at the kitchen island.

"I think that if this is what you want to do, then you should do it. You have a great opportunity. I won't deny that. I'll support you in whatever you do." She walked around the island and kissed his cheek. "I love you. I think I will try to close my eyes for an hour or so."

Nolan turned to her as she started into the hallway. "You, um, you didn't say anything to Lucy about what we talked about, did you?"

Allison stopped and turned to him. "Of course not. I said I wouldn't. But I will tell you, there are others out there who appear to be courting her. I wouldn't wait too long if I were you." Allison disappeared into her room.

She closed the shades and shed the clothes she'd worn since yesterday. But before laying down, Allison checked her phone again. "Damn." Still no call from Shane. She was worried for him, even though the raid was over, and she knew he was safe, there was still that little tickle in the back of her brain.

Allison crawled into bed and with some light already spilling into her room, she closed her eyes and drifted off to sleep.

———

A KNOCK ON ALLISON'S BEDROOM DOOR ROUSED HER. "MOM? Shane's here." Nolan opened the door a fraction of an inch. "Mom? Are you awake? Shane's in the kitchen."

Allison rolled over to face him. "I'm up. I'm up. Tell him I'll be right there." She checked the time on the clock, and it showed 10 am. "Oh my God." Her eyes widened and she quickly hopped out of bed and pulled on sweatpants and a t-shirt before wrapping her hair into a high bun.

She stood in front of the bathroom mirror and splashed water on her face. "Well, I've looked better." Disregarding her appearance, Allison shuffled to her bedroom doors and stepped into the corridor, making her way to the kitchen. "Shane."

"I tried to call you, but I didn't get an answer. Now I see why." He stood from the kitchen stool. "I'm sorry to wake you."

"Don't be. I didn't think I would sleep for so long." She looked him over. "You're okay, though?"

"I'm fine." He smiled. "I won't lie though. It was the craziest thing I've done since becoming a cop. Guns, people yelling, drugs everywhere. It was insane."

She noticed the huge smile on his face and walked to the cabinet to retrieve two cups. "I heard Hernandez was killed. Coffee?"

"Please. It was Agent Reddick. I wasn't there when it happened, but I guess when he and Baylor went inside some office, there was Childers with a gun to Hernandez's head."

"Oh my God." She handed him the mug.

"Tell me about it. Anyway, the guys tried to get Childers to drop his weapon. He wouldn't. Then one thing led to another and Hernandez was caught in the crossfire. Only it was *our* crossfire, not Childers'. He died instantly. One shot to the head."

"Reddick shot him in the head?" Allison asked. "Geez. I guess he must've been aiming for Childers, but that seems very targeted."

Shane raised his hands. "Hey, I wasn't there. I have no idea what went down. Only Childers, Baylor and Reddick know what happened. That's the official word, though."

"What happens now, Shane? I'm worried about Logan and what the gang might do to him. According to your lieutenant, Hardin's storage unit contained some seriously damaging information on Childers and the cartel. Logan said he didn't think he would ever be safe. I think Logan thought if Hernandez said anything, the cartel would come after him. So, he fled."

"Do you know where?"

"No. He didn't tell us anything. I couldn't stop him."

Shane appeared defeated. "Damn it. We could've used his testimony when this thing goes to trial. Well, it's out of my hands now anyway. This belongs to the FBI and the rest of the taskforce."

"So that's it? We're out of it?" Allison asked.

"Unless you know something I don't, then yeah, our job is done. It's all over except for the trial."

"Are you afraid of what the cartel will do now? Two of their shipments were seized. I'd be very afraid if I was a member of the Southside Runners."

"That's not our battle, Allison. DEA, FBI, all those guys. That's what they get paid the big bucks to do. You will just go on and get another client."

Allison nodded. "Sure. No, you're right. It's time to move on and get another gig. I have staff to pay."

———

THE OFFICE WAS OPENED, AND THE STAFF OF ACL Investigative Services returned to work. Lucy sat at her desk and Charlie sat at hers, but no one appeared to be in the mood for idle chit-chat.

Allison eyed her team and finally broke the silence. "I know what you're all thinking. And I'm worried too. I think Childers has a lot of people behind him and those people will make sure someone pays for the loss of yet another shipment."

"It's not just that, Alli," Charlie began. "I'm worried about Logan. I wish he would come back and ask for protection. But I'm concerned about something else too and I think we all know what that is." She eyed Lucy and returned her gaze to Allison.

"Hernandez's murder," Lucy began. "That's what concerns you, right, Charlie? Because I feel it too. We all read the statements given by Childers and Baylor. And we all met Hernandez."

"It was self-defense," Allison said. "Yeah, I read that too."

"I get that no one wants to point the finger at one of their own, but Alli, what if there's more to this than we know?" Charlie asked.

"More to Agent Reddick? He's a Federal agent. Maybe he was just doing his job."

"Then he would've killed Childers too or instead," Lucy replied. "But it was Hernandez."

"Look, the guy was still a drug dealer. He was still a partner to Childers and took Logan hostage. He wasn't innocent," Allison said.

"No, Hernandez wasn't innocent." Charlie held Allison's gaze. "Is there anything we can do?"

"You think we can prove that Agent Reddick killed Hernandez for a reason?" Allison asked.

"I don't know what that reason would be, maybe something that tied him to the government or the FBI or something like that."

Allison shook her head. "I don't know, Charlie, it's a shot in the dark. We're surmising all of this. There's no evidence to suggest Reddick has done anything but his job. None."

"That isn't entirely true." Lucy rifled through her files and retrieved the book former Detective Asher gave her. "In here. It was bugging me when I got home last night and so I had another look."

Allison approached her. "I had my own concerns about just how much we were able to get against Childers in a short amount of time and yet the taskforce had been at this for years. A taskforce Reddick was on. Show me what you got."

———

SHANE WAS AT HIS DESK WHEN HIS PHONE RANG. "HEY, Allison. What's up?"

"Listen, I'm at the office and we're reviewing some details from the book given to Lucy by Detective Asher."

"Okay. Why are you doing that?" He replied.

"Can you do me a favor and look into something for me?" she asked.

"That depends on what it is. Allison, what's going on? This case is over. What are you guys up to?"

"I don't want to say much until I know for sure, but can you look into Agent Dave Reddick?" she pressed on.

"Look into? Like how?"

"Well, he was a cop before he joined the FBI. A cop in New Mexico. He worked in Narcotics."

"How do you know that?" he asked.

"Because there's a brief reference to him in Asher's book."

Shane sat up at attention. "Why would Reddick be in that book?"

"Because Detective Asher apparently never stopped digging. He took notes up until last year when he got the diagnosis. Shane, can you do this?"

"Tell me what you're thinking first. What do you think Reddick did?"

"According to Asher's notes, he makes mention of the possibility Martin Hernandez was an informant for Reddick when Reddick was a cop in Albuquerque. That's all it says, and I don't know if it matters or not. But can you confirm this?"

Shane pressed his hand against his forehead. "Not really. No way could I look into an FBI agent. Allison, you have no idea what you're asking. And what does this have to do with the raid anyway? Even if you're right, what difference does it make? Hernandez is dead."

"And it was Reddick who killed him," she replied.

Shane was quiet as he pondered her implication. He tossed the pencil he held onto his desk and shook his head. With a heavy sigh, he continued. "I can ask around. Christ, I don't know. It's not like I have any pull around here, you know that, right?"

"Anything you can do would be appreciated," Allison said. "You might be right. This might not amount to a hill of beans. But what if it does?"

"I'll do what I can, Allison. But look, keep this to yourself, you understand? The last thing we want is for anyone to think you're digging into the FBI."

"We're going to head down and talk to Detective Archer again about this. See if he recalls anything else about Reddick. I'll wait to hear from you."

"Don't hold your breath," Shane said.

"Hey, Shane. Thanks."

"For what?"

"For believing in me. For believing in my team."

Shane closed his eyes. "I've always believed in you, Allison."

27

W hen the ACL team arrived at the hospice center and walked in to see former Detective Archer, Allison realized he probably didn't have much time left. Maybe news that the second bust was a success would bring a smile to his face. Or that they used his intel to get as far as they had.

"Good morning, Mr. Archer." Lucy announced their arrival since she was the only one who had met him besides Shane. "I brought some friends I'd like to introduce you to. This is Allison Hart and Charlie Wells. We work together. You remember me telling you I work for a private investigating firm?"

Benny Asher turned his head toward them. With a deep, gravelly cough, he cleared his throat. "I remember, Lucy. It's good to see you, kid." He turned his sights to Allison and Charlie. "Lucy spoke very highly of you both. It's a pleasure. So, Lucy, what can I do for you today? As you can see..." he coughed again. "Today's not the best day for me."

"Of course. Benny, we won't keep you, but I wanted to say thank you for letting me use your book. I don't know if you saw the news, but there was another successful raid and well, we had a big part of that and so did the information in your book."

"That is good news, Lucy. Does that mean case closed? You got the Southside Runners and the Columbians?"

"We're close. But that's not exactly the reason why we're here. The bust was a success and one of the main players in the Southside Runners organization was captured," Lucy continued. "That's the good news."

"What's the bad?" Archer asked.

"The other big player, Martin Hernandez, he was killed at the scene."

"Pardon me for saying, but that don't sound like bad news to me. He was a bad dude, Lucy."

"Yes. No question. But the way it happened." She turned to Allison.

"Go ahead," Allison replied.

"The way it happened, according to the FBI and one of TPD's detectives, Hernandez was killed by Agent Dave Reddick. It was, I guess you could say, in self-defense."

"Dave Reddick?" A hint of a smile appeared on his ashen, tired face. "And you saw his name in my book, didn't you?"

"We did," Lucy said.

"We've asked a detective-friend of ours to take a look into Reddick's background when he was with Albuquerque police," Allison began. "Because as we read in your notes, you thought he once had an informant named Martin Hernandez."

"So that's why you came here today?" Archer started into a coughing fit.

A nurse hustled inside and approached him. "How you doing, there, Benny? Come on now, let's sit you up a little bit."

He brushed her away. "I'm all right, woman! I'm all right."

She peered at him and shook her head. "Just trying to help you out, Benny. But I can see you're busy and I'll leave you be. Just sit up and that should help." She smiled at Allison and walked out.

"That's why we came here today," Lucy replied. "Is there anything else you can tell us about Agent Reddick?"

Archer tried to sit up a little but couldn't manage. He slumped back onto his pillow. "Well, I'll tell you. I did my damnedest to keep up to speed on the Southside Runners and their association with the Columbians. I guess you could say it's sort of been my life's work. Was a big part of your father's work too, I don't mind saying."

Lucy nodded.

"But ol' Dave Reddick. Yeah, he was a cop in New Mexico. Narcotics. I did some digging a few years back when I heard Reddick was posted to the taskforce. Man has a lengthy history in Narcotics. Has a whole lot of contacts. I never could say for sure, but I think he came across Hernandez not long before he joined the Feds. I assumed he kept in contact and figured Hernandez was a rising star inside the cartel and had hopes of continuing his relationship with the man."

"Wait, Hernandez was a part of the cartel? The Columbians?" Charlie asked. "I thought he was with the gang?"

"Yes and no. At the time, it was the Sonoran Cartel. You know, the Mexicans. I figured something must've went down and he started working for the Columbians. They're all in cahoots to some degree."

"I'm confused. I thought Hernandez was a member of the Southside Runners?" Allison asked.

"He was a man of many talents. Man had his fingers in so many different pies it was tough to keep track. I started to uncover his background a little, and Dave Reddick's but then... well I got sick and..."

Allison wore empathy as she peered at him. "Dave Reddick was the one who pulled the trigger. Is it possible Hernandez might've had something on Reddick and that was why Reddick killed him?"

"Anything's possible, Allison," Archer replied. "But from what I know about those two men. It wouldn't surprise me none at all if Reddick got himself wrangled into the Southside Runners and the Cartel, trying to play all sides. Look, I'm not saying Reddick was a bad apple. Hell, I don't know that was the case at all. But what I am saying is that Reddick was deep in it, if you know what I mean. There's a very real possibility he killed Hernandez to keep him quiet about something."

"How do we find out what that something was?" Allison asked him.

He furrowed his brow. "Well haven't you talked to Logan about all this?"

"No. He—um—he went into hiding. He said he didn't think the cartel would ever let him be free or the Southside Runners. So he's gone," Allison said.

Asher nodded and pursed his lips. "Well, Allison, you best find him. He might've known what was what in regards to Hernandez's place in the organization."

———

ALLISON STARTED THE CAR WHILE THE OTHERS STEPPED IN. "So all this time, Logan knew Hernandez."

"Sure. He was part of the gang. We just haven't focused on him before and kept our sights on Childers," Charlie said. "I'm not going to convict Logan based on what Benny Asher thinks."

"Charlie, he's been right so far," Lucy said from the back seat. "I don't want to believe Logan did anything wrong. This is just a case where Logan might have information he doesn't know is valuable. And it could be out of fear of Hernandez that he fled."

"So how do we find him and tell him Hernandez is dead?" Charlie asked. "Logan could be in Canada by now for all we know."

"Lucy, why don't you try his cell phone?" Allison peered through the rearview mirror at her.

"Why me?"

"Because he shares a connection with you. Your dad helped him. He was drawn to us because you work with us. I think he'll pick up if you call him."

"Okay. I'll try." She retrieved her cell phone and dialed his number. "Who knows if it's even on or what... Hello? Logan, it's me, Lucy. How are you?"

Allison and Charlie traded glances.

"Yeah, it's been all over the news. It's great. You know that means it's all over now, right? There's no need for you to stay in hiding. Childers is in custody and Hernandez is dead." She listened again.

Charlie closed her eyes and crossed her fingers. "Come on, kid. Tell us where you are," she whispered.

"Logan, we need your help," Lucy said. "We think Hernandez might've been holding something over Agent Reddick. Do you happen to know anything about that? Anything at all that could shed some light on this for us?"

Allison continued to drive back to the office, though she kept an ear trained on Lucy's conversation.

"It's okay. You aren't in trouble. You've done nothing wrong. Please, Logan. We need to know because if Reddick is hiding something..." She began to nod. "Uh-huh. That's what we were told, yes."

Allison pulled into the parking lot of the office and cut the engine. Both she and Charlie listened to the one-sided conversation.

"I see. No, that's great, Logan. Thank you. But I was serious about what I said before. There's no need for you to run away from this. There are people who can help. People who know what good you've done for this investigation," Lucy said. "Of course. You take care of yourself. Thank you, Logan." She ended the call and peered at Allison and Charlie.

"Don't keep us in suspense, kiddo," Allison said.

"Logan had heard rumors about Hernandez being an informant a long time ago," Lucy began. "And apparently, some inside the Southside Runners organization thought that might still have been the case, especially when the Coast Guard made that first bust a few weeks ago. Logan said Julius Hardin sort of filled him in on who he thought was the snitch and made mention of Hernandez. Logan didn't think much of it then and especially when Hardin apparently shot one of his own in the head for being the snitch."

"Oh my God. That still raises the question, if we're making assumptions, as to why Agent Reddick would intentionally kill a former informant who was in a unique position of power inside the gang and possibly the cartel," Charlie said.

"We have to consider the possibility Reddick might have been protecting Mateo Figueroa or the undercover DEA agent inside the rival gang. If arrests were made and if Hernandez suspected these men, word could have easily been leaked." Allison's phone rang. "It's Shane." She pressed the speaker button. "Hey, Shane. Don't tell me you found something already."

"On your question, no. But that makes what just happened all the more intriguing."

"What do you mean?" Charlie asked. "By the way, you're on speaker. We just arrived back at the office and we're sitting in Allison's car."

"You all should hear this anyway. DEA Agent Pierce got word from his undercover operative that Enrique Esteban was found dead in his home. They're pulling out that agent now for his protection along with Mateo Figueroa. There's a whole slew of law enforcement heading to the Esteban compound now."

"What does this have to do with Reddick?" Allison asked.

"Likely nothing, but..."

Allison gripped the steering wheel and furrowed her brow. "Shane, do you know what they found inside Hardin's storage unit?"

"Baylor's handling that but I know they found some damning evidence on Childers."

"Can you find out if there's anything else?" she added.

"This Esteban thing is huge, Allison. I don't know that I'll get hold of Baylor for a while. I'll give it a shot though."

"Thank you. Give me a call if you find out something."

"Allison, why is this so important to you? We got the bad guys," Shane replied.

"I know. But something's bothering me about Reddick. He's been on that taskforce for three years, right?"

"Something like that, I think."

"And only two weeks ago, they got a tip from Pierce's undercover agent that led to the first big bust."

"I follow you," Shane said.

"Before that, there wasn't a lot of movement, is that right?"

"I don't really know. "I'd have to ask Baylor. Look I have to run. I'm sorry. I'll talk to you later." He ended the call.

Charlie glanced to Allison. "What are you getting at?"

"Esteban's dead. Hardin's dead and Sam Childers is in custody," Allison began. "The entire operation that had for years run smoothly is being dismantled in a matter of days." She turned to Charlie. "I don't think that's a coincidence."

———

On their return to ACL's office, Charlie dropped to her chair and stared through the nearby window at the blue afternoon skies.

"What?" Allison said. "You clearly want to say something."

Charlie pulled her attention away from the window and turned to Allison. "I understand why you'd think something was up with Agent Reddick. The events that have transpired over the course of just the last 24 hours would raise alarm bells for anyone."

"But?" Allison returned to her desk.

Lucy walked to the credenza and made a pot of coffee. While it brewed, she leaned against the cabinet and studied Charlie, appearing to wait for her reply.

"We did our part, Alli. What you're suggesting might be true, but if you pursue this—if we pursue this—not only could it jeopardize our business, but it could put us at an even greater risk of danger than we're already in." Charlie pulled up in her chair. "Look, there were only a few people who knew we were hired to help Logan. One of them is dead. The other is in custody. Sam Childers never saw us as a real threat. But if we keep pushing..."

"You think if I push this, and Agent Reddick is involved with the gang or the cartel, it'll come back on us."

"Yeah. That's exactly what I'm thinking," Charlie replied.

The coffee maker finished, and Lucy poured a cup before returning to her desk. "I agree with Charlie, Allison. I'm sorry, but these people are dangerous. I don't want to keep looking over my shoulder if we move on this and we do find something on Reddick."

Allison studied her friends and partners. She considered them family and just as she felt about her own family, she would never want them to feel afraid. "You know, it's probably nothing anyway. Just me and my paranoia. You guys are right. Besides the fact that it's not our job to investigate the investigators, we have a duty to the clients who come to us, who pay us." She pushed back her shoulders and donned a closed-lipped smile. "So, let's get down to the business of finding our next paying client."

———

ALLISON RETURNED HOME LATER IN THE EVENING THAN SHE had expected. The day carried on with the partners repacking and returning Tommy's files for Lucy to put back in storage. They finished unpacking the office and hanging pictures on the walls. No one talked about the Southside Runners, Logan Carr or Agent Dave Reddick.

When she spotted a car pulling onto her driveway as she sat on her sofa in a pair of sweat pants and a long-sleeved t-shirt, she was surprised to see that it was Shane.

Nolan appeared from his bedroom with a plate in his hand. He noticed the headlights shine through the front window. "Who's here?"

"It looks like Shane." Allison pushed off the couch. "I'll get the door." Nolan disappeared into the kitchen when she preempted Shane's knock and opened the front door to see him approach. "Evening."

"Hey, I didn't catch you at a bad time, did I?" He asked.

"Not at all. Come on in. I'm just sitting here in my PJs watching TV." She stepped aside and let him in.

"Thanks." Shane removed his coat and hung it on one of the hooks on the foyer wall.

"You want a beer or something?" Allison asked.

"No thanks. I just wanted to sit down and talk if you have a minute."

"Sure." She headed back into the living room and gestured for him to take a seat.

"Mom?" Nolan appeared from the kitchen. "Oh, hey Shane."

"Nolan. Nice to see you. I hear you're practicing with the team now. How's that going?"

A broad smile danced on Nolan's lips. "Great. It's awesome, man. I couldn't be happier. Listen, I just wanted to say thanks for helping out my mom and stuff."

"I haven't really done anything. Your mom's great at what she does."

"Well, thanks for supporting her then. She deserves it. Mom, I'm just gonna..." He thumbed toward the hall.

"Sure." Allison returned a smile and waited until he disappeared in the hall. "I don't know how I got so lucky with that one."

"He's a hell of a good kid, Allison," Shane said.

"So what brings you by? I thought things would be crazy with all that's happened."

"It has been, but there's nothing more for me to do. It's in the hands of the taskforce now. The reason I wanted to stop by was that my lieutenant said she would recommend me for Major Crimes whenever a spot opens."

"That's fantastic. I'm so happy for you. You've earned it."

"I have you to thank for it, Allison. I really do. If you hadn't gotten me involved in Logan's case, no way would I have had an opportunity to get my hands on the taskforce's investigation."

"I won't take credit for the hard work you put in, Shane. You deserve this." She studied him for a moment. "That's not really the reason you're here, though, is it?"

"You do know how to read people. It's not the entire reason, no. I had a brief opportunity to get my hands on the evidence log from what they pulled out of Hardin's storage unit. Don't ask me how I did it. But um," He cast down his gaze for a moment. "You might have been right about Dave Reddick."

Allison's lips parted slightly, and her eyes widened. "How? What did you see?"

"Look, I haven't said anything to anyone about this because I guess maybe I figured it would find its way to the surface at some point. But I found a receipt of a wire transfer. At first glance, I didn't think much of it, but then on closer examination, I noticed a scribble on the upper left-hand corner of the receipt. Dave. It just said 'Dave' on it."

"That could mean anything, couldn't it?" She asked.

"It could. But when you look at all the pieces. What you talked about. It seems to slip right into place."

"What are you going to do with it?"

He shrugged. "I don't know. I mean, if it is what it looks like that would be really bad."

"Yeah, it would," Allison replied. "And if someone else happens to find it. Someone who has a reason to believe it's there. It could disappear before it's noticed."

He nodded. "Yep."

"The girls and I decided that we weren't going to pursue any of this. That it could put all of us in too much danger. We're just people who want to help clients find their biological parents or help them recover some heirloom. So we're just going back to doing what it is we're supposed to do."

"You're saying it's on me, then," Shane replied.

"We aren't law enforcement. As much as I want justice to be served, I won't endanger them, their families or my own. And I wouldn't want you to face any danger either."

"I should forget about it?" He held her gaze.

"That has to be your call."

He stood. "You're right. I should let you relax. It's been a crazy couple of weeks."

She joined him. "You don't have to leave. We can talk this through."

"No. This is my call and I'll figure out what to do." He kissed her cheek. "Goodnight, Allison. I'll show myself out."

———

SHANE WALKED INTO THE BAR WHERE HE HAD BEEN A FEW days earlier and to see the same man. "Baylor." He pulled out a stool. "Thanks for meeting with me on short notice. I know how busy you are right now."

"Sure. It sounded important." Baylor tossed back a shot and held up the empty glass. "You want one?"

"Uh, sure, yeah. I think I could use one."

Baylor pointed toward the bartender. "Two more shots over here." He turned back to Shane. "What's on your mind, Sully?"

Shane turned his gaze upward for a moment and took in a long deep breath. As he exhaled, he looked at Baylor once again. "How well do you know Dave Reddick?"

———

IT WAS A NEW DAY AND ACL INVESTIGATIVE SERVICES needed a new client. Allison sat at her desk working on the accounts while Charlie organized the files. Lucy was busy entering her father's contact list into the system. But they all still awaited the call that would bring them another client. Hopefully, not one associated with a deadly drug trafficking ring.

The door opened and Logan meandered inside, his hands tucked in his pockets. "Hey."

"Logan?" Lucy bounded from her seat. "You're here."

"Well, hello." Allison approached and offered a hug. "It's good to see you, Logan."

"Good to see you too, Allison." He peered at all of them with a hint of embarrassment on his face. "You know, you three are probably the toughest chicks I've ever known. You took on the Southside Runners."

"It wasn't just us," Charlie said. "But I won't argue that we had a pretty big hand in it."

"I'm here because I started thinking about what Lucy said when she called me a few days ago." He eyed her. "About not being afraid and taking a stand. I'd like to help the investigation. I'll make a statement and do whatever else they need me to do."

"You're doing the right thing, Logan." Lucy hugged him and gave him a peck on the cheek, but she quickly pulled back, her own cheeks flushed.

"It was because of you, Lucy. I want to do the right thing because of what your dad did for me. And because of you."

Charlie walked toward Allison and leaned in to whisper. "Looks like Nolan might have some competition."

Allison grinned. "The good news is that at least the spotlight's off my love life now."

Charlie patted her on the back. "Oh, you think this lets you off the hook, huh?" She laughed. "I wouldn't count on it."

Their attention was drawn away when the office phone rang.

"I'll get it." Lucy hurried to her desk and picked up the line. "ACL Investigative Services. How may I help you? Uh-huh. Sure.

Absolutely. When would you like to come in?" She looked at Allison and gave a thumbs-up.

Allison folded her arms. "Things are looking up, my friend."

Charlie nodded. "Good. Now I won't have to get that second job as a stripper."

THE END

ABOUT THE AUTHOR

Robin Mahle has published more than 30 crime fiction novels, many, of which, topped the Amazon charts in the US, Canada, and the UK. And most recently, she has delved into the world of psychological thrillers.

Also a screenwriter, she has adapted some of her works into teleplays, which have gone on to place in film festivals nationwide.

From detectives to federal agents, and from killers to corruption, her page-turning tales grab hold and refuse to let go. Throw in tense action and thrilling twists, and it becomes clear why her readers come back for more.

Robin lives in Coastal Virginia with her husband and two children.

If you enjoyed Ms. Mahle's work, please share your experience by leaving a review on <u>Amazon.</u>

ALSO BY ROBIN MAHLE

The Kate Reid FBI Thriller Series (17 books)

The Chef (stand-alone psych thriller)

The Man in My Attic (stand-alone psych thriller)

The Compound (standalone psych thriller)

The Remy Fontaine Fugitive Hunter Thrillers (4 books)

The Det. Rebecca Ellis Thrillers (5 books)

The Allison Hart PI Thrillers (5 Books)

The Lacy Merrick Thrillers (4 books)

**Sign up to receive Robin's Newsletter on her website. robinmahle.com so you can stay up to date on her new releases, events, contests and even exclusive new material!

www.ingramcontent.com/pod-product-compliance
Lightning Source LLC
Chambersburg PA
CBHW062129170626
46813CB00002B/622